Barry Trotter
and the
Dead Horse

Also by Michael Gerber

Barry Trotter and the Shameless Parody
Barry Trotter and the Unnecessary Sequel

Not also by Michael Gerber, but listed here in the
hopes that someone will not be paying attention and
that royalties will be mistakenly sent to him, by which
time it will be *too late*! Hahahaha! Whee-ee!!!

The Bible
The Guinness Book of World Records
Quotations from Chairman Mao Tse-tung
Valley of the Dolls

BARRY TROTTER
and the Dead Horse

Michael Gerber

GOLLANCZ

LONDON

As Valumart's writ-shaking ninjas closed in, Barry raised his wand and yelled, *'This book is a work of parody! Any similarities, without satirical intent, to copyrighted characters/material, or individuals living or dead, is purely coincidental! This book has not been endorsed by J.K. Rowling, Bloomsbury Books, Warner Bros, or any of the other entities holding copyright or licence to the Harry Potter books or films! No connection is implied or should be inferred!'* And so the ancient lawsuit-dispelling incantation was cast . . .

The moral right of Michael Gerber to be identified as the author of this book has been asserted by him in accordance with the Copyright, Designs and Patents Act of 1988, but most scholars believe it to be the work of superintelligent yeast.

First published in Great Britain in 2004 by Gollancz
An imprint of the Orion Publishing Group
(which respectfully asks the mice to stop peeing in the water-coolers)
Orion House, 5 Upper St Martin's Lane, London WC2H 9EA

Tpyest yb Deltatype Ltd, Birkenhead, Merseyside

Printed in Great Britain by Clays Ltd, St Ives plc

A CIP catalogue record for this book
is available from the British Library.

ISB 0 575 07630 5

www.orionbooks.co.uk

To

A Note From the Author

Many people ask me (God knows, I ask myself), 'Why do you keep writing these?' The short answer is: I need money desperately. In fact, I am nearly destitute – I'm writing this on a Big Mac wrapper in a bus station in a town so poor it can't afford a name. That's home. Being a writer isn't all it's cracked up to be, and it's not cracked up to be much.

First, let me respond to the rumours. Regardless of what you might've read, I did not spend millions trying to woo Madonna. Madonna and I are both happily married (not to each other). Nor did I pour a fortune into building the world's tallest Lego structure. That seems almost too absurd to refute, but you'd be surprised at how many people ask about it. I did buy a vintage Jaguar to celebrate the completion of *Barry Trotter and the Unnecessary Sequel*, but it is only five inches long and sits on my desk.

My needs are few – give me a roof over my head, the simplest food to eat and a work of children's literature to parody and I am satisfied. After the success of the first two *Barry Trotter* books, I should've been able to amble off into the sunset, living off my royalties and creating my dream, a chain of drive-thru wedding chapels. But like so many in show business before me, I trusted the wrong people. 'People' – yeah, right. If only.

Several years ago, while doing interviews for the first book, I met a group of mice. Their leader was a very charming brownish-grey individual named Timothy. Timothy claimed to be immortal, but all I knew was that he was funny, and full of fascinating stories about the rich and famous. He and I had many long – and, I thought, quite meaningful – conversations; soon we were inseparable.

There were a lot of good times ... *Wild* times. I remember one summer Timothy and I bummed around Europe in a VW microbus. (I'd had it customised so that he could drive.) When Timothy offered to become my agent/accountant/manager, I readily agreed. I am not one to let the fact that someone is two inches tall automatically disqualify them from a management position. I am short myself.

I only found this out later, but within a week everything had been signed over to him; all the proceeds from the first two *Barry Trotter* books had been redirected to the rodent's numbered Swiss bank account. Whenever I'd ask about cheques that never arrived, Timothy would put me off with some excuse. Stupidly, I believed him.

Timothy started getting harder and harder to reach on the telephone. Like a fool, I assumed that he was busy drumming up new projects for me. In reality, he was throwing incredibly lavish parties, getting hooked on designer peanut butter, and running up massive debts with the most expensive cheese shops in London.

Not only that, but Timothy had begun to appear around the world *posing as me*. It was *he* who was courting Madonna; *he* who had the Lego fetish; and *he* who was involved with 'The Muscine Liberation Front'! I have never, and would never, contribute a penny to a group as misguided and hateful as the MLF. I've never been to one of their rallies – if you look at the picture, it's obvious that's not me. I am not covered with fur, even if I am an eighth Sicilian.

I realised what was happening much too late. My only solace has been discovering that many of the famous people who Timothy talked about – people like Benjamin Disraeli, Sonia Henie, Maria Callas, and UN Secretary General Kofi Annan – were also scammed by this minuscule miscreant. At least I'm in good company.

My editor has graciously allowed me to write this book, in the hopes that the proceeds will allow me to fight this mouse in the courts. But it's not going to be easy: every night, around three a.m., the phone rings; when I pick it up, I hear a squeaky voice telling me all the terrible things that will happen to me if I publish this book. I'm sure it's a hit mouse, some of Timothy's hired muscle. 'Hey buddy' (he always calls me 'buddy', which I hate), 'if you publish Barry Three, we're gonna chew up all the pages . . . Then, we're going to tell all our people in bookstores to knock 'em on to the floor – they'll get scuffed up and have to be returned. Your publisher will lose millions!'

Sure I'm scared – who wouldn't be? But Orion assures me that they will spare no expense when it comes to security, and I'm determined to do what's right. Please consider buying this book, if only to keep me from writing others. With your help (actually, money) I can win the fight to clear my name.

Thanks for reading this, and I hope you enjoy the book.

M.G.
Town-With-No-Name, 2004

CONTENTS

THE FOCUS GROUP

᪥᪥᪥

Trivet Row shimmered in the summer heat. For weeks, the sun had been stuck on reverse, its strangely heavy rays sucking energy rather than giving it. Activity under this celestial interrogator's lamp was half-speed, half-hearted, and almost incomprehensibly sweaty. Even the street's insects, always plentiful, had given up biting and stinging as too much effort. Each crispy blade of grass wanted to stretch itself out against the earth and sleep, at least until England got a little further away from the sun.

On this Tuesday afternoon all was quiet, save for the drip, drip, drip of perspiration oozing off frightened homeowners. It was going-home time at school; whole families peered worriedly out of un-airconditioned homes, their doors and windows locked tight. Will my child make it past the zombies today? Or will they make her eat dirt – again?

Outside, two figures moved. Blank-faced and stiff, Vermin and Pecunia Dimsley staggered to and fro, doing the bidding of their obnoxious young ward, the fifteen-year-old wizard Barry Trotter. Insensible to the heat, the pair reeled up and down Trivet Row, letting the air out of the tyres on all the cars, gnawing open plastic bags filled with grass clippings and dumping them out, scooping up kids and putting them face first into rubbish bins.

At the end of the street, a local eight-year-old named Howard appeared. Howard, an imaginative child, meandered along lost in thought, not noticing the zombies converging on him.

Using an action figure, Howard pushed up his glasses, which were forever sliding down his nose. 'You fools,' he said aloud, 'no one can stop my magneto-meter!' This was a major plot-point in the story he was making up as he walked.

'That's what you think,' Howard said in a slightly different voice, indicating the other action figure was speaking. 'I am going to hit you!' He brought the two action figures together with a little crashy sound effect.

Fifty feet away, Howard's mother opened the win-dow a crack. Attracting the zombies' attention might bring several kilos of grass clippings through the letter box, but that was a risk she had to take.

'Howard!' she yelled, pointing a frantic finger through the tiny crack. 'The Dimsleys! Run, Howard, run!'

Howard looked up, saw the neighbours-turned-zombies, and made a dash for his door. He didn't make it.

'Arrghh,' Pecunia said, as she stuffed the struggling Howard into a bin for the third time this week.

'Arrghh,' Vermin concurred supportively.

Howard's mother had finally reached her limit. Broom in hand, she charged down her front steps and made a beeline for the Dimsleys.

'Bleedin' undead!' she said, swinging wildly. 'Get out of here!'

As the Dimsleys retreated, pawing at the air and gnarring, Howard's mother helped him out of the litter bin. 'You two should be ashamed of yourselves!' she yelled. 'And that freaky Trotter boy, too!'

Emboldened by this show of defiance (and already pretty cranky from the heat), Trivet Row struck back. Windows and doors flew open and objects of all sorts began to rain down on the retreating zombies, hurled by sweat-stained residents pushed too far.

'Take that, you bastards,' one homeowner yelled from his step. 'I know you ate my dog!'

Inside, Barry Trotter watched the tumult with deep, deep satisfaction. He finally understood what witch doctors were on about – having zombies was great! Sending away for that kit was the best idea he'd had in years.

And yet ... The strangest feeling came over him. Was he actually looking forward to going back to school? He *had* become a bit of a deity at Hogwash, now that J.G. Rollins's heavily fictionalised *Barry Trotter and the Philosopher's Scone* was flying out of bookstores. Really, when it came to books, people would buy anything.[1] But actually making him anxious for school to begin? Nah, couldn't be. Barry closed the curtains and the room was dark again.

Sprawled across his unmade bed, staring blankly at the football on the television, boredom enveloped Barry like last month's newspaper. Making newcasters belch was only fun the first five hundred times ... And reversing football goals only mattered if one had a bet on the game. Maybe if he did it enough times in a row, he could get France and Honduras to go to war, Barry thought with a smirk.

---

[1] Like I need to tell *you* that.

The puzzling feeling came back again. No, it wasn't enthusiasm for school exactly; Hogwash simply couldn't arouse that much of a reaction, positively or negatively. Giddiness, dread, fascination and an urge to flee ... If he weren't in Trivet Row, he'd swear there were marketors about.

Hearing a noise, Barry walked into the bathroom. Standing on the toilet, he peered out of the window. What he saw stirred nausea tangled with utter delight: fifteen feet below, in the back garden, a cadre of suited marketors were surrounding Dirty Dimsley. Dirty, being a Muddle (and a powerfully dim one at that), couldn't know that marketors were the scourge of the wizarding world and that no one – perhaps not even Barry – could escape a 'focus group', a collection of marketors training their awesome evil on one hapless test subject.

'Mum! Dad! There's some weirdos in the ... garden...' Dirty yelled, already falling under the power of the marketors' stupefying, extremely expensive cologne.

'Argggh,' Vermin emoted dumbly from the front porch, where they had been driven. He and his wife were engrossed in a family bucket of week-old fried chicken.

'Don't run, young man ... We'd like you to answer

some questions,' a marketor said, smoothness belying his menace. 'In exchange, we'll give you this ten-pound note.'

'All ... right.' Dirty, quite groggy now, snatched clumsily at the note.

'Not so fast.' The marketor cleared his throat and said loudly, 'By taking the proffered payment, you are agreeing to participate in our study, and agree to hold this firm and our clients harmless in the event of your injury and/or death.' The boilerplate over, he handed the note to Dirty, who tried to stuff it into his pocket, but missed.

As the note fluttered to the ground, the marketors gathered like jackals. There was no hope for Dirty now – the 'focus group' had begun. 'Which sports star do you like most?' a marketor demanded.

'Only ones with criminal records, now!' another added.

'Cheese-favoured milk,' said a third, clipboard at the ready. 'Yes or no?'

'Would you buy a toothpaste that made your spit look like blood?' the second chimed in.

'Inflatable pants?' a jostling fourth asked. 'Collapsible thigh zones, automatic basket extension, emergency buttock-cushioning action – sound good?'

The first grabbed Dirty by his collar and barked,

'Would you eat feathers? How about with a non-dairy topping?'

Dirty struggled to form words. 'Are they . . . crunchy?' He was pale and his eyes were glassy.

'They can be! Surrounded by nougat, perhaps!' the marketor said ravenously. 'And covered in delicious, hypoallergenic caramel!' The marketor let go of Dirty, and the boy dropped to the ground in a heap.

Another marketor picked him up. Dirty wobbled unsteadily as the marketor asked, 'How do you feel when I say this: "deep-fried cigarette"?'

'I think – I think – I think I'm gonna be sick!' The ring of marketors stepped back, and Dirty vomited beneficially into the flower bed. He then collapsed. Dirty was motionless but not dead; they had sucked him dry in record time. Above, unnoticed, Barry watched in fascinated *schadenfreude*.

'Not much there, you know?' one said to the other.

'These kids today . . .' the other replied. 'It's like they don't even *care*.'

'Splash water on him and we'll start again,' a third said.

'Not *water*,' another answered. 'There's a drought on.' He mimed peeing on the supine knucklehead.

'Nah, forget it, he's tapped out,' the fourth marketor

said, picking up the note that Dirty had dropped. 'Let's go to lunch.'

The marketors snapped their briefcases shut. Barry could hear them plainly; they talked loudly, like people used to being accommodated.

'You know, I had an idea for a joint venture,' one said, turning his mobile phone back on.

'I'm listening,' the marketor next to him replied. The marketors all knelt by Dirty, administering their grisly coup de grâce. Barry couldn't wait to see it.

'If your company introduces a deep-fried cigarette, my company will introduce toilet paper impregnated with nicotine.'

'We hook 'em and you help 'em quit?' the second marketor said, getting up. 'I like it. Send me a memo.'

The first marketor pushed a button on his phone. 'Done.'

The second marketor pushed a button on his phone. 'I've just agreed.'

Another button. 'Now I've floated an initial public offering,' the first said.

And another. 'And I've taken a few million of that money and bribed the right government officials,' the second marketor said. 'It's already been approved. Should be on the shelves by Monday, Tuesday at the latest.'

'Super!' the first marketor exclaimed, then hit another button on his phone. 'Stock's for sale . . . Price is going up . . . Bingo, we're billionaires!'

'Brilliant!' the second marketor said. 'Hey, lads! Drinks are on me!'

As the cheering marketors shuffled out of the back gate, Barry could see what they had wrought: Dirty was covered in the latest trends. Garish and absurd, they had moronic catchphrases and slogans plastered all over them. Dirty would no doubt be delighted. Some might say that he was his own punishment, but Barry didn't agree. He considered punishing the Dimsleys to be his job.[2]

---

[2] Barry had every right to despise the Dimsleys, who (among countless other things) had trained wolf spiders to nest in his hair. However, this was not simple meanness on their part, but the result of secret cooperation between the Ministry of Magicity and the Muddle spy agency MI-6. The infant Barry Trotter was selected out of a national pool of magical orphans to participate in Project TANTRUM. The Project's goal was to create a magical person so annoying that he or she would attract all the free-floating animosity felt by Muddles towards wizards. The Dimsleys' role – which they performed with great relish – was to torment Barry constantly until magical Puberty. By doing this, it was hoped that Barry would develop a massive persecution complex and, once magical, be completely irresponsible. As we know, this portion of the plan worked to perfection. Whether or

Out in the hall, Earwig gave a hacking cough. Barry looked at the clock – he was running late, as usual. He wore a wrist-glass, but it was useless; the sand shifted whenever you moved your hand. Barry had just missed the 'Hogwash Depress', his ramshackle ride to the next term at Hogwash School for Wizardry and Witchcrap.

Luckily Barry didn't need to pack much; most essentials he could cajole from other students (by persuasion or force, it didn't matter to him). Most would give willingly, now that Barry was famous – he positively basked in his newfound piratey popularity.[3] Barry had gone from garden-variety arsehole to internationally renowned bad boy in under a month. God bless that writer, and that book!

Twelve months ago, Barry had been approached by a Muddle journalist, J.G Rollins. Ms Rollins told him

not Project TANTRUM succeeded in its largest goal – preventing conflict between the Muddles and magical people – is yet to be seen. But a case could be made that the Dimsleys, far from being Muddle villains, are three of the wizarding world's greatest heroes. This case would probably be wrong, but it could be made.

[3] Colin Creepy, writing in *The Hogwash Haunt*, the school's student newspaper, had called Barry 'mean, moody, and magnificent'.

that she was looking to write a book drawing attention
to the nihilistic existence of today's magical teens.

'I want to rip the lid off,' she had said, all earnestness
and pens.

'Okay,' Barry said, not sure whether he was the
ripper or the lid.

'Great!' she said, and whipped out a notebook. 'In an
average week, how often do you see your parents?' she
asked. 'Occasionally, seldom, or never?'

'Never,' Barry answered honestly, not telling her
they were dead.

'Excellent! I mean, how sad,' she said. 'So they're not
there for you at all, are they?'

'No.' Barry squeezed out a fake tear.

'There, there – it's okay. We'll find you a nice home, I
promise.' Barry stiffened; J.G. noticed. 'Or not. You're
a big lad – you can probably survive on your own.' She
scribbled some more; Barry deciphered the words
'resists domestication; semi-feral'. She looked up again.
'Starved for guidance and direction, bored by school
and abandoned by the older generation, are your days
filled with illicit drug use and casual sex?'

If only, Barry thought. Apart from whatever expired
potion ingredients they could swipe from Snipe's
cupboard, drugs were unknown at school. Hogwash's
caretaker, Angus Filth, confiscated everything and

resold it in Hogsbleede at a handsome profit. The centaurs did a smashing business selling oregano, much to the delight of students unfamiliar with the placebo effect. And as far as sex was concerned, male braggadocio aside, Barry was currently hung up somewhere between second and third base. But the writer was so hopeful – and there seemed to be money in it.

'I couldn't have said it better myself,' Barry lied.

Barry met with Rollins regularly throughout his fourth year, and three months ago, in May, *Barry Trotter and the Philosopher's Scone* had rolled off the presses. It sold well, especially among adults; no one has ever lost money by telling the older generation that its darkest suspicions about teenagers are right. Within weeks, Barry's name became synonymous with delinquency; naturally, he felt obliged to live up to it. With the Measly twins' encouragement, Barry went wild. He created a spell to magically wrap clingfilm around every toilet in the school. Boiled sweets appeared inside every showerhead. And Barry spent a large portion of each day in various closets, 'getting to know' his fellow students.

'Our fear for the future,' *The Daily Profit*'s editorial page bellowed (magical papers did that), 'now has a name: Barry Trotter.' *The Stun*'s cover simply had Barry's picture on it, with a single word: 'Git'.

With notices like this – along with the boy's triumphantly incoherent appearances on television and radio – the book sold even better. Barry soon strode the dank halls of Hogwash like a god. Albeit one with occasional Acne of Fire and still-patchy facial hair.

Scone was almost fact-free, but in J.G.'s defence Barry had started off fudging and only gathered speed. He thought J.G. suspected something after a particularly graphic story about subduing and buggering 'the biggest dragon ever' in front of the entire cheering, chanting, rioting school. But she didn't question Barry, not once. Not even after she'd spent enough time with him to know just how deep the mendacity ran in Barry.

Factual or not, it had worked out well for both of them: J.G. was constructing a wee bit o' the Caribbean in Scotland, and Barry was looking forward to exercising his first full term's worth of fame. Honesty may be the best policy, but when it came to *Barry Trotter and the Philosopher's Scone* dishonesty had done swimmingly.

Thinking of this cheered Barry up as he locked the house. The Dimsleys were still outside, but they would eventually find their way into Mrs Kegg's cellar (she kept it unlocked, because she could never find the key). There the zombies could guard her massive stores of cheap plonk from the Muddle teens that roved about the neighbourhood in search of drink. Mrs Kegg had been one of those teens, a long time ago. Now perpetually drunk, Mrs Kegg probably wouldn't even notice Vermin and Pecunia shuffling about, gnarring and eating bugs. All summer, she had thought they were coat-stands.[4]

Barry stepped into the fireplace, and took out a tiny paper umbrella. He'd got it at a tiki bar in Hogsbleede during an illegal end-of-term dance. This soirée, which had ended with the time-honoured tradition of Hogwash's gamekeeper Hafwid trudging down from school and fishing several students out of jail, had been organised by Ermine Cringer to impress her new beau, Victor Crumb. Normally, Ermine was a goody two-shoes – or three, or as many as possible – but Barry had noticed that her judgement seemed to worsen markedly whenever certain boys were involved.

Victor Crumb was a grunting, odiferous, semi-literate Quiddit stud from a rival school. At first, Barry disliked him simply because of that; then Barry moved on to other, sounder reasons. During matches, Crumb's favourite trick was to sneak up in mid-air and doodle all

---

[4] Mrs Kegg, a dipsomaniac, was so constantly and emphatically squiffy that she believed herself to be magical. Which was true, but only if 'magical' is another word for 'brain-damaged'.

over you in felt-tip pen. His on-the-spot illustrations were often extremely sexual, scatological and funny, as long as they happened to somebody else.

Ermine agreed. 'He's a teenage Bruegel,' she said.

'Teenage barmpot, more like,' Barry said, angrily scrubbing the back of his neck with a towel.

Victor's scribbles awakened something in Ermine, something new and exciting and not entirely appropriate for younger readers of this book. Ever since she had seen the obscene little drawing Victor had done on the back of Barry's neck, Ermine had been convinced that Crumb was a genius. Furthermore, she just knew that she was *the* woman to warm up the sullen and uncommunicative sociopath.

Good luck with that, Barry thought, looking at the umbrella. This little wood-and-paper geegaw was magically endowed with the power of 'homing'. Once unfurled, it would whoosh whoever was holding it back to the Tiki Shack, the dark and sticky Hawaiian-themed dive where the party had taken place. The bar handed them out as promotional items to patrons (who often didn't know about the 'homing' power until it was too late). It was damned effective – how else to explain the commercial persistence of such a sore on the landscape? The décor was dingy, the service snotty, and

the entertainment – a weatherbeaten she-male imper-
sonator named 'Dawn Ho' – frankly painful to look at.

So the Shack was shabby, even by Hogsbleede's
snake-belly standards. But after four years, Barry was
sick of the decrepit Hogwash Express, all mildew,
chipping paint and sentient sick-making sandwiches. A
good stiff mai tai would be just what he needed to get
through the soporific Picking ceremonies. He could
almost taste it.

Barry unfurled the umbrella, raised his arm and
intoned the magic word: *'Comoniwanaleiya!'*

Nothing happened.

'Must be a dud,' Barry said. Not surprising for a
place where the worms in the tequila were worm-
flavoured plastic replicas.

As he opened and closed the party favour a few
times, Barry heard someone pounding on the front
door. He leaned down and took several steps into the
bedroom – then the umbrella activated. Barry was
dragged effortlessly through layers of plaster, laths and
shingles, bruising freely as he flew.

'Aieee!' Barry shrieked as he rocketed into the air,
narrowly missing a duck. Screaming more deeply now,
sphincter slammed shut, the boy wizard held on to the
umbrella with every available fingertip.

Amazing how powerful this little umbrella is, Barry

thought, watching loose change fall from his pockets and plummet to earth at lethal speeds. Oh well, I suppose I should relax and enjoy th—

At that moment, the umbrella shot a massive spark, and Barry's ascent ended. With a cough and a wheeze, it promptly crapped out. Now the *real* screaming began.

Sometimes, they say, it is better to be lucky than competent; by sheer chance Barry landed in a shrub in the Dimsleys' back garden. Dirty, briefly stirred by the crash, raised his addled head for a moment. Then he passed out again.

Barry sat in the bush, resting. All his major organs – the ones he knew about, anyway – seemed intact. Any broken bones? No, but what he saw next made him suspect concussion: Hafwid, kitted out in a French maid's uniform.

'Hay B'rry,' Hogwash's gamekeeper rumbled alcoholically. 'I've come t'take yeh to scuhl. B'mmlemore sint a car for yeh.'

'Are you real?' Barry asked.

'P'raps,' Hafwid said, then turned thoughtful. 'Butt thin agin, p'raps not. After ul, whut is real'ty? Kin anny one uv us relly—'

'Oh, shut up. I knew you shouldn't have taken those extension classes,' Barry said with exasperation. 'A little knowledge is a dangerous thing, especially when you have nowhere to put it. Help me out of this, would you?'

'Sher,' Hafwid said. He yanked Barry to his feet, splintered branches flying everywhere.

On the ground again, Barry had never appreciated it so much. People didn't think about how useful it was until they were thirty storeys up, about to become guacamole. 'What's with the getup?'

'Thuh whut?'

'The clothes, the uniform!' Barry said, tugging at a sleeve.

'Hay! Watch thuh threds – it's renned! B'mmlmore wanned me tuh dress to blen intuh thuh Mud'le worl',' Hafwid said. 'But all thuh stor had in my size wuz this, or a sexy nurse's otfit.'

'Well, in that case, I think you made the right choice,' Barry said. As they left the garden Barry heard Dirty rousing himself, softly slur-singing a jingle. He couldn't just leave him there, could he? Maybe it would start to rain . . . or hail! Really forcefully! With the drought on, hail was unlikely – Barry couldn't just assume that things would go badly for Dirty; he had to *make sure*.

'Hold on,' he said.

'Barrie, B'mmlmore wants tuh see yeh first thing—'

'It'll just take a second,' Barry said. The enthusiastic-ally vindictive young wizard walked back, pulling out his wand.

Dirty was sitting crosslegged in the scraggly grass, mumbling happily to himself.

'*Adestefidelis*,' Barry intoned, and a bolt of red and green energy shot from his wand, hitting Dirty squarely in his thick neanderthal forehead.

'Jingle bells, jingle bells, jingle all the way,' Dirty sang lustily, rocking back and forth. 'Oh, what fun it is to ride in a one-horse open sleigh!'

'Won't be fun for long, sucker,' Barry said. 'That was for all the chocolate swirlies you gave me when I was little.' Death came swiftly from the spell, usually from the singer's own hand, as he did whatever it took to stop 'Jingle Bells' from playing in his head. The thought of Dirty in psychic torment made Barry very happy. Spirits light, he skipped back to where Hafwid was standing.

'Yeh look like sum sorta d'ment'd elve,' Hadwid said, regarding him with suspicion. 'Now kin we goh?'

'Yes, *si, oui, jawo-o-ohl*!' Barry sang. He suddenly grabbed Hafwid's hands, and began swinging around the giant in triumph. Barry swung round and round Hafwid, round and round, round and round – until he lost his grip and flew . . .

Chapter One

... Barry's head hit the carpeted floor painfully, waking him up. 'Ow! Motherfu—'

'Here, let me help you.' A rangy, balding man in a somewhat decayed tweed jacket reached down. 'You fell off the couch.'

'Painless procedure, my arse! You ought to put a guardrail up!' Barry said woozily. He sat on the couch's edge, rubbing his head, trying to get his bearings. It all seemed ridiculous somehow, like he was a character in some cheesy book. 'I think I have a bloody concussion.'

'We can find out simply enough: how old are you?'

'Thirty-nine,' Barry said.

'What's your wife's name?'

'Headmistress Ermine Cringer,' Barry said. 'She's the one making me do this.'

'Right. And who am I?' the man asked.

'You're Dr Ritalin, the nutbar who hypnotised me, the school's new shrink!'

'Correct,' Ritalin said. 'You don't seem concussed. Want to continue?'

Barry's annoyance momentarily overwhelmed his fear of his wife. 'This'll never work,' he said crossly. 'You're an idiot, and I'm going to look nine years old for the rest of my life.'

'Barry, the human brain is immensely powerful. Furthermore, it has a fucked-up sense of humour,' Dr

Ritalin said. 'As you know, I believe something in your past – something in your mind – is keeping you from aging normally. Hypnotic regression is the only way to find out.'

'Oh, what the hell . . .' Barry said, lying back down. 'I paid for the whole fifty minutes' worth.'

'Just relax.' In moments, Barry had returned to his fifth year, picking up the story several hours later as he steeled himself to face his eternal enemy, the deadly arch-cretin Headmaster Alpo Bumblemore.

Chapter Two

THE PETTING PRAT

⟨∼∙∙∙∙∙∙∙⟩

As Barry trudged up to Bumblemore's office, a pick-pocketing bat came swooping out of the shadows, hungry for booty to take back to its masters in Silverfish House. Barry gave it a glare, and the bat stopped so fast it nearly turned inside out.

'Hey, flying flannels: listen up.' The boy wizard pulled out his wand and intoned the magic word: '*Baddog.*' An ultra high-frequency sound shot from the wand's tip and ricocheted around the room – Barry could feel its vibrations in his palm. Whimpering and smacking into each other, the bats retreated into the shadows.

Barry was in a foul mood again. Unless he'd misunderstood Hafwid – which, after all, was highly likely – Bumblemore wanted to see him immediately about 'a decision of the Wizenedgits'. The Wizarding

High Court didn't meet to discuss Quiddit scores; could he actually be getting *expelled*?

What had he done last year? A lot, so much in fact that it was hard to remember . . . Oh, that's right: he'd been caught in a broom closet with Doris Jackson. Doris, a third-year from Pufnstuf, was somewhat unique in that not only could she turn into a donkey, she'd also let you touch her under the bra for a Sickie.[5] Angus Filth had caught them, and Barry had been forced to cast a Choking Stench spell to escape. Later, he had to bribe Filth not to put the photos on the Witchy Wide Web, but that jerk had done it anyway.

The more details that came back to Barry, the worse he felt. And the ride up from Piddlesex hadn't helped, either; Hadwid had driven him in a ghost limo, which was like travelling in a very cold, very full tissue.

When cars are written off – especially under tragic circumstances – their ghost remains in this world. Many magical folk drive these nether-vehicles, because they require very little physical skill, something that wizards do not have in abundance. And they can be purchased

---

[5] In fact, all you had to do was write the words 'One Sickie' on a piece of paper, and give it to her. It was no big deal to Doris, who had been raised on a commune near Stonehenge and saw nothing special about naked flesh. She was endlessly amused at how much boys seemed to care.

cheaply, because busted-up cars don't really operate properly.

Hogwash had bought several ghost limos after everybody had become good and tired of stepping in invisible thestral poo. Missing the right-front wheel, the axle grinding out a steady shower of sparks, Barry and Hafwid made the trip to Hogwash at a glacial thirteen miles per hour. By the time Barry was mounting the marble steps towards Bumblemore's office, it was well past dark, and the torches cast their usual creepy shadows on the walls.

Barry's scar hurt, as it often did. I ought to take that company up on their offer, he thought. 'Hello, I'm Barry Trotter,' he practised aloud. 'When I want to foolishly ignore scar pain, I take Throbnomore.'

Barry arrived at the Headmister's door, and knocked on it. He heard a scuffling behind him, and instinctively dived for cover; six throwing stars thunked into the door, missing Barry's noggin by inches. Then a loud German profanity, and the sounds of someone large and clumsy scuttling away.

'Lay off, Valumart,' Barry said irritably. 'I just got here. Kill me after dinner.'

Lord Valumart, aka the Dork Lord, aka He-Who-Smells, was constantly trying to murder Barry, for reasons that Barry didn't quite know. Unfortunately, whenever Barry would get close enough to ask, Valumart would try to kill him.

Whenever Barry would tell a teacher about this, they would get a funny, slightly fixed smile on their face and say something like, 'Don't be silly, Trotter. He-Who-Smells cannot enter Hogwash – or haven't you read *Philosopher's Scone*?' They always thought they were so funny. Barry suspected that they wanted Valumart to kill him. There were rumours of an office pool in the staffroom. Pretty rude, Barry thought.

Despite several failed attempts per week, and collateral damage in the millions of Gallons, no one (officially) believed the fifteen-year-old. Barry suspected that now he'd been made famous by a book full of self-serving lies, they'd (officially) believe him even less.

Bumblemore's door swung open. 'No need to pound on the door, you impatient twit.'

'That wasn't me, Headmister. Valumart just whipped some throwing stars—'

'Amazing! Lying's the same as breathing to you, isn't it? Haven't even been here thirty seconds and you're already— What are you doing on the floor?'

'I told you, Valumart—'

Bumblemore gave a spasm of annoyance. 'Come inside, the hall reeks of pee.'[6]

Brushing himself off, Barry entered the stuffy, cluttered office. Alpo Bumblemore, Headmister of Hogwash, was standing in front of a long table filled with pots of ink and scraps of note-sized pieces of parchment. All around, quills darted to and fro, dipping into this pot or that, marking the notes. The air was filled with the sounds of scratching.

'What's that?' Barry said, pointing at the table.

'That, Trotter, is the school's new endowment,' Bumblemore said.

Barry picked up a piece of parchment. It was a preposterous forgery of a Muddle thousand-pound note. 'The Queen looks cross-eyed.'

'Do you hear that, quills? We have to start again – Michelangelo here thinks your rendering of the Muddle Queen isn't up to his exacting standards!' Bumblemore

[6] Whizzing in front of Bumblemore's office, then running away, had become the standard test of admission to the Hogwash Gallstones club. As a consequence, a patch of stone all around the door was eaten away. The house elves, backed up by their Union, refused to do anything about it: 'That's terrorism, that is.' Bumblemore was constantly casting *Scrubadub* spells, but even magic had its limits, especially during the asparagus season.

mocked. The quills tittered spitefully and kept scratching.

'Suit yourself, I don't care.' Barry put the note in his wallet – Bumblemore was probably right; the Muddles probably wouldn't notice. He pulled up a chair.

'No, no, don't sit down. This won't take very long, and frankly, I don't want to have to destroy the cushion.'

'I shower!' Barry said, with maximum outrage. Then, more quietly, '. . . now.'

'As you may recall,' Bumblemore said, 'last year ended with yet another of your petty sexual escapades. Yet another fantastic voyage to the bottom of someone else's knickers.'

'Doris and I were just—'

Bumblemore cut him off. 'I know what you were just – everybody knows what you were just. A special commission of the Wizenedgits has spent an unpleasant summer finding out *exactly* what you were just.'

'Headmister, it hardly seems fair that the whole Wizenedgits would get angry over my fondling one girl.'

'Oh no!' Bumblemore said with a haughty laugh. 'Not just one girl, Trotter – give yourself more credit. Your victims are as numerous as the dandruff on your head!'

A knee-high pile of books appeared out of the air and dropped in front of Barry. He looked down and read: 'The Wizenedgits Select Committee on Immoral Activities Report on Barry Trotter, alias "Doctor Pokengrope".'

'Impressive, isn't it? Two thousand "episodes" in only four years. How many is that a week?'

'I don't know, Headmister.'

'I wasn't asking. It was a rhetorical question. Here's another one: Tell me, Trotter, has all this activity given you strange new calluses?'

'Actually, it's funny that you —'

'"Rhetorical" means don't answer, pillock,' Bumble- more said brusquely. 'Thanks to that blasted *Scone* book – which, mind you, the school doesn't see a penny from! – the Wizenedgits were forced to investigate you. Do you know why every student, faculty member and visitor to Hogwash had to spend a week last May being dusted for your fingerprints?'

Barry didn't answer – he was learning.

'They wanted to make an example of you,' Bumble- more said. 'They wanted to make you *get a job.*'

Barry shuddered. Gainful employment was his Kryp- tonite.

The Headmister continued: 'But I – no doubt to my eventual regret – convinced them to give you another chance.' He started making balloon animals as he talked, a nervous habit he'd picked up during a youthful, disastrous stint as a children's entertainer.[7] I told the Ministry that Hogwash could use a dash of celebrity, even as repulsive a dash as you. I promised that I would come up with a way to rein you in. After insisting that the rest of the student body be given massive doses of antibiotics – and your most frequent partners go through a summer's worth of *Clockwork Orange*-style aversion therapy – they reluctantly agreed to let you stay.'

'Thank you,' Barry said.

'I didn't do it for your benefit, I assure you,' Bumblemore said. 'Hogwash is like a living being, or would be, if living beings ate money. While I'm making great strides in certain areas of fund-raising' – Bumblemore gestured towards the scribbling quills – 'wizards aren't so easily bamboozled. We need Gallons, solid gold, and lots of 'em. Your presence here brings

[7] He made them, the phoenix popped them; the room was covered with smouldering shreds. This was the basis for Bumblemore's irrational fear of blimps – he believed that blimps were the bigger siblings of the little balloons, and were determined to avenge their popped brothers and sisters. What a blimp would or could do to Bumblemore, once it got its hands (?) on him, was not clear. Phobias are like that.

applicants. And applications bring fees – which I've tripled, thank you very much.'

Bumblemore walked to the front of his desk and sat casually on the corner. As he did so, his bottle-green robes gaped embarrassingly; the ravaged old codger wasn't wearing anything underneath. 'However, your systematic blitzkrieg of slap and tickle must end. The infamous "Petting Prat" of Hogwash must hang up his speculum.'

'But if the girl doesn't mind—'

'The Wizenedgits *do*,' Bumblemore said with finality. He waved his hand, and a scroll hopped out of a desk drawer, then marched over to Barry. It unrolled – and unrolled – and unrolled. 'This was just the preliminary list.'

'Okay, I'll admit, some of these are right,' Barry said. 'Chi Ching, Doris, Hannah Rabbit, Hannah and Doris, Gollum[8] – I'd forgotten about that . . .' Barry chuckled. 'Wait! I didn't do anything with Angina Johnson and her friend – I just watched!'

Bumblemore's face was impassive, as if he were holding in wind.

'*Dorco Malfeasance?*' Barry spluttered. 'He wishes!'

'Trotter, perhaps you don't realise how serious this is.

[8] Transfer student.

Naturally, for someone like you, expulsion looms constantly, like clouds or the need for a haircut. But this is different: there's a petition circulating.'

'Is it for-sure real? Have you seen it?' Barry asked sceptically. This sounded just like something Ferd and Jorge would do.

'Seen it? Hell, Trotter – I've signed it! In big, swooping, loopy letters!' Bumblemore said, with a mite too much pride for Barry's taste. 'Approximately eighty-seven per cent of the parents of students currently attending this school have called for you to be expelled – then driven from the surrounding county, for safety's sake. Alumni numbers are, it is true, slightly lower, but one must factor in dementia. Any way you look at it, it's a tidal wave of disgust.' The Headmister scratched at a food stain on his robes. 'They fear for the next generation of magical folk.'

'Since when can't a fellow study for his A.U.K.s in genitomancy?' Barry lied defiantly.[9]

Bumblemore ignored this preposterous gambit,

[9] The noble and ancient art of genitomancy is, as everyone knows, fortune-telling through the size, shape, colour, and arrangement of the genitals. It has never been a subject on the A.U.K.s, a standardised test taken by all wizards during their fifth year. A.U.K. has nothing to do with the bird, standing for 'Accumulation of Useless Knowledge'.

merely sighing and thinking that surely there were easier ways to make a living. 'If it was anybody else,' he said with great fatigue, 'you'd be using your wand to spear rubbish in the park by now. And speaking personally, I think a few terms stirring a safety cauldron at St Hilary's Academy for the Marginally Magical would do you a world of good. But over the summer applications to the school have gone up 20,000%, and that's not including the laughable fakes that Ferd and Jorge send in. Those two are incredible morons.'

'Why?' Barry asked.

'Genetics, exposure to multicoloured fires,[10] who knows?' Bumblemore said. 'Oh, you mean why have applications gone up? It's that book.' Bumblemore got

---

[10] This fad arrived in the wizarding world about the time of psychedelia, and while no one dresses like Jimi Hendrix any more, multicoloured (and even strobe) fires are still fairly commonplace. Unfortunately, the chemicals that wizards use to make these effects give off a gas when burnt that causes hallucinations. As a result, observers believe that at least twenty-five per cent of all the 'magic' claimed by wizards is really their own sad delusions. The gas also makes you very suggestible, which makes the claims of magic irrefutable; if somebody says, 'I've just Immuppetised you!' while you're under the influence of a multicoloured, strobe or black-light fire, you believe it.

that pained, rigid look again. 'People love to read about
someone stupider than themselves.'

'Well, if it makes you feel any better, Lord Valumart
is back.'

'Oh, I highly doubt that,' Bumblemore said. 'You put
him through a wood-chipper last June. We all saw you
do it.'

'He's remarkably resilient,' Barry said petulantly.
'And he's trying to kill me.'

'Oh, come off it,' Bumblemore said. 'Don't start *that*
again.'

'Look!' Barry, angry at not being believed, pointed at
the office door. The throwing stars were steadily
chewing their way through the wood.

'Trotter, even if Terry Valumart could survive being
put through a wood-chipper, which I highly doubt . . .'
Behind Barry, Bumblemore saw Valumart step from
behind a heavy curtain. Bumblemore took a few steps
towards Barry and put his hands on his shoulders,
locking him in place.

'Hey!' Barry complained. 'Hands off, perv!'

'In a moment . . . I'm just being fatherly,' Bumblemore lied, and nodded almost imperceptibly. Valumart
raised a blowgun, and aimed it at Barry's back. 'You're
completely safe here. You always are – GODDAMN-
IT!' The dart missed, thunking into Bumblemore's

desk, which gave a small moan and promptly disinte-
grated.

Barry whipped around, and there stood Valumart, in
full dress regalia.

'There he is!' Barry said. 'There's Valumart! Arrest
him!'

No one moved. Then Bumblemore gave a short,
nervous laugh.

'Trotter, you really need to get new glasses. Can't
you tell a statue when you see one?' Bumblemore
walked over and knocked it on the top of the head.

'Kvit it,' Valumart mumbled, without moving his lips.

'. . . though I grant you, it is amazingly lifelike.'

Barry went over and examined it. 'Since when do
statues smell like Chinese food?'

'Isn't it amazing?' Bumblemore said. 'Even smells
real. I got it at an antiques stall on the Portobello Road.'

'The hell you did . . .' Barry said. Still not sure, he
turned around – then suddenly turned back. 'Look!'
Barry insisted, hopping up and down. 'It moved! He
scratched his nose, I saw him.'

'Did not,' Valumart mumbled softly.

'You see, Trotter?' Bumblemore said. 'He didn't do
it.'

'Aaaahh!' Barry screamed in frustration. He fell to

the floor, and beat it with his fists. 'Son – of – a – witch!'

Bumblemore grew impatient. 'Trotter, stop fooling around. I have things to attend to before the opening ceremonies in the Great Hall. Some second-years have been enchanting Snipe's toiletries again.' Barry stopped pounding for a second and smiled; he was the one who had taught them the *Gumgouger* and *Snarlcomb* spells last year.

Bumblemore saw him smile, and said angrily: 'Think that's funny, do you? You're a frog's whisker away from the streets.'

'Wait –' Barry said. 'Frogs don't have whiskers.'

'That's how close you are,' Bumblemore said.

Our hero made a final bid for clemency. 'But Headmister, I'm fifteen,' Barry said. 'I'm going through a natural period of curiosity and discovery.'

'Natural? Not the way you do it, son,' Bumblemore said. 'You deflower in bulk. You play more doctor than the Royal College of Surgeons.'

Barry wanted to argue the point, but couldn't. He'd spent so much time in the bushes last spring, the centaurs had made him an honorary satyr.

Someone sneezed. Barry whipped around – the statue was wiping its nose.

'*Geshundheit*,' Bumblemore said.

Chapter Two

'*Danke schön*,' the statue said.

'Headmister, *that is no statue*!' Barry was outraged. 'It sneezed! Plus, it knows German!'

Bumblemore thought for a second, then put on his most disdainful expression. 'Of course it does, Trotter. It's magical. We're magical. Your name is Barry. You live on Earth. Now,' Bumblemore continued with a sigh, 'consider this an official warning: you are not to touch another student with unwholesome intent this year. If you do, you will be immediately, permanently, and very cheerfully expelled. Informational posters are already hung in all public places. Furthermore, handbills with your picture and most common aliases will be distributed.'

First Hafwid in a dress, and now this? Could fifth year get any worse? 'But—'

'I haven't finished: completely unbeknownst to them, I have placed a spell on every magical teenager within the nearest hundred miles. If you unzip, unbutton, unbelt or otherwise fiddle with your trousers in their presence, an alarm will go off. It's a sort of variant on the Age Barrier,' Bumblemore said proudly. 'I came up with it myself.'

'You can't do that!' Barry said. 'What about my civil rights?'

'Trotter, you have no civil rights,' Bumblemore said with an evil smile. 'You're a student. Now you may go.'

The office door opened, and Barry turned. 'Grotbag!' he grumbled under his breath. 'Knobless Wonder can't get it up any more, so—'

'I most certainly can, you greasy nit,' Bumblemore mumbled tonelessly in Barry's direction. 'You forget I can read minds in my office . . . magical wallpaper[11] . . .'

Hand on the doorknob, Barry saw a picture of a former Headmister, surrounded by a bevy of tanned, buxom blondes. They were all laughing at him. Barry gave him a rude gesture, and left.

'Oh, Bumblemore,' the tiny picture of Dionysus Hefner said. 'You ought to lighten up. Sexuality is one of our greatest gifts. It's what makes us human. It's—'

Bumblemore walked over. 'Does it hurt when I do this?' he said, flicking the picture.

[11] This wallpaper is actually sentient; it's not exactly telepathic, but every flower on it is actually an ear – and with so many ears, the paper is able to hear the slightest sound. Even chemicals combining in a brain to make a thought.

Chapter Three

THE PICKING CAP'S
RAP

୧୩୩୬

Twenty-four years later, Barry was still angry with Bumblemore. Stretched out on the ratty, stained couch in Ritalin's ratty, stained office, the hypnotised[12] Barry said venomously, 'A good *Kidneystonehenge* spell would sort that miserable geezer out . . .'

'Uh-huh. So you've left Bumblemore's office. Go on.' Dr Ritalin had stopped taking notes and was playing with a desk toy. 'What are you doing now?'

'Writing "Alpo Eats It" on the wall . . . Now, I'm walking to the Great Hall.'

In a foul mood, Barry made his way to the Great Hall, which was filling for the beginning-of-term

---

[12] All right, I know that this isn't exactly the freshest method to set up a prequel. But at least it's better than – wait for it – a magic spell! Or a dream. Or a crystal ball. Remember, a cliché is only a cliché if you're paying attention.

ceremonies. Lon Measly and Ermine Cringer, both newly minted Perfects, herded in the lastest crop of first-years. Dorco Malfeasance, also a Perfect, was making Silverfishers kneel, swear a blood oath, and kiss his ring.

'*Stickum*,' Barry mumbled, and the next supplicant, a hapless second-year, became permanently attached.

'Now say ... Hmm, what's good? ... "Dorco is the most wonderful person alive, and I would consider it an honour to be allowed to eat a big cookie made from his dried urine."'

'Mmph-mmmph! Mmmph mmph mmmmmph!' The second-year began to panic.

'Get off!' Dorco bellowed, but the kid's lips wouldn't budge. Dorco's henchmen, Flabbe and Oyle, each grabbed a leg and pulled. The second-year screamed as his lips stretched; Dorco hollered as his finger was dislocated.

Finally the signet ring slipped off. Flabbe, Oyle and the second-year went flying. They sailed completely through the Bloody Imbecile and into the giant lunch-lady Fistuletta, who was already annoyed at having to clean up the trembling first-years' various accidents. Fistuletta began whomping Flabbe, Oyle and the second-year with her effluvium-heavy mop.

As the hubbub died down, and everyone took their

seats, Barry looked up at the high table. Every chair was occupied except Hafwid's. And speaking of empty chairs, there were plenty of them around Barry, too; apparently Bumblemore's propaganda was already having some effect. Lon and Ermine were the only Grittyflavians brave enough to sit next to Barry.

'Thanks,' Barry said to Ermine.

'Oh, we figure we've already got your cooties,' Lon said.

'Speak for yourself!' Ermine said. She was saving herself for marriage – in her usual very public, very perfectionist way. 'I'm aiming for *extra*-virgin, like olive oil.' Ermine was very goal-oriented.

'Keenie,' Barry said. 'Hey, where's Hafwid?'

'He got lost bringing the first-years over. It took him about an hour,' Ermine said.

'Christ,' Barry said. He shook his head. 'All you have to do is point towards the bloody school and row!'

'I think he was drunk,' Lon said.

'That's like saying, "I think he was alive,"' Barry said.

'Be quiet, it's starting,' Ermine said, but Lon kept talking.

'When he finally got here, I heard Nurse Pommefritte insist he take a breathalyser test,' Lon said.

'Shh!' Ermine said.

'He probably broke the machine,' Barry said.

Ermine laid a quick biffing spell upside both their heads. 'Shut up, you wankers, I can't hear the song!'

The Picking Cap was in fine voice this year – and had added a pre-recorded rhythm track. Two enchanted turntables scratched along, as the Cap sang:

> *'We're aware that it's pointless, inane and divisive,*
> *But spare us your spewings oh-so-derisive.*
> *You all must be divided – we simply insist –*
> *For reasons of plot-friendly prejudice,*
> *Into four Houses, each of ill-repute,*
> *Boasting its own unsavoury attribute.*
> *Radishgnaw, in accordance with its Founder's whim,*
> *Has packed these halls with the exceedingly dim.*
> *Silverfishers are, to a one, grasping and greedy*
> *With no higher pleasure than bilking the needy.*
> *Sir Godawfle Grittyfloor was surely empowered*
> *To sniff out the telltale scent of a coward.*
> *In Pufnstuf's case, it's best to ignore it;*
> *They'll admit anybody with the dough to pay for it.*
> *These are Hogwash's tumbledown Houses*
> *Gestating the next generation of louses.*
> *Each with its own traditions, and scarf.*
> *Let's Pick, and quick, or I'm going to barf!'*

'I don't know,' Barry said, 'but I think the hip-hop stuff's a definite improvement.'

Lon, a hip-hop fan, snorted with disdain. 'Only if we could get him involved in a turf war.'

'Oh, he's just an article of clothing,' Ermine said protectively. 'Barry, is that a trick of the candlelight, or are you trying to grow sideburns again?'

'Maybe.'

'Give it up, mate,' Lon said. 'You just haven't got the testosterone. Even Erm's hairier than you are.'

'Erm's hairier than Fistuletta,' Barry said defiantly. Ermine hit him with a roll, but Barry didn't flinch – his attention had been captured by the first-years being sorted. They were tiny, pre-human, ridiculously beat-up-able. Was he ever that small and mollusc-like? It seemed an eternity since Barry had arrived as a dangerously malnourished and profoundly ignorant first-year.

'Students,' Bumblemore began, 'I have a few start-of-term announcements.'

A groan of irritation came from the student body.

Bumblemore raised two fingers in a gesture of friendliness, then continued: 'I know that some of you first-years spent a couple of hours lost on Lake Eerie, and the Hogwash Express broke down several times as well. So I'll keep it short.

'First, and this is quite important,' Bumblemore said, 'Flatulent Fanny has asked me to ask the person or persons responsible for conjuring certain non-flushable items down the Upper South girls' toilets to, quote, "Stop now or taste my wrath!"

'Having been through Fanny's wrath before, I can tell you none of us wants *that*. There's not enough air-freshener in the world. Anyway, remember that for us it is just a toilet, but it is her home, so let's try to be kind, eh?

'Second, by now many of you have seen the posters, but I'll reiterate it here: all Hogwash students are hereby ordered to refrain from engaging in any romantic, exploratory, or even overly friendly activities with the Grittyfloor fifth-year Barry Trotter. Barry,' Bumblemore said, 'stand up, so people can see you.'

Barry reluctantly rose to his feet, smiling bravely amid the catcalls.

'Lift up that fringe – any other distinguishing marks? No? Thank you, Mr Trotter. You may sit down,' Bumblemore said, plainly enjoying Barry's humiliation. 'If Mr Trotter propositions you, please inform a Perfect or the Head of your House immediately, and we will proceed with magical castration.'

The crowd gave a loud, two-note ascending 'Ooooo!'

'Quiet down, quiet down,' Bumblemore said. 'I know

we're all happy about it, but let's get through the announcements. Now, third: some of you might have noticed that we have a new face amongst our faculty. I'd like to introduce Miss Dolorous Underage.'

A smiling girl of not more than eight stood on her chair, and waved. Her hair was in pigtails, each tied with a frilly pink snake. There were wolf-whistles, and someone threw a grape. In a preposterous bit of luck, it popped into her open mouth and lodged in her throat.

Bumblemore's face crumpled – for once, everything had been going so well. Snipe quickly conjured a plunger, and, fixing it over the girl's face, pistoned the grape out.

'Stop it! Students, can't we have *one* pleasant meal?' Bumblemore asked. A hail of small food was his answer. Others saw this and grew bolder, conjuring and hurling everything from pots full of gravy to joints of beef and whole roasts.

'There are people starving in China,' Lon said angrily, as his brothers took this opportunity to chuck loads of stuff at him.

'I don't think that's true any more, Lon,' Barry said, as a twice-baked potato hit the floor next to him and exploded, spraying melted cheese and bacon bits. 'It used to be China. I think it's Africa now.'

'Well, when Africa becomes Communist, I'll say "Africa",' Lon said, ducking.

'What a shame,' Ermine said. 'The house elves will be up all night cleaning.'

'You could help them,' Barry said pointedly.

'Oh, no,' Ermine said, taking aim at an enemy in Pufnstuf. 'I've got my duties as Perfect to consider.'

'Well, what about Mao Tse-tung over here?' He was referring to Lon, who had recently undergone a political awakening of sorts.

'Nope,' Lon said, deftly avoiding a chair Jorge had flung his way. 'I've got to begin indoctrinating the first-years. Can't let the wrong thoughts take root.'

So much for growing up, Barry noted with satisfaction. The summer had changed nothing. Crude, chaotic, with irresponsibility at every level – Hogwash was eternal. As the faculty cowered under the High Table and a foodstuff maelstrom raged around him, Barry thought to himself, it's good to be home.

'. . . three . . . two . . . one,' said Dr Ritalin. 'When I snap my fingers, you'll be completely awake and refreshed.'

'Okay,' Barry said, sitting up.

'No, no! Wait until I snap my fingers!'

'Okay,' Barry said docilely.

'That's better,' Ritalin said. 'We must do this properly, or we might break your brain.'

'At least I didn't fall off the couch this time,' Barry said.

'Shh!' Ritalin snapped his fingers. 'Now, you're completely awake. How do you feel?'

'Fine, I think . . . wait, something's not quite—' Barry suddenly bolted upright. 'Where's my wallet?'

'Um, I was just keeping it safe for you,' Ritalin said, fishing Barry's wallet out of his own pocket. 'I was, uh, afraid it might come flying out.' Ritalin coughed nervously.

'I bet,' Barry said. 'Where's the money?'

'I kept it here in my pocket – in case it sprayed all around the room.'

'Uh-huh,' Barry said, thinking that this character might not be trustworthy. He would bear watching throughout the rest of the book. 'So, what did I say?'

'"Where's the money?"' Dr Ritalin said. 'Really, Mr Trotter, your short-term memory is quite worrying. I have a drug that—'

'I bet you do. I meant, what did I say when I was hypnotised? How far had we regressed to?'

'You had been made to stand up in front of the entire school,' Ritalin said. 'Bumblemore had just declared you Unclean – or as I like to say, *nosferatu*.'

~ 46 ~

'God, fifth year,' Barry said. 'That was the *worst*. Twelve months of endless, level-five shitstorm.'

'Why?' Ritalin said mildly.

'Because that was the year that Lon got hurt. And that girl . . . The first girl I was really mad for . . .' Barry grasped for words. 'Of course, I was essentially a walking boner at the time.'

Dr Ritalin asked, 'Was that Ermine?'

'God, no!' Barry said. 'No, her name was Bea. She . . . disappeared.'

'Disappeared?' Dr Ritalin asked. 'Do you think she simply decided to date someone else and preferred not to tell you?'

'No, she disappeared,' Barry said. 'Like, winked into another dimension.'

'I see. Did a lot of girls you dated as a lad wink into another dimension? Sounds traumatic.' Ritalin scratched a note on a yellow pad. 'Do you think her disappearance contributed to your conscious decision not to grow up?'

Barry exploded like a tube of toothpaste run over by a truck. 'What do you mean "decision"? This youth-enasia isn't all in my mind! It's not a figment of my imagination that I haven't shaved for six months!' Barry said, fuming. 'I want to get older. It's just that Bumblemore put a spell on me, and now I . . .' His anger gave a last spurt. 'Psychiatry is such bullshit. I never should've let Ermine talk me into this.'

'Oh yes, psychiatry is bullshit,' Ritalin said, taking out a monocle (he wore two) and polishing it. 'Unlike magic.'

Barry swung his legs over to the floor. 'Now, listen—'

'Mr Trotter, I've told you this many times. The distinction between magic and the mind is very blurry. You point your wand and something happens, poof—'

'Very seldom does anything go "poof",' Barry carped.

Ritalin continued, 'What made it happen? Something outside of you, "magic"? Something inside of you – your mind, or will? Or both?'

Barry finally stopped feeling insulted long enough to concede the point. 'So you really think that it's my mind that's causing me not to age? That I've somehow *decided* to stay a kid?'

'I don't know – do you?' Ritalin said.

'I don't know – do you?' Barry parroted back.

'I don't know – do you?'

'I don't know – do you?'

. . . Seven minutes later, with no end to the conversational stalemate in sight, Dr Ritalin held up his hand and said, 'We need to stop. I think that's an excellent place to start for next time.'

Chapter Four

MIND OVER MAGIC

〰️

In the years since Barry had been a student, Hogwash hadn't changed much. Oh, people had tried – Potions classes were now sponsored by Coca-Cola – but that was strictly cosmetic. Real innovation just never seemed to stick.

Some buildings have mice, others termites. The Hogwash School of Wizardry and Witchcrap was infested with *traditions*. Within that lichen-licked, crumbling hulk, there was a time-honoured way to do everything – an inefficient, nonsensical, often dangerous way that had been handed down by ancestral nincompoops too drunk and/or insane to care.

'Peas must always be eaten with a knife; spoon-users receive five lashes, fork-users, ten.' 'First-years must lick light sockets when ordered to do so by a Perfect.' 'Any student caught whistling *The Mikado* faces summary execution.' Were these jokes? Perhaps at one time – now, like so many infected splinters, these traditions were deeply embedded in the school's disreputable history, much to everyone's annoyance and discomfort. But traditions must be respected; as a result, very little got done, and nothing very well.

Not every wizarding academy was like this. Schadenfreude, for example, was ruthlessly modern; the building had just been redesigned by BMW. (As a result, the entire school could go from nought to sixty in under twenty seconds.) Beaubeaux was imperturbably Gallic – occasionally inefficient, perhaps, but impeccably decorated, with delicious food and snappy uniforms. In America, traditions were nonexistent, with six out of every ten wizarding degrees awarded online. But at Hogwash, every important element was stuck in the 1300s. Only there did students have a Flagellants' Club. Only there did they miss class on account of having the Black Death.

'Toughens them up,' Bumblemore used to say, adding with a nasty twinkle, 'Tuition is non-refundable.'

But the winds of change were blowing, and for once, they didn't smell like Hafwid's smalls. Alpo Bumblemore was dead (?), replaced by Ermine Cringer.[13] In

---

[13] For the full story, see *Barry Trotter and the Unnecessary Sequel*, if you dare.

her no-nonsense, always-wear-sensible-shoes kind of way, Ermine was determined to drag the mossy pile if not into the actual present, at least into the Industrial Revolution. It wasn't going to be easy; she wasn't dealing with rational people. Her first step, then, was to hire a school psychiatrist.

It had been known for centuries that every act of magic – potion, spell, or item – releases a special vibration. Even though Muddle doctors had proved (in their absurd 'scientific' way) that long-term exposure to these vibrations caused the human brain to dissolve into soupy glop,[14] school officials had resisted bringing a bona-fide mental-health professional aboard for centuries.

Why? Simple – they figured the first thing any rational psychiatrist would do would be to commit Headmister Bumblemore. This was completely logical and probably necessary, but it raised certain painful questions. Such as: what about the rest of the staff? The Trustees? The students? Once you started carting off lunatics, when did it stop? Nobody needed that kind of trouble. What was the point of academia, if not to be a way for society's malcontents and weirdos to be

---

[14] They called it 'Trotter Syndrome', which Barry didn't appreciate. But such are the wages of fame.

collected and isolated from the rest of society? So a teacher was crazy. Crazy was broadening. 'Plus,' the Trustees argued, 'insane people work cheap.' Professor Bunns, for example, had been paid in pebbles for over twenty years.

But Ermine persevered. Why should every two-bit Muddle school have a shrink to talk to the press whenever a student of theirs went bonkers, while Hogwash had to trot out the Bloody Imbecile? And there was the matter of insurance; after a raving, buck-naked Hafwid attempted to sacrifice a Grittyfloor third-year to the god Lager, the Trustees finally conceded to Ermine's wishes. But on one condition: the psychiatrist himself had to be nuts.

The search wasn't an easy one; the profession seemed to have a definite prejudice against the reality-challenged. But Ernst Ritalin, PhD, filled that bill perfectly; over the last twenty years, he had been defrocked, disbarred, or physically ejected from every professional association on the books, including a few he had made up himself. Balding, grizzled, rangy, Ritalin looked like nothing so much as a stork tangled in several yards of tea-spattered tweed. A while back, he had hit on the idea of wearing a monocle to give himself a distinguished air. Of late, he had begun to wear two.

However, run-of-the-mill eccentricity was not the only thing Ritalin brought to the job. Years ago, as a forgetful graduate student, Ritalin had launched himself from a crouched position into an open filing cabinet above. This sharp blow to the brain put him in a coma for thirty-six hours. His family believed he was going to kick the bucket. Later, they sort of wished he had.

Once marginally promising, Ernst Ritalin emerged from his coma a new man – new, and certifiable. The idea that he had been idly entertaining at the moment of impact had somehow become fixed: namely, that the human brain functioned best at an altitude of no more than three feet above the ground.

This, then, became Ritalin's crusade. He harangued everyone who would stand still about this discovery – in fact, Ermine had initially discovered him at a playground in Hogsbleede, passing out leaflets to seven-year-olds. Now at Hogwash, he scoured the halls mercilessly, monitoring the height of every head that passed him with a measuring eye made keen by practice. Those too high would be pushed to the proper altitude, often painfully, and after a brief chase. In Ritalin's defence, he practised what he preached, shuffling about stooped and crab-like.

Hogwash's students quickly learned to avoid the doctor as they staggered quite glassy-eyed from one class to the next. You never knew when the scuttling, tobacco-rank figure would wade into the mass of pupils, eyes ablaze, randomly identifying this or that offender as the worst, and cranking his or her head downwards with a rough shove.

In spite of these habits – one might go so far as to call them 'symptoms' – Ermine had gradually become convinced that working with Dr Ritalin might be the answer for Barry's youthenasia. 'What can it hurt?' was her opinion, and she voiced it frequently.

Barry was dubious. To him, the subconscious was like an overstuffed closet, and anyone foolish enough to open the door would likely be crushed by an avalanche of bric-a-brac. Using matrimonial passive resistance – bland agreement, then changing the subject – Barry hoped that she would lost interest, but one morning at breakfast Ermine forced the issue.

'I want you to make an appointment with Dr Ritalin,' she said.

'Why?' Barry asked, bluffing.

'What do you mean, "Why"? Because you look about nine, that's why,' Ermine said impatiently. 'I'm sick of having people meet us and thinking I'm a horrible pervert. Anyway, I don't see why you're so twitchy about it – Ernst's been teaching here for almost a year, and nobody's died in his classes. How many of our teachers can say that?'

'I don't know,' Barry said from behind *The Stun*. 'One adapts. I don't think I really mind it any more.'

Ermine burned a hole in his paper with her wand. 'Well, I do,' she said, and gave Barry the 'I'm serious' look. That was that – Barry made an appointment for that afternoon.

Ritalin certainly had plenty of time to take Barry on as a patient. Few took Ritalin's class, 'Mind Over Magic', and none willingly, for it was common knowledge that class included mandatory extra-credit sessions with Ritalin in his office. Barry had walked in on one of these.

'Come in,' Ritalin said in his adenoidal voice.

Barry did so, then stopped; there, in front of the teacher's desk, stood three morose-looking students. They were arranged in stair-step height, but the long hair of the shortest one, a second-year named Edith Phlegm, had been teased and moussed into an impressive brown spike. The hair of the tallest one had been plastered down with grease. The middle student was unstyled.

'Sorry,' Barry said. 'I'll come back later.'

'No, no, now's fine,' Ritalin said. Then, to the

students: 'No more questions for today. We'll finish tomorrow.'

'May I—?' Edith asked timidly.

Ritalin cut her off. 'No, Portia—'

'I'm Portia,' said the middle one.

'Sorry, *Edith*, please leave it. Sleep sitting up, if you have to.' Edith made a face. 'Do it for Science,' Ritalin demanded. He turned to Barry and said, 'I was just testing a hypothesis. Could it be that hair height, not head height, is the key?'

'I see,' Barry said, marvelling at the incredible diversity and richness of human insanity.

Ritalin put away his flash cards. With a wave of his hand, the luminous stopwatch numbers dissipated. The tallest student coughed – he was slightly allergic to magic.

'Stanley,' Ritalin asked, opening the drawer of his desk, 'would you like a cough drop?'

'My parents told me never to take sweets from the insane.'

'Sound advice,' Ritalin said. As maniacs go, he was very well adjusted. 'How about you, Portia? Edith?'

'I just want to forget,' Edith mumbled.

'. . . and a stiff drink,' Portia added. Barry heard it and stifled a laugh.

'What?' Ritalin said.

'Nothing,' Portia said, with a let-me-out-of-here smile. The students trooped out. Turning towards Barry, Ritalin gave a little backwards kick with his heel, and the door closed. He may be insane, Barry thought, but he is jaunty.

Students now gone, the psychiatrist plopped down into a chair, which gave a small moan and a chain-rattle. (All of the school's office furniture was ancient, thus haunted. It was just something that happened over time.) 'Sit.' Barry did so. 'Now, what can I do for you?' Ritalin asked.

Barry took a deep breath, and began. 'I have this disease that makes me look younger than I am.'

'Lucky you,' Ritalin said with a chuckle. 'I thought you just worked out a lot.'

Barry silently commemorated the ten millionth time somebody had made this joke, and went on: 'Uh-huh, yeah, well, I want to cure it. I want to look my age again.'

'Doesn't sound like my line of work,' Ritalin said. 'See all these degrees and diplomas?' He waved his arm at a wall crowded with framed papers.

'They're not real, everybody knows that,' Barry said.

'Quite right, but if they *were* real, they'd tell you that I can only fix disorders of the mind, not of the body.'

'The Headmistress and I have been to every doctor

around. They were able to stop me from getting younger – well, that was because Bumblemore died – but nobody seems to be able to start me aging again . . . I'm only coming to talk with you because Erm's at the end of her tether.'

'Do you mind if I smoke?' the psychiatrist asked.

'No.'

'Thank you.' Ritalin lit some of his hair with a match, then quickly patted it out. 'Nasty habit, I know, but I just can't stop myself,' he said. 'Well, Barry, if there is one lesson that my entire career has taught me, it is this: the human mind is powerful . . . Especially when it is approximately three to four feet over the ground. Can I interest you in a Ritalin S-Curve back brace? It will work wonders.'

'No, thank you,' Barry said. 'I'll stick to the youth-enasia, if you don't mind.'

'Youthenasia – are you sure it's not some type of summer abroad programme?'

'No,' Barry said. He was getting fed up. 'Look, if my wife calls – and she probably will – just tell her I stopped by, and that you couldn't help me.'

'Tsk-tsk,' Ritalin said. 'So impatient, so quick to anger. Classic signs of an improperly elevated cranium. I've never heard of your malady, but perhaps that's because I cannot read.' Dr Ritalin's professional travails suddenly became clearer. 'However, I will check out a magical reading monkey from the school's library, do some research, and get back to you.'

'I thought Madame Ponce outlawed them.' The reading monkeys, though entertaining, were noisy and tended to throw faeces.[15]

'Not for Faculty. With this aid, I shall be able to investigate the appropriate literature. Give me a few days.' He stood up and extended a hand. 'I'll call you when I know something.'

'You mean, in general?' Barry asked.

About a week later, as he and Hafwid stood on the edge of the lake whacking golf balls at the kraken, Barry got a call from Dr Ritalin.

'Hello?' Barry said, putting his wand to his ear.

'I've found something,' Ritalin said, shouting. 'Come over.'

When Barry arrived, he saw the office was a shambles. Every file drawer had been dumped on to the

---

[15] Their own *or* the students', they weren't particular. Also, either Ferd or Jorge had given the entire bunch a Tourette's Jinx. It was distracting, yes, but certainly livened up an ultra-dreary textbook. Even legends of boredom like *Defective Magical Theory* flew by when every third word was a completely gratuitous profanity.

floor; all of Dr Ritalin's souvenirs and curios, collected over a lifetime of pilferage from the famous and insane, had been broken or mangled. Even Dr Ritalin's wall of bogus credentials hung askew. A few had been 'outraged' with something Barry could smell from across the room.

A rhesus monkey perched on Ritalin's head; it was wearing a small red fez, with the label 'English' on it.

'Delousing of the first-years – Cadburied Fluke – September the Nineteenth – Disciplinary Hearing –' The monkey, obviously teetering just this side of complete frenzy, was repeating every word in sight in a random, disjointed fashion. Barry coughed; the air was heavy with a ripe simian flavour.

'Come in, come in,' Dr Ritalin said. He blew the monkey's tail away from his mouth with a puff of air. 'Sit. Have one of these.' Ritalin handed Barry a clothespeg. The doctor's nose was pinned shut. 'I find it helps, especially when I come in from the fresh air.'

'Thanks.' It was painful but effective. Barry smacked his lips. 'Amazing how you can still taste monkey.'

'Are you familiar with the condition "hysterical pregnancy"?' Ritalin asked.

'Is that when the woman gets hysterical and starts saying "My life is ruined" and "I don't even *like* you" and "You're going to be a horrible father", stuff like that?' Barry asked. "Cause Ermine did that when we found out she was pregnant with Nigel.'

'Uh, not quite,' Ritalin said. Barry thought the doctor seemed uncomfortable with something, but Barry didn't know what it could be. Perhaps it was the screaming, drooling creature on his head.

'Doctor, I hope you don't mind me saying this, but your monkey is freaking me out.'

'Sorry,' Ritalin said. He walked over to the office door, opened it, then bent from the waist until the monkey lost its grip. 'Back to the Circulation Desk with you.'

Barry heard the monkey running down the hall, and the screams of students. He didn't want the monkey to wander off and go bad; Ermine had mentioned something about a tribe of superintelligent mice, and a mouse–monkey combination might be formidable. 'Shouldn't we make sure he gets checked in properly?' Barry asked.

'Don't care,' Ritalin said, with a blithe wave. 'My only interest is the human mind, Barry, not the peregrinations of a monkey. His head was too low, anyway. A hysterical pregnancy,' he continued, 'is the old-fashioned term for when a woman wants to be pregnant so badly her body starts to manifest the symptoms of pregnancy.'

'Weird,' Barry said. 'The woman's mind makes her body act differently?'

'Yes.'

'So,' Barry said, trying to put it all together, 'you think I'm pregnant.'

'No,' Ritalin said. 'I think your mind is preventing you from getting older.'

'Really?' Barry asked. 'How is it doing that?'

'Not clear. We can't know anything until I start putting you under hypnosis.'

'Hypnosis, huh?' The idea appealed to Barry; it sounded like a good excuse to do crazy stuff. 'Do you really get concentric circles in your eyes, like in cartoons? Will it hurt?'

'No,' Ritalin said, 'but I can hit you occasionally, if that would give you a greater sense of accomplishment.' As usual, Barry couldn't tell whether Ritalin was joking or not.

The mad doctor continued: 'We must return to your past, to unearth and resolve whatever trauma is hidden there. That may be what's preventing you from ageing.'

'Sounds far-fetched.'

'Don't blame me,' Ritalin said. 'I'm just a character. If you have problems with the plot, take it up with the author.'

'What are you talking about?' Barry was totally confused.

'Forget it,' Ritalin said, somewhat wearily. 'I'm convinced we're all characters in a book, but nobody ever believes me . . . Anyway, are you willing to try it? I make no promises. Hypnotic regression may cure you, or it may not . . . Or I may turn you into a robot assassin, sent to kill world leaders one by one until they agree to my plan of Universal Head-Height. Consider carefully.'

Barry weighed his options. On the one hand, the disease wasn't killing him; if anything, the reverse was true. On the other hand, the pimples and constantly cracking voice were both royal pains in the arse, and he would like to go to pubs without being hassled. On the third hand, Ritalin was a dangerous lunatic, nobody you'd want messing around in your noggin. But on the fourth hand, Ermine would probably get fed up and leave him unless he started shaving one of these years. If things went wrong, Barry thought, he could always blame her. Plus, that robot assassin thing sounded pretty cool.

'Okay, why not?' Barry said.

Those three little words had started a journey – an incredible, impossible, completely contrived journey –

back into Barry's past. From the first session, it became clear that his fifth year, the year of the disappearing girlfriend and of Lon's accident, was the key.

They started from the beginning, Ritalin transcribing as Barry relived the events of the year. It was a daunting task – even idle people have lots of things happen to them – but the psychiatrist seemed to enjoy sifting through the mess that Barry dredged up. 'This is a once-in-a-lifetime opportunity.' Ritalin reminded himself whenever his writing hand cramped. 'True sociopaths are very rare.'

'I resent that,' Barry mumbled from the couch. 'What about Ferd and Jorge?'

'Shh! You're supposed to be hypnotised,' Ritalin said crossly. 'If we aren't disciplined, this will only take longer.'

Barry didn't care; he hadn't anything better to do. Since Ermine had forbidden him from teaching classes, he had become a gentleman of leisure. And the more he thought about getting his grown-up appearance back, the more he looked forward to it – sharing clothes with Nigel was embarrassing.

Still, it was a gruelling process. After weeks of work, they had only reached October. Thank God I'm paying him in pebbles, Barry thought.

Chapter Five

QUIDDIT, SPORT OF
TWITS

ᏚᎷᎷᎧ

One October afternoon during his fifth year, Barry was staring out of the window of the Grittyfloor Common Room, picking at a pimple, thinking about some queer dreams he'd had lately. In each one, he'd been a snake. Since the beginning of school, he'd been run over by a car, eaten by a dog and chopped up by a lawnmower.

As Barry watched Dorco Malfeasance sling a Pufnstuf first-year's jacket into a tree, Lon Measly sidled up.

'Comrade –' Lon was fomenting a Communist takeover of Hogwash. Barry blamed this on meagre circumstances whilst growing up. Then again, Ferd and Jorge were rabidly, almost anarchically, capitalistic, so perhaps Lon was simply odd. Unable to wear a Mao-style quilted jacket due to the school's 'Fascist dress code', Lon had to be content with irritating rhetoric and a bowl haircut. '– I need you to make a sacrifice for the Revolution.'

'Bite me, Trotsky,' Barry said. 'I gave all my money to Serious.'

'I don't want money – I need to ask you a favour,' Lon whispered.

'Why are you whispering?' Barry said. 'And stop sidling!'

'Could you –' Lon looked around nervously, then pulled Barry into a dusty corner. There was one other Communist in Grittyfloor, a fey sixth-former named Sloane. Thanks to a few minuscule differences in dogma, each considered the other a dangerous counter-revolutionary.

'I promise not to let Sloane get you,' Barry said.

'He's got secret police, you know.'

'As if. Sloane doesn't even have *friends*,' Barry said crossly. 'Spit it out.'

'Could you help me practise Quiddit?' Lon asked. 'Now that Woode's gone, I want to try out for goalpost.'

'Goalkeeper, you mean.'

'No, goalpost,' Lon said firmly. 'I know my limitations.'

Barry felt a great weariness steal over him. 'Lon, if you know you're going to be crap, why put yourself through the hassle? Plus, I've got a hundred Gallons on Grittyfloor to win the House Cup.'

Lon whipped out his dogeared copy of Mao's Little Red Book. 'The Chairman says that there is only one way to prove that a youth is a revolutionary—'

'How irritating he is to his mates?'

'– whether or not he is willing to integrate himself with the masses,' Lon said. 'Here, the masses play Quiddit. Hence, it is my revolutionary duty to do so. However, I will be crap. We both know this. So I have decided to participate as an inanimate object. I will be politically correct, but athletically useless. But my increased visibility will allow me to gain support for my Five-Year Plan.' Lon was convinced that, in addition to schoolwork and Quiddit, every suite of students should smelt their own iron, till their own fields, et cetera.

Barry felt his eyes rolling back, deep into his head. Politics always had this effect on him. He made a sound like he was swallowing his tongue. 'Gahhh . . .'

Lon had seen it before. 'Come on, Barry,' he said. 'I can't ask Ferd or Jorge. They're cheesed off with me for stealing munitions from them.'

'Well, you're a Perfect,' Barry said. 'Do you think you should be stockpiling explosives? What sort of an example does that set for the first-years? What would your mum say if she knew you were plotting the violent overthrow of Bumblemore?'

'Don't pretend you wouldn't love that,' Lon said. 'Anyway, Ferd and Jorge are running-dog imperialists. They must be liquidated.'

'That's a little harsh.'

'They used to twist my ears when I was small.' Lon sniffed. Such psychodrama fed the fires of revolution.

'Dirty Dimsley used to tie my shoes together behind my head, and you don't see me getting all political about it,' Barry said.

'Look, all I'm asking you is to wing a few waffles at me.'

Barry considered. It was a fine day, a quick flight might be fun. And he could set it up, make things difficult so that Lon lost heart quickly.

'All right, Lon.'

'Thanks, Barry!' Lon beamed. 'You'll be the last motherfucker up against the wall, I promise!' As they left the Common Room to get their mops, Lon asked, 'Could you do me a favour and not tell Ferd and Jorge?'

'Sure,' Barry said, making a mental note: tell Ferd and Jorge.

As they walked to the Quiddit pitch, Lon amused

himself by explaining to Barry all the ways that the conflict between him and Lord Valumart was a manifestation of the larger struggle between the owners of property and the proletariat.

'. . . and that's why you're still alive, comrade. No matter what they say, the reality is that the owners of property *need* the proles to run their factories, buy their goods, and such.'

'I hate it when you call me that.'

'What?' Lon asked. 'Prole? There's nothing to be ashamed of.'

'No, "comrade",' Barry said. 'It makes me sound like Nikolai No-mates. Plus, don't know if you've noticed' – Barry lifted his fringe – 'but that's an interrobang, not a hammer and sickle.'

'Might as well be, com— Barry,' Lon said. 'Because whether you know it or not, you're a symbol of the downtrodden masses.'

'We're here,' Barry said gratefully. 'Wanna warm up first?'

'Oh, no,' Lon said. 'Can't do it here. Ferd and Jorge might see. Also, I think Sloane's behind that stanchion.'

Barry threw his hands up. 'Where in Christ should we do it, then? In my room?'

'I've been meaning to ask you about that,' Lon said,

'How did you manage to finagle your own private *bog d'amour*?'

'It's anything but,' Barry admitted. 'Bumblemore wanted to quarantine me.'

'I'm still jealous. Let's go over there.' Lon pointed towards the Forsaken Forest.

'Okay,' Barry said. 'But you know how pissed off the centaurs get when you hit them with a waffle.'

Soon, Barry and Lon were aloft. The Forsaken Forest glowered greenly below.

'Ready,' Lon said, not ready.

The onslaught began. Barry smacked waffle after waffle at the hapless pinko. The beating intensified, yet Lon sat up on his mop, motionless. He's brave, I'll give him that, Barry thought.

'Good,' Barry said, as yet another ball careened off a wincing Lon. 'Try not to catch it with your face.'

'Sorry,' Lon said. 'That was how Ferd and Jorge always told me how to play.'

'Don't say "sorry" to me, it's *your* face,' Barry said. 'Let's make this a little more interesting.' With a wave of his wand, Barry created a whole team of Trotters and a matching team of Measlys. 'Remember, you're a goalpost,' Barry said. 'No matter what happens, don't move.'

The Trotters approached the goal with speed and

skill. The Measlys, on defence, attempted to engage
their opponents in political debate. Goal after goal was
scored in rapid succession, the waffle ricoheting off
Barry's defenceless chum.

When his breath returned, Lon smiled weakly and
said, 'I really think I'm getting the hang of it— Whoa!'
Another waffle whizzed past, this time quite close to his
head.

'Think so?' Barry smirked evilly to himself. 'Try this
on for size.' the boy wizard gave the ball a mighty
whack. The waffle screamed through the air, going fast
enough to leave a small vapour trail.

Simultaneously, a basher on Barry's squad smacked
a brainer towards the goal from Lon's blind side. A
basher on Lon's team ineptly tried to protect the goalpost, but it was in vain. Just as the waffle approached
the goal, the perfectly timed brainer smacked Lon right
in the side of the head.

As the brainer fractured Lon's skull, he gave an
involuntary kick, neatly deflecting Barry's shot. Then
he fell off his broom. Barry's annoyance at being
thwarted by his inept friend turned to horror as he
watched Lon fall.

'Lon!' A blizzard of thoughts rushed through Barry's
brain. What a bad idea! What a terrible, shitty idea! He
just didn't *think* sometimes. What if Lon died? What

would he say to Mrs Measly? How would he hide the corpse? Could he pretend that Lord Valumart had taken over his body for a second? Maybe . . .

Kicking his broom into high gear, Barry swooped over in time to see Lon splash directly into a large hot tub. In the middle of the Forest.

'Thank God!' Barry said aloud. 'What a completely absurd, idiotic stroke of luck!' Barry zoomed down. 'If I read this in a book, I'd never believe it . . .'[16]

Many feet below, school armourer Zed Grimfood and Red-Arse Moody, two ex-Errors of ill-repute, sat in said hot tub, discussing the issues of the day.

'What I'm asking is,' Zed said, 'what I wanna know is, in your opinion, is McGoogle a lezzie or not?'

' 'Course she is, Zed,' Red-Arse said, taking a swig from his beer. Hafwid lay comatose several feet away.

'What do you mean, ' "Course she is"?'

'I've got proof, you tit,' Red-Arse said. He was, as his name suggested, extremely foul-tempered. 'Utter, incontrovertible proof. Look, last year – you remember last year?'

'Vaguely,' Zed said.

'What do you mean "vaguely"?'

---

[16] Watch it, myrrh-for-brains. I'd like to see *you* try to write one.

'I was preoccupied.'

'Preoccupied? With what?' Red-Arse said.

Zed considered a moment. 'Matters of the heart,' he said.

'Well, that was the thing about last year, Zed – love was in the air.'

'You know, I think I remember that . . . I think I saw it in the Farmers' Almanac!'

'That would be the place to read it – farmers are great cocksmen.'

'Particularly chicken farmers.'

'Yes. But not exclusively chicken farmers, Zed. The skill is widely held among men of the agricultural persuasion. Do you know what their secret is?'

'No.'

'Dung. Women love the scent of dung. Oh, they'll deny it . . .' Red-Arse said.

'Deny it up and down! "Get that stuff away from me! Get it away!"'

'. . . but it's a fact. Last year smelled like dung, bloody reeked of it. So, not surprisingly, love was all over the place. You couldn't walk ten feet without bumping into a great pile of it,' Red-Arse said. 'People got injured. Children were lost. Lost for ever in a pile of steaming, fly-covered love.'

'Terrible way to die.'

'Naturally, in conditions such as these, I was keen to exercise the ferret.'

'Naturally,' Zed said. 'What did it look like?'

'It's a figure of speech, Zed. I don't possess an actual ferret; they carry mange.' Red-Arse took a swig of beer. 'Has anyone ever told you that your conversational skills are lacking?'

'No,' Zed said. 'I meant the love. What was it like?'

'I take it you've never seen the airborne variety?'

'No, I haven't.'

'That's because you're cooped up in that school. You should get out more, I'm always telling you.'

'You are, that's right,' Zed said. 'No matter where I am, you're always saying, "Get out! Get out! Get out of here, you poncey—"'

'Happy to do it, Zed. That's what friends are for.'

'That's what friendship *is*. To friendship.' They clinked pints.

'Anyway, the airborne love was like a sort of brownish mist, hanging about, getting into your clothes, into your hair. My dog stank so bad, I had to have him destroyed.'

'Did he get along with the ferret?' Zed asked.

'Oh, famously. They were real chums, boon companions – on account of the love. Everyone noticed how

they acted,' Red-Arse said. 'Led to some unpleasant
questions.'

Zed saw Barry and Lon practising far above them.
'What's that?'

'Don't try to change the subject,' Red-Arse said
irritably.

'This love sounds like smog,' Zed said. 'Can't be good
for the lungs.'

'It wasn't, Zed, it wasn't! Doctors say it's worse than
working down a coal mine. That's why I was looking
for a helpmeet, to nurse me through my time of need.'

'So why didn't you go after Nurse Pommefritte?'

'Because, Zed, she is reputed to be the marrying
kind. I am not the marrying kind. I am the one-night-
standing kind.'

'Very sensible,' Zed said. 'If more men knew themselves so well, we wouldn't have so many divorces.'

'Or marriages, either,' Red-Arse said. 'That's always
been my solution: the only way to reduce divorce is to
stop allowing marriages. People must start living in sin
– the moral fibre of this nation demands it!'

'Hear, hear!' Zed said, and took a swig.

Hafwid's recumbent form slipped down further into
the water. Red-Arse's very bloodshot magic eye swivelled to take it in. 'Should we haul him out?' Zed asked.

'I'm not touching that great furry berk,' Red-Arse

said firmly. 'Anyway, getting back to last year: I had a few pints, ten or twelve quick ones to screw up my courage and blur my vision, and then I asked Minolta McGoogle to the movies.'

'It never gets any easier,' Zed said. 'When you're a lad, you always think it will, but . . .'

'Oh, it wasn't hard, Zed. I just asked the middle one.'

'And what did it say?'

Red-Arse closed his eyes, remembering word for word: '"I would rather be consumed by weevils."'

'Blimey,' Zed said, 'what do you think McGoogle meant by that?'

'I think she was trying to send me a signal,' Red-Arse said.

'Saying what?'

'I am a lesbian,' Red-Arse said.

'You are?' Zed said, shocked.

'Not me, McGoogle. It is a little-known fact about lesbians that they cannot perceive the cinematographic process. Taking her to a movie would be useless.'

'I never heard that,' Zed said. 'You learn something new every day.'

'Not if you're careful . . . Thomas Edison worked to solve the problem his entire life,' Red-Arse said. 'But much to the regret of the world's Sapphic filmgoing community, some things lie beyond the reach of any man. This is also why Italians cannot hear radio broadcasts. It's elementary physics.'

'I never took that in school,' Zed said.

'Well, you should've. It's very useful.'

'Was that all she said?'

'She also asked me what that horrible smell was.'

'No!'

'Yes,' Red-Arse said gloomily. 'There I was, filth smeared behind each ear, faced with that rarest of creatures, a female resistant to dung. Luckily I kept my head. I blamed it on Flatulent Fanny, who had been seen wafting through the vicinity.'

'Good thinking.' Zed knitted his brow. 'I think she should wear a hat or carry a placard or something, saying "Move along, boys – I am resistant to dung. And don't like movies, if you know what I mean."'

'Sadly,' Red-Arse said wistfully, 'we do not live in such enlightened times.'

'Ahh, don't be so hard on yourself,' Zed said. 'I mean, people can't be responsible in a bloody great mist. It's like Jesus said: "Forgive them, they know not what they are doing."'

'Words to live by, Zed. That's why I gave her another chance. Ten more chances, actually. "Do you want to go out with me?" "No." "Do you want to go out with me?" "No." Ten times in a row, until she hit me on the head with a broom.'

'Playing hard to get,' Zed concluded.

'She finally put me off with some cock-and-bull story about her and Bumblemore doing it.' Red-Arse belched loudly. 'Some people's ferrets get too much exercise,' he said bitterly.

'I'll drink to that,' Zed said.

'You'll drink to anything, Zed,' Red-Arse said. 'That's one of your—' His magic eye swivelled upwards; before he could warn Zed, or perhaps position him under it, something large fell from the sky.

There was a tremendous splash. Lon had plummeted into the middle of the tub like a massive ginger-haired coconut. Water sloshed out on to the centaurs, who complained (in a baked sort of way). Yet the tableau in the hot tub did not stir. Hafwid remained unconscious; brains fogged by lager, neither Zed nor Red-Arse moved.

Barry swept in on his broom. 'Have any of you seen my—' He saw Lon, crumpled in the middle of the nearly empty tub, and ran over to pull him out.

After some delay, Zed and Red-Arse realised that their surroundings had changed. 'Hey,' Zed said angrily, 'your pal wrecked our hot tub!'

'Fuck you,' Barry said in a strained, herniating voice, as he hauled Lon out and laid him on the ground.

'Is he—?' Zed asked.

'Nah, he's breathing,' Barry said.

'Step aside, gentlemen. I know what to do,' Red-Arse said. 'I learned this as part of my Error training.'

'Oi!' Zed said with a bit of wounded pride. 'I'm an Error too, you know!'

'Yes, but only a few of us were selected for the Subtle Sodality,' Red-Arse said. 'We considered you carefully. And then rejected you. Sadly, you did not meet the height requirements.'

Barry stepped aside and Red-Arse knelt tenderly over the body. With no warning, Red-Arse started pummelling Lon with great vigour.

Barry leapt in, blocking Red-Arse's fists. 'What the fuck are you doing?'

'Acupunchure,' Red-Arse said, slightly out of breath from the effort. 'The Chinese swear by it.'

'Well, I swear at it! Bleeding stop!'

'Look, Barry, if you don't want your friend to get better . . .' Zed stepped in. 'Red-Arse knows what he's doing. He's a very clever man; did you know that Italians can't—'

Errors were a special kind of crazy, and Barry had already reached his limit. 'Look, just help me load him on to my mop, okay?'

Lon was too big to be draped over Barry's shoulders.

Red-Arse sprang into action. 'We'll steal the great git's clothes,' he said. They fashioned a makeshift hammock out of the clothes which Hafwid had piled neatly by the side of the tub.

'What's his problem?' Barry said, jabbing a thumb in the gamekeeper's direction.

'He ate all the centaurs' brownies,' Zed said.

'Uh-huh.' Barry felt the stupidity levels growing toxic. With Lon in tow, he flew off to Hogwash and the Infirmary.

'What shall we do now?' Zed asked. 'The beer's gone.'

'I have an idea,' Red-Arse said. 'This was also something I learned in the Subtle Sodality...'

Giggling, Red-Arse and Zed conjured an indelible marker, and covered their comatose friend in rude words and phrases. Then they gathered up the rest of Hafwid's clothes and started home. Not only would the giant have to walk back with a tree branch covering his droopy person, he had things like 'Centaurs Can BLOW ME' written all over him.

'Hey cats – dig Slick's crazy tats,' said a voice, when Hafwid stumbled into a clearing six hours later.

Hafwid suddenly found himself surrounded by centaurs. They looked pissed off. He recognised a few of them, but not enough. 'Hay, Trane, Fluenze,' Hafwid slurred. 'Sum guys rote this shite on me. You no I'm kool . . .'

'No good beatin' your chops, Jim,' Trane said, cracking his hoof-knuckles.

Hafwid got righteously beaten up by the proud hipster/guardians of the Forest. The next morning, Hafwid passed Zed and Red-Arse in the staffroom. The pair stopped defacing a motivational poster long enough to stare.

'Whut're yeh lookin' att, ginger knob?' the giant rumbled, holding a beefsteak to his eye.

'Nothing,' Zed forced through tight lips. the moment the door swung shut, he and Red-Arse nearly shat themselves laughing.[17]

[17] Most of Zed and Red-Arse's pranks ended badly, but that never stopped them. For example, for all of Barry's fifth year, they had enchanted the teapot so that whenever Professor Snipe made tea, all that came out was coffee. This was very embarrassing for a Professor of Potions, and became doubly so after Bumblemore demoted him to Professor of *Notions*; there's simply not that many magical things that have to do with sewing. When Snipe found out what had happened, he cursed Zed with an infestation of pixies. Red-Arse denied that he'd had anything to do with it, and Snipe believed him, the prat.

Chapter Six

A GIRL AND
HER PIG

ᕼᑌᗰᑙᕯ

'Sorry I'm late,' Barry said as he slid on to the couch in Ritalin's office. 'My daughter turned my chamberpot into a Portalpotty. Two seconds into my morning pee, I found myself draining the dragon in the hair-care aisle of the Boot's on Corleone Street!'

'How alarming,' Ritalin said. 'Is that the Chamberpot of Secrets? How nostalgic for you. Are you going to punish her?'

'Nah. I figure it's just genetics,' Barry said resignedly. 'I've always been an arsehole, and Ermine's good at jinxes – it's natural that Fiona would combine the two. Did you know that I spent two months with a small planet circling my head?'

'Really. Let's get started.' Dr Ritalin held a coin on edge, and flicked it so that it spun. The coin immediately rose into the air and hovered in front of Barry,

~ 82 ~

who lay on Ritalin's leather couch. 'Barry, fix your eyes on the coin,' the doctor said. '*Lumosino*,' Ritalin muttered, and the office lights dimmed. 'I'm going to count back from twenty. By the time I reach one, you'll be dead.'

Barry sat up, alarmed.

'Ha, ha,' Ritalin said. 'Just a little hypnotist humour. Lie back down. When I reach one, you will transport yourself back to the time when you first wanted to stop ageing ... the first time you stopped yourself from growing up ...'

By ten, Barry felt as if he was made of limp linguini. Ritalin's voice was a magnet pulling Barry down, down. Or up, up. Or something.

' ... one,' Ritalin said. 'Now, Barry, where are you?'

'You forgot "seven",' Barry mumbled.

'It's not important. How old are you?'

'I'm fifteen.'

'And where are you?'

'At school ... I'm with the guys in the Order of the Penis.'

'The what?' Dr Ritalin said, making a note.

'Order of the Penis. We get together and drink beer and watch dirty movies in a secret room. Don't tell Bumblemore.'

'I won't.'

' 'Cause we stole them from his office.'

'Oh.' Ritalin rubbed his cheek wearily. The relentless tattiness of Hogwash just beat one down.

'I keep trying to get Ms Rollins to put the Order in the next book, but she always says, "I don't think the world is quite ready for that,"' Barry said. Then his voice changed – Barry was now fully regressed, talking to the people from his past.

It was Friday afternoon, and the Order of the Penis was in full swing. Barry got up from one of bean-bag chairs they had smuggled into this secret room, the Room of Recreation. 'Guys, I'm going to go and walk Lon . . . Stop throwing popcorn at me!'

'Shut up and take it!' Ferd said, throwing more. 'Dance, puppet, dance!'

'This beer is revolting,' Jorge said, looking at a bottle as if it had just bitten him.

'I aim to disgust,' Barry said, dodging popcorn. Every week, a different member of the Order was responsible for conjuring another candidate for the World's Worst Beer.

Projected life-size on to the blank wall, a pneumatic blonde in a filmy red nightgown answered the doorbell. 'Ho, ho, ho,' a bare-chested man in a Santa hat and jeans said. 'I've come to fix the plumbing.' He was carrying an oversized wrench.

'I bet you have!' Ferd said, to general hilarity.

'According to the box, this guy's name is Peter Rod Johnson,' Lee Jardin said. 'So the brown-haired guy must be Dick Turgid.'

'Head-hair, you mean?' Jorge asked.

'I bet Mrs Turgid is very proud,' Ermine said with a laugh.

'Start the clock,' said Shamlus O'Stereotype. Ferd pointed his wand at the wall, and large numbers made of white light began to count up. This was an Order tradition – a weekly pool on how many seconds elapsed from the flimsy, inept set-up of the scene until actual penetration took place. Everybody bet on a number. The winner didn't have to drink any more beer and the person who made the worst guess had to take home whatever was left.

Obviously, a penis wasn't necessary to be in the Order; a functioning liver was. Ermine was a founding member, and whenever she brought a movie, as she did this week, it was inevitably much raunchier than any of the boys' highly conventional offerings.

'I'm subverting gender stereotypes,' Ermine said proudly.

'You're subverting my digestive system,' Barry retorted. On the screen, an elf was doing something deeply unhygienic with an oversized stick of rock.

Chapter Six

Some inane dialogue involving 'naughty' and 'nice' was burbling along, but nobody was paying attention.

'There! The stick of rock! I win!' Shamlus said.

'Nah,' Ferd said. 'Sweets don't count.'

'What, do you think she's hiding it for later?' Shamlus said. He was always spoiling for a fight.

'Simmer down, Shamlus . . . Now *that* is an excellent place for mistletoe!' Jorge crowed, pointing at the plumber.

'Ouch,' said Lee. 'Those leaves look pointy.'

'Erm,' Barry asked, 'what would Victor say if he knew you were watching this?'

'If he was smart, nothing. He's no long-distance boyfriend, not my dad. Anyway, what's the harm?' Ermine said with a shrug. 'He's not here, and all I have to choose from is you lot.'

'And what's wrong with us lot?' Ferd said defiantly.

'Ask your mirror,' Ermine said. 'I'm sure Vic's doing the same thing with his mates. Everybody thinks about sex.'

'I bet Underage doesn't think about it,' Lee interjected.

'Her bits haven't kicked in yet,' Ermine said. 'Sooner or later, she'll be as hormone-addled as the rest of us.'

Barry was getting very uncomfortable. The undeniable thrill of having an actual living female share the lascivious proceedings was immediately overwhelmed by the knowledge that, his hours of 'doctor' aside, Ermine was much more comfortable with this stuff than he was. And if girls were just as dirty-minded as boys ... it was too intimidating to contemplate. 'Uh, I have to go and walk Lon,' he said.

'You're still here?' Jorg was transfixed by a sex toy with jingle bells on it.

'Forgive me if I don't show you out,' Ferd said. Two new actresses had appeared wearing nothing but reindeer antlers.

'Get help,' Barry said. 'Come on, Lon – I gotta get my raincoat first.'

Lon, just a few weeks out of the infirmary, lay curled up on the floor oblivious to the titillation coursing around him. As he stood up and stretched, Barry said, 'Let me know if I win the pool.'

'I already won it,' Shamlus hollered.

'No, you didn't,' came the chorus, but by then Barry and Lon were gone.

Ten minutes of arse-pain shifting stairways later, the pair were in Barry's private quarters. This room used to be where they'd confine any Grittyfloor students who went bonkers during the term. (Time was, every House had one; now they simply gave the students *Sedatio* spells and shoved them into the Flue Network.) Barry thought the bars on the windows gave the room character, but the soft rubber walls made hanging posters difficult.

Lon had slept here, on a pallet at the foot of Barry's bed, until Barry grew tired of the two a.m. barkfests. Now Lon mostly slept with Ermine and her friends. They gave him a lot of attention, smuggling food out of the dining halls for Lon to eat while they practised hairdressing spells on him.

Fondling Lon's leash absently, Barry stared out of his bedroom window. He saw the kraken snatch a screaming first-year from a window below.[18] Looking to the left, Barry saw the lawn stretching out vast and green in front of the school. He had never seen it less than lush because it was always pissing down with rain.

The students called it 'water torture': even when the

---

[18] This was a traditional Hogwash game; students would loiter by an open window, tempting the kraken to snake a tentacle their way, then scurry out of reach at the last minute. Sometimes they were too slow, and Hafwid would have to send their personal effects home in a box. Professor McGoogle discouraged the game, being vehemently opposed to anything the students found amusing. But Headmister Bumblemore encouraged it – such stuff kept the school's waiting list down.

sky was blindingly blue, rain fell on Hogwash. Beau-beaux had cast a spell so that their rival school was always wet, and as yet nobody had figured out quite how to break the clammy whammy. Through the damp, Barry saw two blobs moving across the lawn, one small and yellow, the other even smaller and pink.

Lon barked, impatient for his walk. For the first weeks following Lon's brain transplant, he had to be walked extremely frequently. 'We don't want him to turn feral,' Nurse Pommefritte said. 'We have to get him used to people.' Given how destructive Ferd and Jorge Measly could manage to be while solidly within human society, a animalistic Lon prowling outside of it was a fearsome thought.

'No! Bad face rub!' Lon said, when Barry brought out the leash. The dog-boy dropped to all fours and began running around the bedroom, barking.

Barry retrieved his raincoat, a hippie-style multicol-oured poncho once worn by his father. It hadn't been cleaned since before Mr Trotter's death; by now it was gummy with the filth of ages. Ready to leave, Barry stood in the doorway. Lon had stuck his head under Barry's bed, trying to extract a rawhide bone he'd left there.

'Come on, Lon,' Barry said. 'I want to get back for dinner. It's steak and kidney night.'

Chapter Six

'Want it! Want it!' Lon looked back at Barry questioningly, and whined. 'For the first several months,' Nurse Pommefritte had said, 'Mr Measly's speech will be intermittent, simple, and annoying.'

'Mrs Merlin's merkin!' Barry said crossly. After he went over and fished the bone out, he drew the leaping Lon out of the room carefully – unfortunately, not carefully enough to avoid Lon knocking down Barry's quite substantial beer can pyramid.[19]

'Bollocks!' Barry said. 'You know, you're just as clumsy as you were before.' He closed the door. 'Fetch,' Barry said, and tossed the chewbone down the stairway to the entrance hall below. Lon took off down the shifting stairs.

'Look out,' Barry yelled to a group of third-years trudging up the stairs. Too late – Lon knocked several of them sprawling in a blizzard of homework parchment.

As Barry went down after Lon, Lon sprinted back up the stairs, bone in mouth. He zoomed straight past.

'Lon, stop!' Barry yelled, as the red-headed half-human flashed by. Chasing was a fool's game. 'Fine,'

[19] In fact, prior to the Rollins book, Barry's only taste of fame had been an article on said pyramid in *The Hogwash Haunt*: 'Fourth-Year Drinks, Wastes Time,' by Colin Creepy.

Barry said. 'I'm going for a walk. If anybody wants to join me . . .'

Soon Lon was up at the top of the stairs looking down at Barry, who was now at the bottom. Whenever Barry made a move to climb upward, Lon moved a bit further away.

'Lon, come,' Barry said, trying to use the friendly-but-firm voice that Nurse Pommefritte had recommended. *'Come!'*

Lon simply looked at Barry, occasionally giving a quizzical turn of his head, as if to say, 'Are you talking to me? Because if you are, I now have a secret name that only I know.' This was enraging. Barry finally resorted to a spell.

'Ticklarimus!' A magical hand shot from Barry's wand, and began scratching Lon in a particularly choice spot, right below his rib cage. Lon immediately dropped to the ground, rolled on to his back and began jiggling his left leg.

Barry climbed up the stairs wearily. Dog ownership was no picnic; sometimes he would actually prefer to have the old Maoist revolutionary back – but it didn't help to think about that. Barry slipped the halter around Lon's face and head. Lon, as usual, sneezed. Ermine said that it was because the halter pressed on the end of Lon's nose, but Barry was convinced he did it on purpose.

'Yuck,' Barry said, wiping his face with his hand. 'Come on.' Following a jerk,[20] Lon stood up and trotted towards the stairs. Some Silverfish students pointed and laughed, so Barry took Lon on the scenic route – through the Silverfish Common Room, where Lon was being trained to pee on the leather couch.

'Good boy,' Barry said, giving Lon a piece of sirloin-flavoured gum.

By the time they got outside, Barry could make out the two figures he had seen in more detail. One was human shaped, and the other seemed to be a dog or something. But pink?

Whatever it was, Lon was certainly interested. He tore off towards it, unwinding Barry's fifty feet of spooled leash in an eyeblink. Barry tried to keep up, but was woefully out of shape – when you have magic to do every little thing for you, physical exercise is a rarity. Eventually Barry ran out of slack, and the leash went taut; instantly he found himself skimming over the rain-soaked, oozing sod like a water-skiier behind Lon's motorboat.

---

[20] Pun entirely intended.

'Look out!' Barry cried to the figure in the oilskins looming ever closer.

'What?' a high, slightly scratchy voice replied. 'Oh!'

Giving a terrified squeal, the pig that was in front of her stopped sniffing the ground and took off.

'Desmond! Come back here!' the girl in the oilskins yelled.

Hmm, Barry thought. A girl. Pig-owner, so she likes homely pink things. About my age, conscious – but there was that pesky Age Barrier. 'Don't worry! He's friendly!' Barry cried.

Barry was checking her out – two arms, two legs, a head, all systems go – so he didn't notice the small chunk of rock sticking out of the ground in front of him. His right toe caught it and he went sprawling.

Meanwhile, Lon had caught up with the pig and had scooped it up. 'I got ya, I got ya, I got ya,' Lon sang. The pig squealed, struggled and shat. 'Eww,' Lon said, letting the pig go. He wagged his finger. 'People who do that have to wear nappies!' he scolded, repeating something Nurse Pommefritte had drummed into him. The pig scurried off to a safe distance, then began recollecting its dignity.

Barry was no cleaner, although his problem was less smelly – just mud. The girl in the oilskins walked over and hoisted him to his feet.

Chapter Six

'Up you come,' she said cheerfully. She had small hands, and three different colours of nail polish on.

'Thanks,' Barry said. He rubbed his arse. 'I think I landed on my wand.' The girl laughed.

'Your what?' she said.

'My magic wand.' Barry pulled it out. 'I'm a wizard.'

It didn't register. She took off her hat, revealing bob-cut auburn hair. She shook the moisture off the hat, and some droplets hit Barry.

'Sorry,' she said. 'Why do you carry a stick around? Is it a keepsake or something? My grandfather used to carry around a piece of metal,' she said. 'He told everyone it was shrapnel they took out of his head, but Gran told me it was just a bit of scrap,' she confided. 'Grandpa said he Indian-wrestled Rommel, but that was a lie, too. He was in the entertainment brigade. All he had to worry about was rotten tomatoes.'

Lon was walking back. He had made friends with the pig somehow, and had it in his arms again, sniffing and licking it in an overly familiar way. Barry suddenly felt embarrassed.

'Lon, no!' he said. 'That pig's not yours.'

Lon looked up. 'I'm going to call it Bacon!' he said, beaming.

'No, you can't, Lon. It doesn't belong to you,' Barry

said. 'It's this girl's. Drop it.' Barry switched to a voice he hoped sounded very butch. *'Lon! Drop!'*

Lon stopped and cocked his head about fifteen degrees, but made no other movement. More of the 'secret name' treatment.

The girl put her hands to her mouth and yelled, 'Drop!' in an even gruffer voice. (Girls, after all, mature faster than boys.) Lon dropped the pig, who wandered off.

'Impressive,' Barry said, ego twingeing.

'Thanks,' the girl said, brushing some hair from her forehead. 'You just have to teach them who's boss.' She held out a hand. 'I'm Bea,' she said. 'What's your name?'

Barry was taken aback – it had been so long since somebody around here hadn't known who he was. He just stood there.

'In my country, shaking hands is a form of greeting,' Bea continued. 'The open palm means, "I am friendly," or, in more dire circumstances, "I am carrying no weapons."' She paused. 'You *aren't* carrying any weapons, are you?'

'No,' Barry said, returning to his senses and smiling awkwardly. 'Barry Trotter.'

'Pleased to meet you, Barry. You have a nice house,' she said, pointing at Hogwash.

'What? Oh, nah, I go to school here.'

'Then you have a nice school,' Bea said. 'I don't go to school. My gran wants me to get a classical education, so I stay at home and teach myself.'

'That sounds great. Can I come live with your gran?' Anything had to be better than life under Bumblewank.

Bea laughed, sounding a bit like a squeaky toy. 'Depends,' she said. 'Are you a Parthian? Or a Goth?'

'You mean, do I dress in black and—'

'No, I mean "a member of several barbarian tribes which, after being driven from their homes in the steppes by the Mongols, settled in the area north of the Black Sea, and were responsible for hastening the fall of the Western Roman Empire thanks to persistent incursions beginning in the third century AD".'

'What?' Anything that sounded like schoolwork made Barry's brain seize up. 'I'm from Piddlesex,' he said, hoping that this made sense somehow.

It did. 'Okay, then.' Barry's silence encouraged Bea to add, 'Gran and I are Romans.'

'So, you're, like, Italian? I had a neighbour who was from Italy,' Barry said. 'His mum didn't shave her armpits.'

'Not Italians,' Bea said. 'Romans, as in Empire. My last name was originally Thrasyllus, but Granddad changed it to Thompson when he joined the Army.'

Normally at this point in the conversation, Barry asked a girl if she would consider taking her shirt off. Somehow, that didn't seem appropriate, but his dangerously atrophied conversational skills remained. Since he had no idea what to say, Barry was grateful to see Desmond dawdling off towards a lonely copse at the edge of the Forsaken Forest.

'You better not let your pig get too close to those choak trees,'[21] he warned.

'That's where I want him to go, oak trees,' Bea said. 'I'm teaching him to be a truffle-sniffing pig.'

'Huh?'

'Surely you've heard of truffles, Mr Large Impressive School?' Bea said, teasing. '"A flavourful fungus used in cooking that grows on the roots of oak trees"?'

Barry stared back blankly.

How could one go through the world so utterly clueless? Bea wondered to herself. 'What do they teach you, anyway?'

---

[21] The bloodthirsty foliage in the grounds of Hogwash – the Buggering Birch, choak trees, et cetera – were the work of an insane, itinerant botanist who called himself 'Johnny Demonseed'. Dressed only in a discarded antimony sack, and wearing a battered cauldron for a hat, J.D. travelled the wizarding world during the 1700s, planting lethal trees. Nobody knew exactly why he did this, but they all agreed he was a dick.

'Magic,' Barry said.

Bea laughed.

'No, really, I'm not kidding,' he said. As he said this, a choak tree was reaching a lethal branch down towards the pig. 'Watch. *C'mere*,' Barry said, pointing his wand at the pig. Desmond disappeared, then reappeared at Bea's feet. The tree balled its small branches into tiny fists and shook them angrily.

'Oh! How did—?' She took off her rain-fogged glasses, and wiped them. 'Must be the specs,' she said, half to herself. 'Time for a new prescription . . .'

Muddles, Barry thought to himself. How could they go through the world so utterly clueless? 'What are you doing around here, anyway?' Barry asked.

'Like I said, training my pig,' she said, as if that was the most natural thing to be doing in the grounds of Hogwash. 'Gran says that Des isn't the right kind of pig, but he's always struck me as gifted, and I'm the type of person who, if you tell them no, well, they just—'

'Where's my dog?' Barry asked, suddenly afraid that Lon had gone to piss on the Buggering Birch, or had some other brilliant idea.

'You mean your friend?' Bea said. 'You really ought to be nicer.'

'You don't understand – he's sort of half and half,' Barry said. 'It's a long, gross story.'

'There he is, over—' Bea said. Lon was crouching under the Quiddit stands, licking himself. 'Oh. I see your point. He *is* flexible, isn't he?'

'Listen,' Barry said, 'he's a good chap. He can't help it, he's got the brain of a golden retriever.'

'Wow. Weird,' Bea said. 'But I guess "wizards" have weird friends.'

He was being teased. After all the adulation, it was actually kind of fun. 'Bea, you oughtn't to hang around here. It's dangerous.'

'Dangerous? What's so dangerous about it?' Bea said merrily. 'Desmond doesn't look it, but he can be fierce.' He was sniffing around her feet, and she leaned down and scratched between his ears. 'I've taught him some karate. Slightly modified, of course. I got a book called *Karate for the Extremely Short*, and—'

'Right, right,' Barry said, cutting her off. 'But it is dangerous around here, particularly after dark. There's the choak trees, and the Buggering Birch, and the kraken . . .'

'The what?'

'It's a giant octopus that lives in that lake over there.'

'O-kay, "Barry Trotter".' Bea said, smiling and clearly not believing a word. 'Did you know that octopi are as smart as house cats?'

'Oh, for Chrissake,' Barry said, exasperated. 'You've

gotta get out of here! Don't you see him reaching into the windows? Look, there!'

'Where?'

'Over *there*!' Barry pointed with his entire body. 'Just follow the screaming. Do you see it?'

'Maybe,' Bea said. 'Are you sure it's not a trick of the light?'

'*Screaming?*'

'Dusk can be like that. You know, just yesterday I read that some pilots said they saw a dragon.' Bea laughed. 'Can you believe it?'

Barry suddenly realised how late it was, and that he'd better get back for dinner. But he felt a strange protectiveness towards this Muddle. 'How did you get here?'

'Walked up the Hogsbleede Road,' she said matter-of-factly. 'We live in Hogsbleede. Gran's lived there all her life.'

'Poor her.'

Bea shrugged. 'It's cheap.'

'I'm glad you didn't stumble into the Forest. It's Forsaken,' Barry said, enjoying the rare opportunity to be the teacher and not the dunce. 'That means it's full of beatniks and jazz musicians and all sorts of stuff.'

'Ooh, how bohemian.'

Bea's vocab was a real problem. 'Uh . . . yeah. And if

you happen to escape the centaurs, there's giant spiders. Those are awful. The spider-sized giants aren't so bad, though.'

'Interesting. I'll have to come back and explore it some time.'

'No!' Barry said. 'No, you shouldn't, Bea. You'll be killed, and made into bongo skins or something.'

Bea gave Barry a sly sort of smile and said, 'So I might need a guide then?'

Barry blushed. Once again, he felt an unfamiliar, not unpleasant feeling – this time it was of being the hunted, not the hunter. 'Well . . . yes, if you put it that way. In fact, Bea,' Barry said, 'I should probably walk you back to the road.'

'Well, come on, then,' Bea said, and began walking. 'It's getting dark. There might be dragons.'

'Don't worry,' Barry said gravely. 'I can take care of those.'

'Excellent,' Bea said. 'You handle the dragons, and I'll protect us from Bigfoot, Nessie, and their friends the extraterrestrials.'

Barry didn't see what was so funny; Bigfoot was a really unpleasant, sarcastic drunk, and Nessie was even worse. He whistled, and Lon came galumphing up. Lon was followed by Desmond, who was beginning to truly reciprocate this affection. Lon had a way with animals, being one.

When they reached the road, Barry didn't especially want to turn back. 'I'll walk you to town,' he said. 'If that's all right.'

'Fine with me,' Bea said. 'Wizard schools aren't too particular about where their students wander off to?'

'Generally they are. Generally, they're pretty strict, but' – Barry paused to give this its proper weight – 'I can do pretty much whatever I want.'

'Uh-huh,' Bea said, with a disbelieving grin. 'And what makes you so special?'

'I'm famous.'

'Let me guess: you're a famous dragon-hunter,' Bea said.

'I've tangled with a few in my time,' Barry said, pompously. 'A dragon's weak point is its thighs. Dragons are very sensitive about their weight, so if you point at a dragon's thighs and say, "I can see every cupcake you've ever eaten," they will start to sob. And they can't cry and breathe fire at the same time, because of wet sinuses.'

'Where do you come up with this stuff?' Bea said, laughing. 'Are you a comedian? Or an escaped lunatic? I can't believe I've never heard of you.'

'You should get out more,' Barry said, with injured

feelings. 'I'm the only person ever to be attacked by Lord Valumart and live.'

'Never heard of him, either,' Bea said. 'Does he live around here?'

'He's the most powerful Dork Wizard of all time,' Barry said. 'He's trying to kill me constantly.'

'I see,' Bea said, humouring him. 'But you always get away, huh?'

'Obviously.'

'Obviously,' Bea parroted. 'That must be boring. Don't you ever try to kill *him*, just to spice things up a little?'

Barry thought for a second. 'Strangely, no,' he said. He thought this was such a good idea that he took out a pen and wrote on his right palm 'Try to Kill Valumart.' This girl was smart, maybe even as smart as Ermine, but (he noted with satisfaction) less furry.

They were entering Hogsbleede. Lon and Desmond lagged behind, picking through the plentiful street rubbish.

'No offence, but one has to wonder how powerful he is, if he can't even polish off a schoolboy,' Bea said. 'It's not just Volde . . . what was his name again?'

'Valumart. Lord Valumart.'

'Oh, he's a *lord*, is he? Couldn't be just Jeremy Valumart, or something.'

'It's "Terry", actually.'

'Well, what's wrong with that name? My grandpa was named Terry, he didn't need to be a lord. *Everybody*'s so puffed up these days. You can't believe anything. I blame advertising.' She pointed upwards. 'Look at that aeroplane, for example.'

A dragon circled low overhead, dragging a banner that read on the one side, 'Eat More Myrrh!' and on the other, 'Morty's Myrrh Makes Muscles.'

'If you actually believe that, I feel sorry for you. It's all lies.' Bea was agitated, and Barry was happy to listen. 'I hate aeroplanes!' she said angrily. 'So noisy and awful! And they make you want to be everywhere but where you are. Think about it – right now, wouldn't you rather be somewhere warm?'

'Sure,' Barry said.

'But if you were there, you'd want to be, I don't know, somewhere less humid or with a nicer view or something ... Everybody's always flying everywhere, and never staying in one place,' Bea said. 'It's unnatural. I wouldn't like to fly. Would you?'

'Oh yeah,' Barry said. 'I love to fly. I do it all the time.'

'Really? How do you pay for it?'

'It's free,' Barry said.

Bea gave a smirk. 'Because you're so special, right?'

'No,' Barry said defensively, 'because I have my mop.'

'YOUR MOP?' Bea had to stop and lean against a lamp-post, she was laughing so hard.

'Yeah,' Barry said flatly. 'Everybody at my school can fly. Even him.' He pointed back at Lon. He and Desmond looked as though they were hatching anti-human plots together; all it was in reality was a shared appreciation for the many flavours of refuse.

When Bea regained her composure, she said, 'I've never flown. Bit frightened of it, actually. My parents died—'

Barry leapt at the connection. 'My parents are dead, too!'

Bea was taken aback by Barry's enthusiasm.

'– uh, unfortunately,' Barry added.

'I'm sorry. My parents died when I was small. That's why I live with Gran.'

Barry looked for something, anything, to change the subject. 'Oh, you'd like the kind of flying I'm talking about. It's easy, you just—'

'Let me guess: put a bunch of glue or petrol into a bag and start inhaling it. I don't like that kind of flying either.'

'No, you don't understand – it's magical—'

'Yes, the "magic" of asphyxiating brain cells. Whee!'

Chapter Six

They had reached a particularly down-trodden corner. 'Well, here's my turn-off,' Bea said.

'You live here?' Barry asked. They were in front of a real sleazy strip bar, the Lamia's Titty. Ferd and Jorge were constantly nattering on about this place, thinking that if they talked about it enough people would finally believe that they'd got past the troll at the door.

'No, silly, down the road,' Bea said.

'I'll keep walking,' Barry said reflexively.

'You're going to be terribly late for dinner.' Bea smiled. 'Sure you have enough clout for that?'

'Bumblemore – he's the Headmister – wouldn't care if I never came back, but I'll probably turn back Time with a spell,' Barry said. 'Tonight's steak and kidney night. Wouldn't want to miss it!' Barry rubbed his stomach, angling for cuteness points.

Bea laughed. 'No, that's all right,' she said. 'I'd prefer to walk the rest by myself.'

'Are you sure?' Barry said. 'I thought I saw some rough characters around the corner ... Bigfoot ...'

'Nice try, Sir Lies-a-lot.' She stuck out her hand again. 'Thank you for the company, Barry Trotter.' Bea thought for a second. 'You know, maybe I have heard that name on television or something.'

Barry rolled his eyes. 'I keep telling you – there's a book about me, too.'

'Uh-huh,' Bea said. 'Gran doesn't allow us to have a TV – so I have to watch whatever I can through the window of the Titty here. That reminds me, I really should be going, she's probably wondering where I am . . . And coming back with no truffles! It's a bitter pill.'

'Wait, Bea,' Barry said. 'I can conjure you some.'

'If you mean by "conjure", "go to the supermarket and buy" . . .'

'No, no,' Barry said impatiently. 'Hold on.' Barry turned his back to Bea, performed a quick *C'mere* and turned back around with a large, black truffle in his hand.

Bea was confused but impressed. 'How—?' She suddenly figured it out. 'I knew you were kidding about not knowing what truffles were. You were protecting your stash, over by those oak trees!'

'No, I wasn't, I just—'

'Oh, stop lying. You have to promise me that you'll show me where it is.' Bea grabbed his ear and pulled. 'Promise!'

Bea's attack – and her touching him – seemed to paralyse Barry, like electricity was flowing through him. His tongue sprawled uselessly in his mouth.

'I'll take that as a yes. When? Next Saturday? Or do "wizards" have school then, too?'

Things had not improved, tongue-wise.

'I'll take that as a yes, too,' Bea said. Then, suddenly, she stood on tiptoe and gave Barry a friendly peck on the cheek. Barry nearly fainted.

'Thank you. You're a weird person, Barry. But I like you. It was very gentlemanly of you to walk me home, especially since you're missing dinner. See you on Saturday,' Bea said. 'We'll meet here. Come on, Desmond.' The girl turned decisively, whistling for her pig, which trotted over to its mistress. They then walked down the street.

A gentleman? Barry thought. Me? The young wizard felt like his insides were filled with Rhutastic. He didn't know what it meant. He just wanted Saturday to come *now*.

Barry leaned against the wall of a shabby outbuilding containing magical waste. Maybe it was the toxic fumes making him feel this way, or maybe . . . In the midst of Barry's reverie, Lon sauntered up behind him and jammed his nose into Barry's arse.

'Aieggh!' Barry shouted. 'Where do you keep that thing, in the freezer?' he said, whomping Lon on the head. Lon yelped; fifty feet away, Bea looked back.

'Perfectly fine! Everything's perfectly fine!' Barry shouted, waving. 'Just this idiot . . .' he mumbled.

Bea turned back and continued walking; Barry stood and watched her until she, now a yellow speck in the twilight, approached a house and went in. So that's where she lives . . . He looked at his watch.

'Damn, dinner's almost over. Come here,' Barry said, grabbing Lon. 'Rewind spell – two hours ought to do it. I think I remember . . .' A few words and a subtle jitterbug later, Barry and Lon found themselves two *days* in the past.

Back at school, Barry looked at what Fistuletta plopped on his plate. 'Son of a *witch*!' It was such a simple spell, and yet Barry could never get the hang of it. Not only did he now have to wait two more days to see Bea, it was tofu night. Barry hated tofu.

Chapter Seven

BARRY TROTTER,
POET

ᏩᏍᏬ

'How do you feel?' Ritalin asked after he had drawn Barry out of the dream.

'Okay,' Barry said. He smacked his lips. 'My mouth tastes like paste.'

'People often say that about hypnosis. That's why it's so good for losing weight,' Ritalin said. It was amazing how authoritative one could be, when actual facts didn't enter into it. 'So that was Bea. Interesting girl.'

'I thought so,' Barry said rather blankly.

'Was she really so ignorant about wizards and magic and such?'

'Nah,' Barry said. 'She was playing dumb. Her grandmother told her never to talk about magic with a stranger. I found that out later.'

'I see,' Ritalin said. 'Why was this traumatic for you,

I wonder? Were you ashamed that you liked a Muddle?'

'Don't be a dope,' Barry said. 'Mum was a Muddle. It makes perfect sense that—'

'Then perhaps you were ashamed that she lived in the ghetto?' Ritalin said.

'The what?'

'The Muddle ghetto.' Ritalin smiled. 'Come now; don't tell me you never noticed the Muddle ghetto in Hogsbleede? Just past the zoo. Only they don't call it that. After a certain number of visitor deaths, it's against the law,' Ritalin said. 'As I remember, it's called the "Hogsbleede Municipal Menagerie of Despicable Animals".[22] I still remember the first time I endured the

---

[22] The Hogsbleede Municipal Menagerie of Despicable Animals was filled with some of the least delightful creatures that five hundred million years of evolution had conspired to produce. The city hadn't started out to create such a collection, but after a chronic lack of funds forced them to stock their facility with vicious castoffs from other zoos, they decided to turn this negative into a positive. For twenty years, they'd been actively seeking dangerous denizens. 'Nature, red in tooth and claw!' was their slogan. (The general public supplied the red.) One might think that this might suppress attendance, but the reverse proved to be true: making it all the way through the HMMDA was a badge of toughness and cunning prized by hooligans of both sexes.

Hall of Stinging Insects ... I just read there's a new "big cats" exhibit called "Valley of the Stink". Really amazing facility,' Ritalin said. 'Terry Valumart bought it several years ago, and it's been a fine investment for him. It's a place families can really enjoy, especially if they don't like each other.'

Barry just sat there, mouth open, so Ritalin continued: 'No idea about the ghetto? Selective perception, we all have it. I myself am black/white colour blind . . .'

Barry finally caught up. 'Wait – there are *Muddles* living in Hogsbleede?'

'Oh yes,' Ritalin said. 'For centuries. First there's the wizarding part of town – it's the nicest – then there's the HMMDA, which acts as a sort of cordon sanitaire. Then there's the Muddle section. You can tell by the hairdressers.'[23]

'Wow,' Barry said.

'Indeed. Makes perfect sense once you think about it. Most magical people have – I'm looking for the kindest way to put this – a problem with reality. They need help. Somebody to put nappies on the hellspawn, to wash up after the witches' brew. They can perform the rites, they just can't remember where they keep the

---

[23] Magical folk don't need haircuts. They just shrink it an inch or two whenever necessary.

aconite,' Ritalin said. 'For every magical person in Hogsbleede, there are three or four Muddles doing the shit jobs.'

'Wow,' Barry said again. 'Don't they have house elves?' he asked, trying to alleviate some of the guilt.

Ritalin laughed. 'House elves are great for plot twists, but what society would possibly be stupid enough to employ *magic slaves*? That makes no sense. We use them here because the Faculty can control them, sort of. Brainwashing. That whole clothes thing – it's what's called a "trigger". Mind Control 101.' Ritalin liked to let his monocles drop into each palm and replace them as he talked.

'Would you stop that? It's distracting.'

'Sorry,' Ritalin said. 'Stupid habit. Don't even realise I'm doing it – the brain knows not what the hand is doing. Anyway, the Muddle ghetto is grim as hell, but there are some really good restaurants if you go with a native.'

'Fascinating, but I don't see what this has to do with anything,' Barry griped.

'Nor I,' Ritalin said. 'But we'll find out. Shall we begin again?'

Barry found himself standing in front of Bea's door, having decided to skive off the entire afternoon. His truanting had become epidemic once he realised that Bea was home all day, getting home-schooled – or really just teaching herself, since her grandmother worked full-time as an alchemist's assistant.

Some progress had been made on the magic front. 'What you call wizards, Gran calls hippies,' she said.

After much convincing, Bea had finally admitted that such a thing as magic existed. But she still thought it had nothing to do with Barry. This frustrated the young wizard no end, and coaxed more and more spectacular demonstrations from him.

'I think you're just being obstinate to make me do things,' Barry said, levitating a piano grumpily.

'Do what? Talk funny and waggle your stick around?' Bea shot back. 'I think it's daft, but it seems to give you pleasure, so I turn a blind eye. Who am I to judge?'

'But I've levitated your piano! And your cat!' Barry said. 'Look – she's hanging there in mid-air!'

'So perhaps *she's* magical,' Bea said. 'I don't see where you enter into it.'

'But I'm pointing my wand—'

'I think you're just trying to weasel out of learning the Emperor's Song,' Bea said. 'That's very hurtful, Barry. I wrote it myself.'

~ 114 ~

With a short, close-mouthed cry of frustration, Barry put down the cat and piano. 'Okay,' he said wearily.

'Good,' Bea said. 'It really helps you remember.'[24] After singing it seven times running, Barry had to agree.

Bea was also making some headway – Barry's brain wasn't exactly crammed with facts, but through Bea's kind efforts now some occasionally bumped into each other. She was continually amazed at the depth and breadth of his ignorance; one day, as they sat on a park bench, she hoped to use it to her advantage.

'Would you look at a poem for me?' Bea asked.

Barry winced. 'Will it hurt?'

'I've been analysing it all morning, so I'm not the person to ask,' she said, rubbing her temples. Her hair, usually a neat bob, was a little messy; this was a sure

---

[24] Bea's song was a list of the Roman Emperors, set to the tune of 'Major Bogey'. It went like this:

> First Augustus, then Ti-ber-ius,
> Gaius, followed by Claudius –
> Nero, who was quite queer-o,
> Galba and Otho, who both-o,
> Died quick.
> Vitellius, then Vespa-si-an . . .

. . . and so on. Barry thought it extremely wet, but sang it anyway. Liking somebody makes you do things like that.

sign of thinking hard. She handed over a sheet of paper. 'Give me the layman's opinion.'

'Huh?' Barry said. 'Lay' 'man' – did she just come on to me? Barry thought moronically. Bea's vocabulary remained a constant stumbling block.

'Just read it.'

'I'd really rather animate that postbox,' Barry said desperately. 'It's really funny when a bird lands on it, trust me.'

'You can do that after,' Bea said.

'"On Poet-Ape, by Ben Jonson,"' Barry said aloud.

'To yourself, please,' Bea said. 'If I hear it once more I'm going to spew.'

'Sorry,' Barry said. Then, to himself:

> *Poor POET-APE, that would be thought our chief,*
> *Whose works are e'en the frippery of wit,*
> *From brokage is become so bold a thief,*
> *As we, the robb'd, leave rage, and pity it.*
> *At first he made low shifts, would pick and glean,*
> *Buy the reversion of old plays; now grown*
> *To a little wealth, and credit in our scene,*
> *He takes up all, makes each man's wit his own:*
> *And, told of this, he slights it. Tut, such crimes*
> *The sluggish gaping auditor devours;*
> *He marks not whose 'twas first: and after-times*

May judge it to be his, as well as ours.
Fool! – as if half eyes will not know a fleece
From locks of wool, or shreds from the whole piece!

After he finished, Barry sat there, trying to think of something to say. It didn't seem to be in English. 'It's a poem, right?' Barry said in a groping tone of voice.

'A sonnet,' Bea said.

A what? Barry thought. He already felt powerfully stupid, so he tried a little trickery. 'I think it's pretty obvious what he's – it is a he, right? – what he's trying to say. What did *you* think it meant?'

'The poet is cheesed off at someone who is making money by ripping off other, more talented writers.'

'What, copying?' Barry prided himself on not having written a single original word in his entire Hogwash career.

'Yeah,' Bea said. 'Plagiarising.'

Barry shrugged. 'Big deal; people at school get the plague all the time.'

'No! No! This is totally different!' Bea said, getting exasperated. 'Copying is the worst thing a writer can do.'

'So every time I cast a spell,' Barry said defensively, 'I'm "plagiarising" whoever invented it. Every time I put jam on a scone, I'm "plagiarising" the first person who . . .'

'It's not the same,' Bea said. 'Writers—'

Barry pressed his advantage. 'I think whoever wrote this was high,' he said.

Bea gave a dinosaur-like squeal of frustration. 'Ask an idiot, get an idiotic answer,' she said, snatching the paper back.

Barry continued to needle: 'I mean, put down the bong, dude. Just *put it down*!'

Bea collected herself. 'You're thinking of Coleridge,' she said after a deep breath. 'Jonson was a contemporary of Shakespeare.' Then, seeing that name cause no answering echo in Barry's noggin, she added, '*William* Shakespeare.'

'Is he from around here?'

'Oh my God,' Bea said. 'You don't know who William Shakespeare was? The greatest writer in the history of the world?'

'Look,' Barry said defensively, 'I told you: all they teach us is magic. If this Shakesfear bloke—'

'Shakes*pear*e! With a "p"!'

'Whatever – if he was a wizard, I'd know all about him. they teach us spells and fortune-telling and stuff like that,' Barry said. 'Did he play Quiddit?'

Bea didn't dignify that with an answer. 'I can't believe they don't teach you English.'

Barry laughed. 'Of course not – I already know how to speak English.'

'Maths?'

'No. I remember some from Muddle school,' Barry said, referring to his vague sense that (for example) seven was more than three. Wizards could leave such details to house elves and Muddles. 'What's that stuff called?' Barry searched for the word. 'Admission?'

'Oh my God. You can't even add,' Bea said. 'What's three plus—' She stopped. 'Forget it, I don't want to know. Any science?'

'Um . . . a little whatchacallit – alchemy.'

Bea snorted. 'Do me a favour: if you ever meet Gran, don't get her started on alchemy. She thinks it's a waste of good lead. Canadian Bacon – that's her boss – is no Einstein.'

Barry gave Bea a particularly vacant look.

'Einstein was a very clever Muddle,' Bea added.

'If he was so clever, why is he dead?' Barry said. 'Anyway, you don't have to know all that stuff to be a great wizard.'

'You'd better hope so,' Bea said.

They spent the rest of the afternoon helping Barry relearn addition. When he got back to his room, he realised that the effers at G'ingots had been stealing hundreds of Gallons out of his account every month.

'Dear Bea,' Barry wrote. 'I just relearned maths, and my life is already worse. You know what they say: "Ignorance is . . ." Some word, I can't remember.'

The letters travelled fast and furious between Bea and Barry. They used Muddle post rather than owl; not only did Barry have no interest in sharing Bea's letters with the others at the breakfast table, Bea thought owls were 'starey and creepy'. Barry could see where she was coming from, especially now that Earwig had begun to smoke cigars.[25] But he thought Muddle post was damnably slow, and expensive, too – owls didn't require stamps, and would nip you if you tried to use one. But it was better than nothing – at least until the poor postman got buggered or choaked or dragged off to a watery grave.

Ermine insisted on seeing Bea's letters – and editing Barry's, too.

'I don't see why . . .' Barry protested, after she'd whipped one from under his quill.

---

[25] Thanks, of course, to Hafwid. Though the gamekeeper's expertise with animals was largely his own delusion, no one could teach an animal bad habits faster than Hafwid. He could teach a snake to pick its nose in a single afternoon.

'In addition to writing like a Cro-Magnon, you've got the emotional intelligence of a two-year-old,' she said. 'Trust me – you need my help. Look here,' Ermine said. 'This part's a perfect example. Never, and I mean never, suggest that a girl is acting a certain way "just because it's your period".'

'Why not?' Barry said. 'Maybe it is.'

'Because it's incredibly rude! It's like saying to a ghost, "You're just cold because you're dead." That may be, but it's unkind to bring it up – maybe it needs to put on a jumper. People's periods are their own business. Here.' Ermine handed back Barry's letter. After all her erasing, it was four lines long.

'Hey!' Barry said. 'Now I have to write a whole new one.'

'Poor baby. If you really like her, it should be easy,' Ermine said. 'Victor's letters are usually six or seven feet long.' She was carrying on her own torrid correspondence. While Barry rewrote his letter, Ermine read one of Bea's old ones.

'Is this her?' Ermine asked, holding up the small picture Bea had enclosed. 'She's nice looking. What is she doing . . .'

'Gimme that,' Barry said, and stuffed it in his wallet.

Ermine read Bea's description of the Muddle schools in Hogsbleede. 'It must be terribly degrading to be a

Muddle,' Ermine said soulfully. 'It's bad enough they
have to endure the world without magic – the least one
can do is educate them properly.'

'She doesn't go to Muddle school any more, she
teaches herself,' Barry said.

Ermine paid no attention – she was on a roll. 'The
poor girl probably doesn't even know pastomancy!'[26]
She shook the piece of notebook paper. 'We purposely
keep them ignorant so they can do our dirty work! This
kind of thing makes me ashamed to be magical – don't
you feel ashamed?'

'In a sort of general sense, yes,' Barry said. 'But it
may just be that cartoon of Victor's.' He pointed
towards one that lay open in front of Ermine. A smiling
man was emerging from a woman's bottom, where he
apparently lived.

'He's just accessing his subconscious. Victor's probably healthier than you are! That reminds me, I ought
to write to this girl,' Ermine said. 'It seems only sisterly
to warn her about you – or at least suggest which
injections to get in advance.'

Barry snatched Bea's letter back. 'Don't you dare,' he
said.

[26] A very rudimentary form of fortune-telling using noodles.
Wizard children are practising pastomancy by the age of seven.

Barry had to agree with Ermine on one count: the schools for Muddles in Hogsbleede were awful. From what Bea had told him, the facilities were post-apocalyptic, and most of the teachers criminally indolent, inept, or both. But even if things had been better, it was considered inappropriate (and possibly dangerous) to teach Muddles anything that might encourage them to rise above their station.

'In those schools, the whole point was to keep us stupid, to keep feeding us folderol about "magic",' Bea wrote, 'which is of no use to anybody who isn't magical. No offence, but I wish that magic had never been invented. As long as there's magic in the world, I'll always be second-class, or worse. For you, it's a toy. For me it's a jail I can never break out of.'

Barry had never thought of it that way.

Depth of feeling comes easily to some people, but Barry wasn't one of them. The young wizard habitually reached his greatest emotional peaks and valleys while playing video games. The rest of the time, he remained comfortably shallow.

As a result, Bea's well-meaning applications of literature had no effect whatsoever. Exposing Barry to the Classics was like teaching an elephant ballet: the optimism is admirable, but sooner or later something bad is bound to happen. In Barry's case, this was deciding to write poetry. Certainly he would do better than that Jonson berk.

Instinctively, Barry realised that the right look was more than half the battle. So he walked down to Phake and Affektid's. This cramped little shop, which claimed to have been 'Serving Hogbleede's Histrionic Teens Since 684 AD', was a great favourite of Hogwesians; magic tended to make the students self-important and prone to drama. In fact, 'P&A's' was the unofficial second home to the Hogwash Players, the school's dramatic club, which specialised in the kind of teens who spontaneously develop outlandish accents. Barry had briefly considered joining – rumours said that the Players were constantly crawling all over each other – but it seemed like an awful lot of work. Laziness trumped every emotion, even lust.

The Players travelled in a pack, pumping out equal parts smoke and disdain for the rest of the student body, who they considered 'sheep'. Every weekend, P&A's would be packed with preening, posturing thespians. Barry was forced to go midweek to avoid the crush (and being poked in the eye by some idiot using her new cigarette holder).

Hunting among the canes, opera glasses and spats – all second-hand, discarded after the wearer moved on to the next exciting identity – Barry looked for writing equipment that expressed the new, tragically articulate him. He thought a notebook with black paper struck the right tone, but after the shop assistant explained certain practical problems, Barry decided on one bound in a suitably melancholy shade of mauve. The cover read simply 'My Agony', in a tastefully decorative script. Barry felt his wank-o-meter going off, but he ignored it, like so many throbbing scars.

Sure that poetry was the way to Bea's heart (or at least under her bra), Barry skipped back to school. Then, about halfway home, he remembered that poets were miserable; he put a pebble in his shoe, and for the rest of the way tried to walk through puddles whenever possible. I never realised being tormented was such work, Barry thought.

He passed Ferd in the Entrance Hall.

'How is it outside?' Ferd asked. Lon stood in front of him, on a leash.

'Wonderful,' Barry said, then caught himself. 'I mean, terrible. Somewhere, someone is crying.'

'What the fu– Why are you limping?'

Barry didn't answer, save for a small moan. He hoped it would sound pitiful, but it sounded bovine instead.

'Moo to you, too!' Ferd said, and stomped off.

I'm not very good at this, Barry thought. Maybe the writing will be easier.

It wasn't. First, it took Barry ages to figure out a topic. Valid Tumour Alarm wasn't really love-poem material, and if he ripped something off from Led Zeppelin there was a chance that Bea would recognise it. That would be just like her – she seemed to take pleasure in knowing stuff you'd never expect her to know. And there was her whole 'originality' fetish, too.

Just as Barry was about to drop-kick his notebook out the window, a line came to him. 'My heart is like a broken cauldron,' he wrote. Then, much to his amazement, something else emerged.

'Sold to me by that douchebag—'

Hmm. 'Douchebag' was probably too harsh, especially when you're writing to a girl. He activated the thesaurus function on his wand, and tapped the word. 'Blackguard', the wand suggested. Barry didn't know what that meant, but he trusted the software.

'Sold to me by that blackguard Serious
Practically useless, made in a . . .'

What's a really awful place? Barry thought, then wrote:

'. . . sweatshop's sweatshop
So cheap it leaves bits of black paint on your hands.'

'Okay, that'll do to begin with,' Barry said aloud. 'Now, on to the emotion.'

'My tears fall like . . .'

He was stumped. What is wet and falls? A gob was the first thing that came to mind. Jorge was always doing this ultra-disgusting thing where he spat straight into the air and caught it in his mouth. Unfortunately, this image became stuck in Barry's head, and he had to stop writing, or throw up.

The next day the same thing happened again. Barry realised he needed help.

Ermine nearly choked on her sandwich. 'Poems?' she laughed. 'Jeez, you've got it bad – the only time I've ever seen you write is when you're practising your signature. Anyway, I'm no good at that kind of thing. You know who you should get?'

Barry was stabbing some haggis, which didn't seem quite dead. 'Don't say "Tuna Lovecraft",' he said.

'Tuna Lovecraft,' Ermine said.

In a school full of weirdos, fourth-year Tuna Love-craft was the Queen of the Bizarre. Pale to the point of actual translucence, not only did she talk funny, she also smelled faintly of fish, thanks to a perfume she (but no one else) favoured. Add to this that her father ran a magazine called *The Unnameable*, and you had a world-class oddball.

The one thing Tuna could do was write; the school's student literature magazine, *Abracadabra*, was filled with her byline. So it was natural that Barry go to her for help with his poem, and it was equally natural that she make him regret doing so almost immediately.

Despite her unremitting weirdness, Tuna never came in for any teasing from the other students. This was thanks to her familiar, a 250-foot-tall winged octopus-headed demon/god named C'thulu.

'Did you have to get him neutered?' Barry asked. The Ministry of Magicity insisted that all familiars be fixed, have tags and so on.

'He's not a familiar-familiar,' Tuna said. 'He's more like a friend of my dad's.'

Tuna glanced at Barry's poem. 'This is totally worthless. I'm going to have to start from scratch, and that's going to cost you.' Barry nodded. Hundreds of feet above, C'thulu filed his nails malevolently. 'So you're going for a sort of lurking dread, I assume?'

'No, I—'

'Really?' Tuna was surprised. 'Unspeakable insanity, then? Cosmic horror?'

'No,' Barry said. 'Look, Tuna, I just want to write something that will make this girl like me and think I'm deep.'

'Wow, that's asking a lot,' Tuna said. 'Also, rhyming'll cost you extra.'

'Don't worry about it rhyming,' Barry said. 'Just make it nice and romantic.'

'Okay,' Tuna said. 'But I've always said, "The quickest way to a girl's heart is unadulterated cosmic horror."'

Barry began to protest, but Tuna cut him off. 'I'll do what I can. When do you need it?'

'The You'll Ball?' Barry said, a note of pleading in his voice.

'I've got a lot of unholy activities between then and now,' Tuna said, 'but since you're a friend, I'll do it.'

Chapter Eight

WHEN IN ROME . . .

൭ഝ൭

Though she was only eight, the school's new Dork Arts and Crafts teacher[27] Dolorous Underage was precociously mean; she combined the intellectual curiosity of a lump of suet with the broad-minded conviviality of Hitler. However, Bumblemore considered this a small price to pay to keep his job.

The Minister of Magicity had been wanting to remove Headmister Bumblemore for a long time, after

---

[27] Every summer, Alpo Bumblemore put the same classified ad in *The Daily Soothsayer*: 'ARE YOU AN IMPOSTER? A psychotic? Or merely incompetent? If you answered "yes" to any (or all) of these questions, you're just the person we're looking for! Ancient, vigorously unsafe magical academy with lax standards and even dodgier Faculty seeks disreputable individual to join team, drive plot. Full-time position in Dork Arts and Crafts MUST BE FILLED before this year's crop of

the scandals had reached triple digits. Since changing the locks on the school hadn't worked, and sending him on fake holidays to far-flung, dangerous locations had become too expensive, compulsory retirement was their latest gambit. Bumblemore's precise age was not known, but estimates ranged from 150 to approximately six million.

Alpo Bumblemore was no more interested in entering the work force than Barry Trotter was. Sweating bullets, he dug something out of Hogwash's original charter: it was not the age of each teacher that was measured for compulsory retirement, but the average age of the staff. (The school charter was full of such nonsense – it could be interpreted to allow or forbid almost anything.) And so a secret, nation-wide search was undertaken. Dolorous Underage was found in the nick of time – a group of angry villagers were burning her at the stake.

horrible nits arrives, so no candidate too absurd. Criminal record encouraged, but not essential. Must be able to keep mouth shut. Do you have what it takes to warp minds? Send owl with résumé, salary requirements, and non-refundable application fee to A. Bumblemore, Hogwash School for Wizardry and Witch-crap.' Some years, when the barrel required even harder scraping, the Headmister resorted to placing rudimentary pictograms in *The Stun*.

'Why are you burning this poor girl?' Minolta McGoogle asked. 'Don't you know that burning doesn't kill a witch? Didn't you read *Barry Trotter and the Philosopher's Scone*?'

'She's a witch?' a town elder asked with surprise. 'We thought she was just a pain in the arse.'

'Well, can I have her?'

'Only if you promise not to give her back,' the elder said.

McGoogle managed to smuggle the child back to Hogwash, keeping one step ahead of other groups that Underage had annoyed, all looking to destroy her. Inside and safe, Underage was hired, lowering the average just enough so that Bumblemore could live to swindle another day.

She was a nightmare; her exploits at Hogwash would fill a many-hundred-page book.[28] But as long as Underage bothered the students, and not the Faculty, firing her was out of the question. 'I actually find her quite witty,' Bumblemore said. 'Taunting is a lost art.'

One Saturday in the late October of Barry's fifth year, everyone woke to find the following notices

---

[28] Specifically, the pondered-but-never-released *Barry Trotter and the Order of the Penis*, the only book in the history of written language to be banned before it was even composed.

posted all around the school (right next to the ones with Barry's picture on them):

BY ORDER OF
Dolorous Underage, Dork Arts and Crafts Teacher
All Hogwash students must answer the following question:
'Are you PT?'
(touch one)
( ) yes
( ) no

If you pressed 'yes', Underage's head materialised and sniggered, 'You're a pregnant teenager?' then gave an irritating laugh. If you pressed 'no', Underage said, 'You're not potty-trained?' and laughed twice as hard.

'Oh shut up,' Jorge said, when he pressed it.

'I don't shut up,' the head said, 'I grow up, and when I see you I throw up.'

'Idiot!' Jorge barked.

'You have something on your shirt,' the head said.

'Where?' Jorge looked down.

An ephemeral finger reached out and flicked him in the face. 'Burned you!'

Like so many pranksters, Jorge could dish it out, but

couldn't take it. He lost his cool and began trying to tear down the poster.

'That's not going to help, mate,' Barry said. 'It's magical. Let's go for a fly.'

Robbed of his usual outlet by Bumblemore's unfair edict, Barry had thrown himself into Quiddit. He tried, in vain, to replace the physical contact of broom-closet petting with the rough bumps and whooshing wind of the ancient, idiotic game. Actually, this was the key to its popularity: to the young and sexually frustrated, Quiddit was a harmless, mindless balm. Barry still had occasional sickly memories of the brainer ploughing into the side of Lon's head, but he reassured himself that Quiddit injuries were rare. Well, not exactly, but usually quite entertaining.

Practice was chaotic and brutal, and messed up everybody's hair. Bowlegged and with aching taints, the Grittyflavians straggled happily into the locker room. Barry brought up the rear, goosing people with the handle of his mop, chaffing and being chaffed.

'Stop it, Barry. I think I'm having a heart attack,' Angina Johnson, the new team captain said, clutching her chest.

'Ahh, you always say that.' She split off into the girls' side, so he turned to Ferd. 'You know, Ferd, I know a penis enlargement spell, if you're interested. Totally natural.'

'No way, not after what happened to Woode,' Ferd said. 'Haul a log like that around? No thank you.' The previous term, Oliver 'Morning' Woode had primped for a hot date with a bootleg spell picked up on a Hogsbleede streetcorner. Designed to increase one's manhood, the spell had worked much too well, increasing Woode to an outlandish size and perpetual turgidity.

'Poor Morning has to pee on the carom,' Jorge said, padding off to the shower. In the corner, Lon scratched his ear with a foot.

'Hey, wait for me,' Barry said. 'Last time you used up all the hot water.'

Barry quickly hopped out of his trousers. Suddenly, there was an ear-splitting sound: the entire team froze; as soon as Barry had dropped his trousers, each person's mouth had opened in a horn-like scream. Eyes wide, rigid fingers pointing, the team continued its otherworldly bellow. Barry realised that Bumblemore's spell had been engaged, and quickly pulled up his trousers again. The bellowing stopped, and the team continued on as before, ignorant of what had just happened. Madame Cootch didn't really understand why Barry insisted on showering after everybody else had gone, but she acquiesced without comment. After all, Barry was a celebrity.

Barry was now the school's hood ornament. He had to show up for a certain percentage of classes, no more than six out of every ten. And he would have to take the A.U.K. exams, of course – even Bumblemore couldn't handle three hundred trainee wizards in full-on rebellion. But book-work was strictly optional. 'Just sit at the back and try not to get stupidity all over the other students,' McGoogle had said.

According to *Barry Trotter: Even Satan Couldn't Write This Poorly*,[29] Barry's fifth year was 'the absolute nadir of scholarship in the school's already-chequered history ... Students in name only, these pea-brained, shiftless turds meandered about, scratching themselves and poking each other with their otherwise useless wands.'

---

[29] This quickie exposé. ghostwritten by Filth, was released during the height of Trottermania. It was quickly pulled off the shelves after parents complained about the photos of Bumblemore's vinyl sex dungeon. Ever since it has circulated *sub rosa* among the more depraved and devious Trotter fans. The author obtained his copy from a very shady character on eBuy; it is obviously authentic, because it occasionally emits sex-type sounds.

Several students did so poorly in their A.U.K.s that the Ministry felt obliged to put them to death.

In the years since, it had become fashionable to blame Barry for all of this. But as with other titanic human calamities – like World War One or platform shoes – an unlucky confluence of history was responsible. While Barry's example certainly didn't encourage scholarship, that year marked the introduction of cheap wand-projected video games. Hogwash students spent thousands of formerly productive hours manoeuvring pixellated versions of themselves, in the false belief that this was a real-world accomplishment.

As befits a sparkling, fantastical world where dragons appear on TV hawking heartburn medication, wizard video games can strike outsiders as incredibly tedious. But when one can conjure any object, fly about, and change one's sexual organs at will, going to the shops to pick up a loaf of bread is the stuff of dreams. Starting that year, everybody in the mouldering castle walked around with aching thumbs, their eyes watering from countless hours staring at a bedroom wall, upon which the picture was projected, life-size.

Not everybody was afflicted; Ermine Cringer remained aloof, and absurdly active in school affairs. Mrs McGoogle, who operated on the same rigid go-getter frequency, had noticed this and asked Ermine's help planning the school's annual Halloween party.

It was a thankless task, doomed to failure. For magical folk, the entire concept of Halloween is irritating and useless. Ghosts, goblins, a rotting hand reaching up through a fresh grave to drag you down to Hell – all these things were quotidian details for witches and wizards. For them, Halloween is like a holiday celebrating public transport, or skin. The only people who attended the school's annual Halloween party were Muddle-born first-years – and those devoted to making fun of them.

The parties were invariably wretched, boys huddled on one side of the Great Hall, girls on the other, and great puddles of punch and flat fizzy drinks in the middle. Even the sound system was awful, an ancient set of palm-sized squawkboxes installed high up on the walls some time before World War Two. Music was intermittent, and always punctuated by random bursts of ear-splitting static.

Yet there were heroes. Occasionally some brave lass or lad would pretend to be so taken with whatever crappy pop tune that was oozing out into the ether that she or he would risk a syncopated sally out into No Man's Land, only to return, alone and blushing, before the end of the song. Ah, the humanity!

There had been periodic attempts to do away with the holiday altogether, not because of the deaths – those were unremarkable, simply part of the school's annual cull – but on the grounds that it was demeaning to magical folk. Dorco Malfeasance and his cronies were circulating a petition (in blood, of course) to abolish it.

One day during lunch, the Malfeasance clot slimed over to the table where Barry and his pals were sitting.

'Anybody w-want to sign our p-petition?' Panties Parkinsons quavered.

'No way,' Ferd said. 'The last time I signed one of those, Ermine forced me to save my own poo for a term.'[30] He shuddered at the memory of it.

Dorco pushed forward. 'Sign my petition, Trotter, or I'll give you a demerit,' he demanded. Snipe had made Dorco a Perfect, and the pointy-headed ponce wielded his new authority like an electrified club that shot bullets. 'We're outlawing Halloween.'

'Hand it over,' Barry said. 'I won't be here for it anyway.' As Barry signed, he tried not to notice the palpable interest that this last comment had generated.

---

[30] As you doubtless know, Ermine's crusade to fertilise the school's greenhouses with human excrement is exhaustively documented in *Barry Trotter and the Acne of Fire*. A limited scratch 'n' sniff edition published for charity sold out almost immediately.

Chapter Eight

After Dorco had left, Jorge asked, 'Won't be here? Where are you going? Don't you know that's Order night?'

'Well, the Order will have to survive without me,' Barry said. 'I've got a date with an actual girl.'

'What am I, chopped liver?' Ermine asked, mock-huffily. 'How did you manage to get around Bumblemore's alarm?'

'I didn't,' Barry admitted. 'She's a full-Muddle.'

'Wow!' Ferd and Jorge exclaimed. It was every magical boy's greatest fantasy to find out if all the legends were true. Muddles were reputed to be incredibly well-endowed, sexually voracious, all the usual dopey malarkey.

'You'll tell us all about it, won't you?' Ferd said.

'We'll prepare a list of questions,' Jorge said.

Barry shrugged. 'Who knows if I'll get anywhere with her?'

Ferd gave a dismissive puff. 'You? The master of the spells of seduction?'

'Hell, even I'm afraid you'll slip something into my drink,' Jorge added.

Ermine stepped in. 'Shut up, you animals. Barry, I understand. Maybe she's not that kind of girl.'

'Then why on Earth is she dating Barry?' the twins chorused.

These guys are arseholes, Barry thought, and not for the first time either. 'Get stuffed,' he said, and left to general taunting.

Actually, it wasn't a date – Barry had agreed to eat dinner over at Bea's house so her gran could meet this strange boy that had been sending all the letters. On the night, Barry was nervous and distracted; Valumart took advantage of this to try to knot Barry's tie into a noose and hang him with it.

'Hey, *Schweinehund*! *Halt!* Knock it off !' Barry said as the Dork Lord ran into the closet. Barry felt a little remorseful for speaking so sharply. 'Sorry, Terry, I'm just really busy at the moment. If my date goes badly, then you can hang me.'

As Barry rolled out of the school and into Hogs-bleede (he was wearing some new seven-league roller-blades), an early death didn't seem so bad. Bea had told him that her gran hated Visigoths, Ostrogoths and Parthians. He didn't know what any of those were – should've listened in Professor Bunns's class – but they all sounded vaguely wizardy. And he, Barry, was only the most famous wizard since that dude from Oz. How could she not hate him? Nevertheless, Barry was determined to do his best; he rolled up to the house right on time, which was nothing short of miraculous – Barry had been born late, and become tardier from there.

Bea opened the door. 'Hi, Barry! Come in.' She was wearing a nice outfit, and for the first time Barry noticed her figure. This had the effect of 400,000,000 volts of electricity[31] coursing through his body.

'Stop talking and kiss me again,' Barry wanted to yell, but instead simply slumped against the doorframe as he rolled inside.

'Are you okay?' Bea said. 'Aren't you feeling well? Too much steak and kidney?'

'I'm . . . fine . . . it's just that . . . your . . .' Your what? Breasts? Hips? Legs? Barry tried to think. 'Your house . . . is amazing . . .' This was the perfect cover for his clumsiness; he was genuinely shocked by what he saw inside – and it takes a lot to shock someone whose world is filled with dragons and assassination attempts and talking fruit.

Behind Bea was a large room with a pool in the middle of it. Lush vegetation hung everywhere; below, the floors were cool marble and intricate tiling. In one corner, behind the pool, a tall old woman wrapped in a

---

[31] Give or take a couple.

bedsheet stood over a sheep that looked like it had been
attacked by a leopard.[32]

'How do the auspices look, Gran?' Bea called.
'Dinner still on?'

'Not good,' came a slightly scratchy voice – now
Barry knew where Bea had got hers from. 'I don't like
the look of this liver, but since he's here, he can stay.'

'You're such a worrier,' Bea said loudly, then turned
back to Barry 'That's Gran, obviously,' she said. 'She
was reading the auspices. Can I take your coat?'

Barry offered it, then Bea said, 'Could you take off
your shoes? Gran doesn't want the tiles to get damaged.
They cost a packet.'

Barry looked down and saw a mosaic of a watchdog.
Above it was written, *'Cave Canem'*. The dog looked a
little like Lon.

'It means, "Beware of the dog",' Bea said. 'We don't
have one, but robbers won't know that.' Barry hadn't
moved. 'What's the matter, Barry?'

'Er . . . I'm not wearing socks.' Suddenly, Barry's feet

---

[32] It should come as a surprise to no one that persistent reports of
a big cat in Gloucestershire have a connection to the Measly
twins. All I'm really at liberty to say is this: some teenagers aren't
responsible enough to have pets, and if you don't want a pet any
more, you should find a proper home for it, not just dump it out
on the M5 outside Tredington.

struck him as the most disgusting objects in the universe. I must really like this girl, he thought.

'Hm.' Bea considered for a moment. 'I know. You can wear some of my grandpa's. Be back in a second.'

Before Barry could cry out, 'Don't leave me here with your weird gran!' Bea had skittered off. Remain calm, Barry thought. Must remain calm. But his serenity crumbled immediately when the old woman finished smearing Nutella on a small statuette, turned and called, '*Salve*, young man.'

What was that, Latin? The only Latin Barry knew was the garbled kind used in spells, and that might actually be dangerous to speak. So he waved, and hoped that the cretinous smile plastered across his face did the trick.

'How do you like my decorating?' she called across the pool. 'I couldn't afford a bigger house, so I bought this one and hired a hippie to expand it magically. Got it for a song – nobody wanted it. Gingerbread is expensive to maintain, so I got vinyl siding. And there had been some unpleasantness, too – apparently an old she-hippie used to cook children in the kitchen ... Until she got cooked herself, the Parthian!' She gave a papery sort of laugh, which Barry took as a cue to smile even harder. 'I didn't care, I'm not superstitious ... Where's Bea? She shouldn't leave her guest. Anyway, you two make yourselves at home, I'm just sacrificing to the household gods.'

After an eternity, Bea returned with some thick oatmeal-coloured socks.

'Thanks,' Barry said, then added quietly, 'Is your gran ... sane?'

'Oh, yes,' Bea said. 'I mean, no, not really, but she's not dangerous. Unless she decides you're a Parthian or an Ostrogoth or something.'

'And how does she decide that?' Barry asked.

'I've never been able to tell ... Anyway, here are your socks.'

Barry put them on. He immediately felt like his feet were covered in chilled oyster meat; no doubt about it, the socks were haunted. But Barry was determined to appear a man of the world, so he kept on smiling.

'We're eating right away,' Bea said. 'After about nine, my gran's a zombie.'

'Excellent!' Barry whispered excitedly. 'Do you make her do stuff? I made my first ones this summer, out of my aunt and—'

'What are you talking about? You say the strangest things sometimes,' Bea said as they padded left, to the dining room. 'I mean, I knew that wizards were weird – once I figured out what Gran meant by "hippies" – but I think you're particularly so. Are you? Be honest.' She

Chapter Eight

saw the pained look that leapt on to Barry's face, and added hastily, 'Don't worry. I think I like it.'

Thank God, Barry thought, feeling his stomach settle back into his body. 'It's not my fault, it's what we learn in school.'

'I think you add your own special something to it.'

'Hey, Bea?' Barry whispered.

'Yes?'

'Why is your gran wearing a bedsheet?'

Bea laughed. 'It's a toga, silly. Roman clothes, doubles as a blanket or, in a real fix, a sail. by the way, that's my grandfather,' she said, pointing to a marble bust standing in an alcove. 'He ran a chemist's.'

'Okay, then, why is your gran wearing a toga? Is there going to be an orgy?' That sounded too hopeful, Barry thought. Or judgemental, maybe? *Christ.* 'I mean, I'm okay if there is – or isn't – I mean, I'm cool with whatever.'

'No!' Bea blushed.

'Orgying is all I really know about Romans. And vomitoriums.' Bea suddenly looked like she could use one of those. Changing the subject was suddenly the most important thing in the universe. 'Tell me about your grandfather,' Barry pleaded.

'I don't know very much,' Bea said, as they entered

~ 146 ~

the dining room. 'Grampy Thompson died when I was small.'

'Like your parents?'

'Yes, everybody seemed to,' Bea said matter-of-factly. 'It was a mortar-and-pestle explosion. Tragic, really – the odds against something like that are astronomical.' They entered a big room. Oil lamps stationed every few feet gave a flickering, smoky light; Barry could make out some couches surrounding a low table. Bea gestured to a saffron-coloured couch. 'Take a seat.'

Barry sat.

'Lie down, I mean,' Bea said. 'We eat Roman-style, big surprise.'

'Oh.' Would he do the right thing even once tonight? To cover up, he said, 'So was your grandfather magical? It sounds like it.'

'No, he was just a druggist. But he knew a lot of hipp— wizards, I mean,' she said. 'They'd come in, and he'd mix things for them. He was mixing something for your school's armourer when the explosion took place.'

'Something for Zed exploded? There's a surprise,' Barry said, then thought it seemed a little too jolly. 'Sorry – I didn't mean to joke. Zed's a bloodthirsty prat.'

'Yes, well, it killed my father, too. He was upstairs,

asleep,' Bea said. 'No magic in our family, just a marked laziness.' Barry found this immensely attractive.

'Me, too,' Barry said, laughing. 'Maybe we're related?' The conversation suddenly got weird again. In his desperation, Barry picked the worst conversational gambit imaginable. 'So, what happened to your mum?' He realised the true horror of asking this the moment it left his mouth.

'She fell down a manhole when I was four. We were walking down the street together, and down she went. I don't remember it. We're lazy, and also a bit distractable.'

He was just a clod, that's what he was. 'I'm sorry,' Barry said. 'And I'm sorry I mentioned it. My parents are dead, too, so I know how it feels.'

'Oh yeah?' Bea asked, picking at a tray of olives that sat between them. 'How did they die? I mean, under normal circumstances, I wouldn't ask, but given that you did, I think it's only fair.'

'Of course,' Barry said. He'd never been so glad to share this information. 'They were killed by Lord Valumart, in his quest for world domination. Valumart's the most powerful Dork wizard there ever was—'

'Yes, I remember you talking about him,' Bea said. 'World domination, now. You didn't tell me that part before. He's the character who's always trying to kill you, right?'

'Right. He tried to kill me then, too, but it didn't work. I just got this scar, see?' Barry lifted up his fringe to reveal the now-famous interrobang.

'Oh, wow,' Bea said. 'I assumed that was just bad acne.'

'I had that, too,' Barry said, without thinking. 'Acne of Fire.'

Bea's smile grew a bit brittle. So many difficult topics. 'Oh,' she said.

Just as the conversation had ground to a complete halt, and both Bea and Barry's skins seemed to be getting a little smaller with every passing moment, Mrs Thompson arrived. Seating herself at the remaining couch, Mrs Thompson clapped her hands. Immediately a train of people carrying salvers streamed in. They placed them on the table, removing silver tops to reveal dishes that Barry had never seen before (and the smells were new, too). They poured goblets of wine, and handed one to each.

Mrs Thompson pointed to each dish in turn. 'Swallow cloacas ... Roasted tips of goat's penis ... Lamb's thymuses ... Wren toes ... Pig vulvas ...'

'Yum,' Bea said, then to Barry, 'Gran's really pulling

out all the stops, Barry. We *never* have pigs' vulvas. Not even at Christmas.'

'Dig in,' Mrs Thompson said. Barry noticed that she was wearing her hair in weird, tight little curls he'd never seen the like of before. Everything was so strange – the clothes, the couches, the servants lurking in the shadows, the bizarre paintings on every wall. It was as if Bea lived on Mars.

Barry looked confused. 'Mrs Thompson?'

'Yes, Barry? Here, try some twice-baked goose anus.'

'Thank you,' Barry said, taking an oozy morsel and trying to look enthused. 'Where's the cutlery?'

'In the kitchen!' Gran said. 'You're eating with Romans, Barry!'

Bea raised a greasy hand, and wiggled her digits. 'Use your fingers!'

'Okay,' Barry said. Muddles!

'Bea,' Mrs Thompson said, 'help our guest with his napkin.'

Bea reached over and spread Barry's napkin out in front of him. 'Here, Barry. That way you won't stain the couch. And you can put especially good bits in it, to take home for later.'

'Sorry, Mrs Thompson,' Barry said. 'We eat differently at school.'

'I'm sure you do,' Mrs Thompson said, her face

already smeary with fermented fish sauce. 'Barbarians with twigs, the lot of you.'

'Now, Gran, that's not fair,' Bea said, working over something visceral with obvious relish. Then she said to Barry, 'I bet they don't feed you like this at Hogwash!'

'No, they don't!' Barry forced a smile as he tentatively prodded something that looked like a deflated eyeball. He had never wanted a ham sandwich so much in his life.

'Barry,' Mrs Thompson said. 'I'm sure my granddaughter has told you that I dislike hippies – *wizards*. That is only partially true. I dislike Ostrogoths, Visigoths and Parthians. Standing up in chariots shooting arrows! It's unmanly!' Mrs Thompson seemed to lose her train of thought, then got it back. 'But wizards, I pity. They aren't responsible for their disgusting customs. And it's clear that they suffer grave deficiencies in the brain department.'

Barry tried to keep his face a pleasant mask, but some outrage must've slipped through. Bea noticed it.

'Gran, that's a bit sweeping, don't you think?'

'I mean no disrespect. The gods give each of us strengths and weaknesses, and it's clear that magic is the gods' consolation prize for when they have run out of intellect.

'What's worse is how irresponsible they are. Wizards

~ 151 ~

fix sporting events, they make people fall in love with people they shouldn't. They're always throwing around curses, willy-nilly,' Mrs Thompson said. 'That doesn't create goodwill, you know.'

'I'm sure Barry's never done anything like that,' Bea said. 'Have you, Barry?'

Mrs Thompson's quick reply saved Barry from the lie. 'I have met some good wizards and I've met some bad ones,' she said, 'but I've never met one who didn't use his unfair advantage whenever it suited. That's what magic is, unfair, and if you don't mind me saying so, I think the world would be a better place without it. Fairness doesn't exist in nature, and that's why we have to work for it in human society. On the one side there's civilisation, and on the other there's magic.'

'Not that Gran's above hiring a spell, when it comes to decorating,' Bea said.

'Only when there's no other way,' Mrs Thompson said. 'This isn't just blind prejudice, I know what wizards are like. I work for an alchemist – perhaps you've heard of him: Roger Bacon's great-great-great-great-great grandnephew, Canadian. Horrible, deceitful, disgusting twit,' Mrs Thompson said. 'He blows his nose into his cauldron. Care for some pheasant embryos?'

'Never heard of him,' Barry said, mouth full. He was trying to fill up on bread.

'You're fortunate.'

'Gran,' Bea said. 'I keep telling you: not all wizards are like your boss.'

Mrs Thompson appeared not to hear her grand-daughter. 'Barry,' she asked, 'do you believe in prophecy?'

'No,' Barry said, and had four years of classes with Madame Tralala to prove it.

'Well, I do,' Mrs Thompson said. 'But one doesn't have to read the entrails to know that trouble's brewing.'

'Here it comes,' Bea said, rolling her eyes.

'What's coming? Valumart?' Barry asked.

'History teaches us,' Mrs Thompson said, 'that any group that tries to hold itself apart from everybody else – to lord it over them – is heading for trouble.'

Barry didn't follow. Bea said, 'She's talking about wizards.'

Mrs Thompson nodded. 'Sooner or later, this system of separate and unequal must come to an end. And when it does, there will be great bloodshed. The skies will crack open, the rivers will turn to Lucozade. The beasts of the field and the fishes of the sea will change places. A mother in Surrey will give birth to a baby she doesn't really like. Sleazy parodies of children's books will appear on the bestseller lists. All this and more has been foretold.'

'Yeah, right,' Bea said, making the 'she's crazy' sign. 'Parodies.'

'I don't know,' Barry said sceptically. 'Look at Hogsbleede. Muddles have been living peacefully with magical people since – well, for ever, probably.'

'I agree with Barry,' Bea said. 'I think you're being a pessimist.' Barry didn't know what that word meant, but he liked the first part of the sentence.

The old woman seemed to become disheartened. '*Virginibus puerisque canto*,' she mumbled, giving a wave expressing 'I give up.' Mrs Thompson held up her goblet, and a man stepped out of the shadows to fill it. She saw Barry's confused look. 'Are you surprised that I know Latin?' she asked.

'Was that what that was?' Barry said. 'I thought my ears were drunk.'

Mrs Thompson laughed. 'Taught myself. Picked it up off the streets. It's useful – kept me working all these years. A Muddle that knows Latin is rare indeed, the wizards see to that.'

Barry harrumphed; the wine had made him a bit bold. 'Wizards don't care—'

Bea leapt into the breach. What Barry didn't know[33] wouldn't hurt him. 'I'm learning it,' she said proudly.

'*Book* Latin,' Mrs Thompson sniffed. 'Barry, do you know any?'

'Latin?' This question was like asking a goat if he knew badminton. 'Just whatever they teach us for spells.'

'Would you like to learn some?'

Well, no, Barry thought, but it was probably better than eating. 'Okay,' he said, and tried to look happy about it.

Mrs Thompson pulled a spiral notebook from between the cushions of her couch.

'Gran! You planned this!' Bea scolded.

'Maybe I did,' Mrs Thompson said, with a sly smile. 'It would be very helpful to have a young wizard as famous as Barry—'

Finally! Barry thought, but resisted the urge to tease Bea.

'— involved in our group. He can spread the word; surely some of the eggheads up at Hogwash are smart enough to realise that it's their only hope for survival.'

---

[33] – that the last boy she had brought home for dinner had been crucified –

'Group?' Barry asked, with unpleasant memories of the old, Communist Lon.

'We're going to re-establish the Roman Empire,' Mrs Thompson said. 'I'll explain it later. First, some Latin.'

'Gran, I've told you, you learned it wrong—'

'Shh, Bea. You stick to your fancy Latin, and I'll teach Barry the living, breathing tongue of the people. He's going to have to learn it after we take over, anyway.'

'Is that foretold, too?' Barry asked.

'Well, practically,' Mrs Thompson said, then showed Barry a handwritten page. 'Have a look at this. Nouns – people, places, things – are arranged in something called "descensions". Because when you write them in a list, they descend down the page, you see? And verbs – words for actions – are organised into "conflagrations", to commemorate the Great Fire of Rome. Dear Nero was framed, the gods rest his soul.' She stopped and looked at Barry. 'Is any of this ringing a bell?'

'Gran, give Barry a break,' Bea said. 'He goes to school all day, sort of.' Then, 'Sorry – sometimes she gets like this.'

'I think Barry's enjoying it. Aren't you, Barry?'

What was the right answer? To escape, Barry did something by accident-on-purpose. 'Sorry, I think I got food on your book,' he said.

When in Rome . . .

'That's all right, a little rotting fish sauce never hurt anything. All nouns have cases, which determines how they're used in a sentence. The cases are Normative, Dated, Accusatory, Aberrative, Vocational and Locational. The Normative case is the common one, what everybody uses normally.'

'What Gran means by "everybody" is actually "nobody",' Bea said. 'She's the only one who speaks Latin around here.'

'That's not true,' Mrs Thompson said. 'Many of us in the group speak it during meetings.'

'That's why nothing ever gets done,' Bea said.

'Bea doesn't approve of my activism,' Mrs Thompson said. 'Although she'll benefit along with everybody else when the Empire is re-established. Where were we?'

'The Dated,' Barry said. At least it was saving him from having to eat the food.

'Right. The Dated is simply that – you never use it unless you want to sound old-fashioned. The Accusatory case – that's nasty. If you're in a fight, you use the Accusatory.'

Barry thought for a second. Some of this information was getting in, in spite of his best efforts. 'So, like, any word could be a swear word? If you put it into the Accusatory, right?'

'Right!'

Chapter Eight

'Gran,' Bea piped up, 'what's the Aberrative case used for? I always forget.'

'Oh, I hope you never have to use that, Bea,' Mrs Thompson said. 'That's reserved for insane people.'

'Ah.' Bea tucked into another pig's vulva.

Mrs Thompson turned back to Barry. 'Now, the Vocational is rare – it's like jargon, or technical talk. And the Locational is just for maps. Now,' Mrs Thompson said, shutting the notebook, 'about this group.'

'Great,' Bea said, plainly embarrassed over how her grandmother was hijacking the evening. 'If anybody needs me, I'll be asleep over here.'

'It's called People United for the Return of the Empire, or PURE. If you have to be told which Empire is worth returning to, you're not PURE material,' Mrs Thompson said.

'Interesting,' Barry said, by which he meant 'crazy'.

'I founded it several years ago. The group's goal is obvious: to avoid the coming battle between Muddles and magical folk by bringing back the Roman Empire as quickly as possible, by any means necessary.'

'So far the only means necessary have been weekly dinners,' Bea said, smirking.

'Bea is a cynical youth,' Mrs Thompson said. 'But I

~ 158 ~

have a feeling Barry's not so cynical. I have a feeling that you, Barry, are a high-minded young man.'

Barry stopped himself from laughing out loud by stuffing a large bread pellet into the back of his throat. He nodded, eyes watering.

'Magicians existed in the Roman world – but they were like plumbers, tradesmen. They didn't hide them-selves away in their own secret world . . . Don't worry, Barry, magical people would have their place – but they would be punished, too, if they did anything wrong. As it is, you people monitor yourselves; which is to say, you don't monitor yourselves at all! Under the Roman Empire it was different; magicians were respected, but they knew their place. Now, they secretly run the world, and anybody can see what a cock-up it is.'

Barry felt obliged to voice some sort of objection. 'Well, Mrs Thompson, I don't know—'

The old woman didn't let him finish – which was lucky, because Barry hadn't gone so far as to actually form a thought. 'Do you like the way the world is? You must be joking! Do you honestly think anything from our current time will last? Of course it won't. We build cheaply and furtively, like thieves in the night. We use up everything in the pursuit of trifles. We waste everything and leave nothing but rubbish behind.'

Now it was Bea's turn to interject. 'But Gran, most of

the world is built by Muddles. How is that the fault of magical people?'

'Magical people are lazy – no, Barry, don't try to deny it.'

'I wasn't,' Barry said, in vino veritas-ing.

'It's not their fault. Who wouldn't get lazy, if you could conjure up anything you'd like, just like that?' Mrs Thompson snapped her fingers, and a fleck of partridge testicle hit Barry in the neck. He decided not to notice. 'That's fine, I don't mind. But your laziness has infected us Muddles . . . That school of yours is the only thing around here that will last, and I bet we'll find some way to blow that to smithereens, too.'

'Gran, I think you've had too much wine,' Bea said.

'And I think you've had too little!' Mrs Thompson said.

'Don't be like that in front of our guest,' Bea said, a pleading note in her voice. 'I read a joke today, Barry. Would you like to hear it? It's about magic.'

'Okay,' Barry said.

'A fraud magician went on a trip to Greece. When he got back, a man asked, "Hey, how's my family back home?" "They're all fine, especially your father." "But my father's been dead for ten years!" the man said. So the magician said, "Ah, clearly you do not know your *real* father."'

Mrs Thompson collasped with laughter. 'That's a good one,' she panted. 'Three hundred AD. That's when people really knew how to laugh.'

A small brown owl flew into the room, alighting on the back of Mrs Thompson's couch. It began to peep.

'Oh, Hades, that's my peeper,' Mrs Thompson said. 'I wonder what Canadian wants at this hour.' She unwrapped the message. 'A rush.' She turned to Barry. 'Apparently your school armourer and gamekeeper have got into a fight, and the gamekeeper's a bleeder.'

'As long as he's not a breeder,' Barry said. No one laughed. 'You'd laugh if you knew him. You wouldn't want Hafwid reproducing. His half-brother is a giant pile of trail mix named Gorp.'

Nobody quite knew what to make of this. 'I'm afraid I have to go into work,' Mrs Thompson said, 'which means that Barry has to go home.' Mrs Thompson gave a signal, and the people around the room started clearing the table.

'You'll come back again, won't you?' Bea asked. 'Gran hasn't scared you away, has she?'

'Yes,' Barry said. 'I mean, no. I mean: I'll come back.'

'Good. Practise your Latin and next time we'll translate something a little dirty.' Mrs Thompson wiped her hands on a napkin, then shook Barry's hand. 'Nice meeting you, young man.' Then, as she left the room,

'Maybe I'll invite you to a PURE meeting some time. Would you like that?'

'Gran! Give it a rest. *Please.*' Mrs Thompson smiled and walked out.

'Do you want to take anything home?' Bea asked.

'No!' Barry said, with just a trifle more emphasis than was strictly necessary. 'I mean – I'm really full.'

'Well, then . . .' Bea and Barry stood nervously for a moment, until Bea said, 'I'll walk you to the door.'

They stood in the atrium. 'So,' Barry said, hopping as he put on a shoe, 'what are you going to do tonight?'

'Study, I suppose,' Bea said. 'Gran's quizzing me on chemistry tomorrow.'

'That's like alchemy, right?'

'Yeah, except no religion.'

'Rather you than me,' Barry said.

Bea suddenly thought Barry might think she was too clever for him, so she added, 'First I'm going to watch *Wizard's Funniest Home Videos*.[34] There's this one where a

---

[34] Barry and Bea's voluminous correspondence had convinced Mrs Thompson to lift the ban on television. She'd rather have Bea obsessed with TV than with rascals like Barry; and whatever Bea might learn from the box, it might counteract or dilute whatever pernicious rot Barry was telling her. Of course the best thing would be a return to more wholesome activities like training Desmond, but Gran knew that once the hormones

wizard tries to use a cashpoint, but he thinks it's going to eat his hand. The first time I saw that, I nearly wet myself.' That was perhaps a little too salt-of-the-earth, Bea thought. 'Not that that's a problem for me or anything.' Oh God, that was worse!

For the first time that night, Barry felt like he wasn't the only uncomfortable one. Bea had probably been just as nervous as he was! He tried to think of something both funny and comforting to say, but as usual his mind was filled with one thought that he couldn't say. So he leaned over and kissed her.

Bea, surprised, gave a small cry. Luckily, most of it went into Barry's mouth. She knocked over an umbrella stand in the shape of Justinian's head. They both scrambled to pick everything up.

'Whoops,' Barry said, holding up a piece of the nose which had chipped of.

'It's okay!' Bea said, thoroughly flustered. 'It's a modern reproduction.'

'Everything all right?' Mrs Thompson called from another room.

'Yes!' Bea and Barry chorused, a moment too quickly.

kick in, everybody goes insane. And stays that way until age 55 or so.

Bea opened the door; she wanted Barry to stay, but she also wanted him to leave before something happened that was really embarrassing.

'Thanks for coming!' she said. 'I'll write!'

'So will I!' Barry said, and the door closed. His heart leapt and fell at once; he had made it through the evening in one piece – but he wanted the night to go on, too. I bet she'll love Tuna's poem, Barry thought as he tightened up his rollerblades.

He hadn't gone far when he nearly ran into a street person selling newspapers. J.G. Rollins had ploughed some of her new riches into founding a weekly paper that Muddles down on their luck could sell to make a few pounds. It was boring as all hell – the pictures didn't even swear.

'Hey!' the guy said. 'Watch it!'

Barry's good cheer had swelled into unfamiliar feelings of compassion. Skidding to a stop, he pulled out his money-bag. 'How many do you have there?'

'About ten,' the man said.

'I'll take 'em,' Barry said, and handed over twice as much gold as necessary.

'Thanks,' the man said, handing him three papers.

'You're welcome,' Barry said, noticing with an inward chuckle that he'd been scammed. 'Get inside, okay? It's dangerous out here.' The Muddle ghetto at night was no place for carbon-based life forms.

'I will,' the man said, sniffing. The night was clear and chilly. He pulled out a new stack of papers.

Whistling, Barry rolled into the night. He did his best with the constant potholes, nearly face-planting more than once when a streetlamp was out. And he noticed that Hogsbleede produced an incredible amount of dog poo for a town its size. Barry heaved a sigh of relief when the zoo was behind him, and he was safely in the magical side of town.

Rollerblading uphill to the school, Barry stopped for a moment and looked back at Hogsbleede. So many sleazy bars, pawn shops and cheque-cashing stores. So many prostitutes and hustlers, drunks and homeless. So many Muddles trying to squeeze a life's worth of pleasure in their nights, when their days were filled by working for people like Barry – people who could change their lives with a wave of the wand . . . What a tip Hogsbleede was – they should probably just nuke it and start again. And yet, Barry thought, for that night at least a small part of it was beautiful, and her name was Bea.

Chapter Nine

POWER OF ATTORNEY

꩜

From the moment they'd seen Underage at the beginning-of-term feast in the Great Hall, the students had been licking their chops. Barely three feet tall, and just under five stone, Underage was in no position to exercise any authority, and the students knew it. Tormenting teachers was a grand Hogwash tradition, and anything, up to and including lethal force, was tolerated, as long as it was truly witty.

Underage had ratcheted student hatred up steadily further with a series of decrees. These infantile pronouncements appeared in more and profusion; some were taunts, others stroppy demands. After every girl in the school was forced to let Underage plait their hair, the students had gone into overdrive. As a team of sixth-years was investigating whether child labour laws indeed ended at the school's grounds (as Bumblemore had insisted), the rest of the students were enchanting every portrait in the school to call Underage 'diarrhoea-head'.

Still, Underage had proved herself a worthy adversary, matching every student prank with an even more childish one of her own. A student might give her a spit-bubble jinx, causing her to dribble one out every third word. Then the class would sit down at the beginning of the next class, only to find that their chairs had been booby-trapped with an *Incontinentio* hex.

'Oh, this is awful,' Ermine said one class, as Underage ran around the room being chased by a flaming paper aeroplane. 'Don't you agree, Barry?' Ermine pointed her wand and evaporated the plane, to a lusty chorus of boos.

'Whatever,' Barry said, not looking up from his comic book. As long as he wasn't bothered, he didn't care. Dork Arts and Crafts was a useless class, always had been. Like his prowess on the Quiddit field, eluding Valumart came naturally.

'But what if you meet up with He-Who-Smells?' Ermine said.

'Like this morning, you mean?' Barry said, flipping the page. 'I was shaving, and when I went to squirt some lather on my hand, a cobra came out.'

'Did it try to bite you?'

'No, it was a friendly cobra,' Barry said sarcastically. 'Of course it did! I killed it with my toothpaste cap.'

'Nice one,' Colin Creepy said, edging his nose in the direction of Barry's rectum.

'I don't know if I believe you,' Ermine said.

Underage had begun to natter on about one of her obsessions: how to tell if a boy likes you, using the letters of his name. Nobody paid much attention. It started to snow directly over Cyril Broadbottom, and some Silverfish students laughed.

'Class! Class!' Underage, all knees and elbows topped by frizzy blonde hair, attempted to re-establish order. 'Lee! Get back in your chair! Sit down!' This was nearly impossible, since Lee Jardin had been turned into a dolphin. (Luckily he was wearing a reverse-scuba outfit.) 'Farters! Tinkle-bottoms!' Underage swore clumsily, then ran over to the closest student and kicked him.

'Ow! Son of a witch!'

Barry looked up, annoyed. It was so loud, he couldn't follow the plot of his comic.

Ermine saw the look on Barry's face. 'Whatever you're about to do, please don't.'

'Too late, I'm already waving. If I stop now, I might

pull a muscle,' Barry said, pointing his wand at Underage, who disappeared in a flash of light.

'What did you do?' Ermine said angrily. 'She was just a kid.'

'She's being raised by the centaurs now,' Barry said.

'Oh, she'll like that,' Colin gushed. 'She always liked horses. Perhaps she'll become another Catherine the Great.'

As Ermine fumed, Barry stood up and bowed from the waist. After the clapping died down, the class was presented with a dilemma: faced with freedom, what should they do? Run outside? Mass-evaporate to Hogsbleede and go on a spree? Play strip Top-Trumps? They were, as people often are, utterly unnerved and paralysed by their options. So the rest of that class period was spent in nervous titters and uncomfortable fidgeting.

The next time they filed into Dork Arts and Crafts, Headmister Bumblemore was sitting at the head of the room. There was an unnatural hush. After everyone had taken their seats, Bumblemore began to speak.

'Class, it is very immature – and wasteful – to keep burning through Dork Arts teachers like a cheap pair of trainers. At this point, I'm seriously considering setting up a work-release programme with Aztalan.'

Chapter Nine

'Cool!' Dorco Malfeasance said.[35]

'What on Earth do you *do* to them? Don't answer, I already know. There are hidden cameras installed throughout the school.' Bumblemore went on, paying no attention to the gasp that echoed throughout the classroom. He was lying, but they didn't know that. 'I know this is the way things have always been done at Hogwash. We torment you, you torment us, the Cycle of Life continues. But I tell you that teachers do not grow on trees! Torment them, yes; expose them as weretrouts if you like; but teleporting them to the Forsaken Forest to be raised by centaurs – even though that's a nice bit of magic, I admit – is going too far. Do you know that when we found her, Professor Underage had plaited the hair of every centaur in the Forest? They were enraged; it will be centuries before they trust wizards again.

'Hogwash isn't just about magic,' Bumblemore said. 'We are also trying to teach you about life. Now, during

[35] His dad had recently been sent to Aztalan's minimum-security wing, after using a Time-Twister to manipulate the stock market. Mr Malfeasance's letters home were filled with details of the place, which was more like a hotel for the slightly naughty than an authentic prison. 'It's quite broadening,' Ludicrous had written. 'The old adage is true: "Cellmate" really *is* just another name for a friend you don't know yet.'

Power of Attorney

life, will you be able simply to teleport someone? Plainly not – ours is not a consequence-free world, no matter who we are.' Bumblemore looked squarely at Barry, who had given up trying to look blameless and was reading his comic book. 'On that note, I'm forced to admit that Professor McGoogle has awarded five points to Grittyfloor because she thought ex-Professor Underage was "a noxious little rugrat". But that doesn't excuse it!'

Bumblemore's empty hands mimed making a balloon animal. Barry looked up, thought it looked like some form of palsy at a very advanced stage, and went back to reading his comic. The old wizard continued to talk.

'It is very difficult indeed to come up with a competent replacement at such short notice. However, I have been informed that your new substitute is extremely well qualified, and will prepare you excellently for your A.U.K.s, which are approaching rapidly. I also hope that he will make you more aware of the consequences of your actions. Whether or not this is the case, please do not destroy him as the cupboard is bare,' Bumblemore said. 'I'm giving you fair warning: do not make me teach this class myself.'

With that, Bumblemore strode out. There were several voices in the hall; the entire class stared at the door to see who – or what – might emerge. Even with

~ 171 ~

all his experiences battling Valumart, and all the creatures that Hafwid was constantly taming (a polite way of saying 'being consumed by'), what walked into the room was utterly beyond Barry's ken.

It was a lawyer.

'Hello, class,' the man said cheerfully, swinging his briefcase up on the desk. He was nearly bald, except for a few brown strands combed over from one ear to the other. About the size and shape of a cigarette machine, he wore thick, tinted glasses. 'My name is Allen Goinkman, and I'm a magical solicitor,' he said, as he shot open the clasps and removed some papers. He handed the papers to Cyril. 'Mr—'

'Broadbottom,' Cyril said meekly.

'Mr Broadbottom, please hand these out to every member of the class.' Mr Goinkman took his gold-plated wand out of his shirt pocket and wrote his name on the board. 'Before we begin, I'll need everyone to fill out this form. It states that, in the event of any injury to me, each one of you is personally liable.'

'What does that mean?' Lee asked.

'It means I can take you, the school and your families for everything they've got,' Goinkman said. Ermine raised her hand. 'Yes, Miss . . . ?'

'Cringer, sir. What happens in the case of your death?'

'You don't want to know, Miss Cringer.' A churlish mumble of annoyance went through the class. Barry slumped down in his seat even more. The best way to deal with this Goinkman dude was to avoid him as much as possible.

As everybody had expected, Cyril tripped, sending the papers flying. There was a single titter. 'Detention, Mr Malfeasance.'

Dorco was outraged. 'Do you know who my father—'

'Yes, and he'll join you on the scrotal press, if you're not careful,' Mr Goinkman said. 'I'm going to be your Dork Arts and Crafts teacher until Christmas, and possibly after. That will be my choice, not yours. I have boned up on all your tricks, and will tolerate none of them.' He opened a desk drawer and stepped back. 'If any of you currently have in your possession anything the least bit objectionable, I'd ask that you deposit it here, where it will be kept until the end of term.'

Barry saw his chance to score points. He felt in his pockets – amazingly, this was the one class of his entire Hogwash career that he didn't have something incredibly alarming on his person. He stood up, marched to the front of the room and dropped the comic into the drawer.

The class was flabbergasted.

'Thank you, Mr . . . ?'

'Trotter,' Barry said, and turned back towards his seat.

'Wha . . . ?' Ermine couldn't believe her eyes.

'Already read it,' Barry whispered, and sat down. Barry's deposit created a stampede. Soon the drawer was filled to overflowing with knuckledusters, zip-guns, homemade shivs, and even some C-4 Lon had swiped off his brothers because it picked up newspaper cartoons.

'Thank you,' Mr Goinkman said, shutting the drawer very carefully. 'On to today's lesson. Notebooks out, please. Write this down: "The most powerful weapon in the magical world is a competent, properly trained lawyer."'

'That's ridiculous,' Peppermint Patil said. 'What about your wand?'

'What about it?' Mr Goinkman said. 'So you kill someone in a duel. Then you go to jail. Sounds to me like you both lost.'

Patil was dubious. 'Doesn't sound very honourable . . .'

'Look, if you want to end up being some tough old witch's familiar, be my guest,' Goinkman said.

Barry raised his hand. The rest of the class remained dumbfounded at his manners.

'Yes, Mr Trotter?' the teacher asked.

'But, Mr Goinkman,' Barry said, 'I'm sure you're right, but I've been fighting Lord Valumart —'

The class gasped at the mention of his name.

'Oh, grow up, people!' Barry said impatiently. 'It's just a name.'

'B-b-but it's copyrighted,' Cyril squeaked.

'By a lawyer!' Mr Goinkman said.

Barry pushed on. 'Valumart's always trying to kill me. What can a lawyer do about that?'

'Sue him!' Mr Goinkman said. 'That son of a witch will think twice if he knows your heirs will take fifty per cent of his assets!'

Barry hadn't thought of that. Suddenly, this made a lot more sense than trying to smack somebody in the breadbasket with a bolt of fuchsia fire.

'Students, write this down. "If anybody tries to kill or injure you, if they try to steal your property, deny your interest, prevent you from working, or even cause you emotional distress, don't jinx 'em – sue 'em!"'

'How about regular wizards?' Dorco said. 'Or instructors? Can you sue them, too?'

'Certainly!' Mr Goinkman said. 'Mr Malfeasance, in exchange for your promise not to sue me over the grievous and entirely inappropriate level of force entailed in your detention, to wit, the application of a scrotal press to your testicles, I will cancel the rest of your detention. Do you agree?'

'Sure,' Dorco said, smiling.

'See how powerful?' Mr Goinkman said. *'That's* Dork Arts and Crafts.'

Goinkman looked at his watch (Barry noticed it was an expensive one). 'Our time is up for today. For the next class, I'd like each one of you to have identified at least one classmate you'd like to sue. Then we'll serve each other papers, and really start learning.'

'This is very odd,' Ritalin said, handing Barry a yellowed piece of parchment. 'You actually sued Dorco for defamation of character?'

'Yeah. He kept saying that Valumart didn't exist, and wasn't trying to kill me. We settled out of court,' Barry said, taking the paper. 'I got to pick five issues out of his collection of *Satyr*.'

For Barry's next session, Dr Ritalin had asked him to look through his personal belongings to see if he had anything relating to his fifth year, or Bea Thompson. As far as Bea was concerned, all Barry found was a single sheet of paper, tucked into the very bottom of his old school trunk.

'This is all you found?' the doctor asked.

'Yes.'

'Seems a little odd, don't you think? No snapshots, no keepsakes ... Personally, I can't help but accumulate that kind of thing. Unless,' Ritalin said, 'it's something I'm trying to forget. Is there something you're trying to forget?'

'That's an idiotic question!' Barry said. 'Even if there was, I would've forgotten it!'

'Touché,' Dr Ritalin said. 'I must ask you to keep in mind that I am not a real doctor and, furthermore, that my brain does not always work properly.'

'That I remember,' Barry said. 'I get fairly constant reminders.'

Ritalin pulled out his pair of reading monocles. 'Let's take a look at this, shall we? "Dear Barry,"' Ritalin read, ' "This is just a short note to acknowledge receipt of your idiotic forgery. Bea would never have 'run off and joined the Visigoths'. Regular bathing was too important to her. Plus, calling me 'Mrs Thompson' throughout was a bit of a giveaway.

"'I know what happened, and I know that you are responsible. It was foretold, in the guts of an ant the evening of the You'll Ball, and many times before. I mistakenly crucified several boys before you, thinking that they were the ones in the prophecy. Oh, well. You can't make an omelette without breaking a few eggs.

"'Bea and I are the last descendants of the great

Thrasyllus, who interpreted the stars for the Divine Augustus. I, too, have the gift of sight; this is how I know that the wizarding world and that of the Muddles must collide. Do not doubt it – what is written by the stars cannot be altered, even by celebrities such as yourself. Many, many wizards will die; my only hope of survival is keeping my magical nature secret.

'"Your future is . . . clouded. However, if you reveal our family secret to anyone, at any time, for any reason, I'll make it my personal mission to clear it up, if you catch my drift. If you do not immediately expunge all traces of your association with Bea and/or myself, I will be forced to tell the whole sordid story to my old boy-friend, Alpo Bumblemore, as well as send a letter to the Armed Forces indicating your immediate availability.

'"To close on a personal note, it pained me deeply to be foretold of your clumsy make-out technique. Stand-ards surely have fallen since I was a girl. Yours truly, Drusilla Thompson."

'Wow,' Ritalin said, after a pause. 'The old lady writes one hell of a letter.'

Chapter Ten
THE YOU'LL BALL

൭ᔕᕽᓗᕽ൭

'So you finally grew a pair and invited her, I see.'
Ermine was reading Bea's latest letter aloud, much to
Barry's embarrassment, and commenting on it. She
continued:

"'At first, Gran didn't want me to go. She slew an ant,
and said that its internal organs foretold real trouble,
especially its liver. Well, I never even knew ants had
livers,'" Bea wrote and Ermine intoned.

"'I cried and threw a tantrum, but nothing worked.
Finally, I threatened to run away, so she gave up,
muttering about omens and how you 'can't outwit the
effing stars'. What a dark old bird she is! Anyway, then
she said, 'You can go, but if he asks you to perform any
spells, mumble something about your period. Men are
always stymied by that.'"

'It's true,' Ermine said, pausing for an observation.

'My father truly believes that letting me borrow the car helps with cramps.'

She parried Barry's grabbing hand and continued reading. '"As soon as I heard that, I was sure Gran liked you. She usually tells me 'Just kick 'em in the crotch and run'! Barry, try not to judge her. It's probably all the mercury she's handled over the years—"'

'Give it back, Erm.' Barry made another grab for his letter.

'Too slow!' Ermine laughed, jumping out of reach. Barry made like he was going to cast a spell. 'No fair! No magic!' Ermine said, laughing and ducking. Ever since Barry had refused to divulge the details of his hot date on Halloween – what they didn't know, they couldn't make fun of, Barry thought sensibly – curiosity had built. Now, at Christmas, it was running at fever pitch.

That was the last thing that Barry wanted. His friends might scare her away – Hell, his friends practically scared *him* away. Ermine might whip out a Mensa test. Lon was sure to sniff her somewhere impolite. Ferd and Jorge might even blow her up; they had done it before, at last year's You'll Ball.[36]

---

[36] The Hogwash You'll Ball was an annual event. It had to be – by the time Christmas rolled around, the student body had been

'Sorry, mate,' Ferd had said, examining the blackened crater where Barry's date had been sitting. 'These nuclear whoopee cushions are more powerful than we thought.'

'Yeah, our bad.' Jorge was going over everything with a Geiger counter. 'On the other hand, there's not much radiation.'

Though Nurse Pommefritte had been able to (mostly) reconstitute the girl from a scrap of flesh blown into the punch bowl, Barry liked Bea too much to risk history repeating itself. So he had kept everything hush-hush. He hadn't intended Ermine to know anything until the dance itself but, as usual at Hogwash, secrecy was impossible.

Christmas Day had started out wonderfully, with a load of presents. Serious had sent him a card with a Gallon in it, which nearly covered the postage due. Ermine had got him a self-help book called *Thirty Days to Not Being an Arseface*, but that was nicely counterbalanced by Hafwid's present, a universal churchkey. This

edified to the very edge of rebellion. It was either a school-sanctioned blowout, or rape and pillage. This was only logical; the You'll Ball, like every other red-letter day in Hogwash's calendar, had originally been the date of a massive town–gown riot. Tradition said the name came from cries of 'You'll be sorry!' uttered by angry townspeople.

magic doohickey meant that no container of liquor –
bottle or can, foreign or domestic – would be able to
resist him. And Mrs Measly had shown that there were
no hard feelings about Lon's accident by knitting him a
knobbly macramé thong.

'I think my mum fancies you,' Ferd had said, after
Barry had worn it down to the Grittyfloor Common
Room.

'Your mum fancies everybody,' Barry said with a
laugh.

'What's the "B" on it for?' Jorge said. 'Having
showered next to you, we know it can't be for "big".'

Barry made a 'you-think-you're-so-funny' smile and
tossed Jorge what he'd received from his Dimsley
zombies: the head of someone who used to bully him in
year two.

'Yahh! Shit, Barry, that's awful!' Jorge said.

'*He* used to tease me, too,' Barry said darkly. Jorge
flipped him off, and left to wash his hands.

'Merry Christmas,' Ferd said, and gave Barry a small
foil package. 'Hot pepper condom,' he said. 'I thought
we could slip it into Dorco's top drawer. That'll make
Panties Parkinsons *really* tremble. Dorco, too!'

After Ferd had left to go and check on Lon (who had
brought Barry a stick), Barry opened Bea's latest
missive – perhaps better called a 'massive' owing to its

great length. Inside was a little gift, a slightly broken chocolate in the shape of a wand, which Bea had made herself. Barry gnawed off the tip; even though it tasted a little weird, it seemed to be part of the chocolate family.

Barry now tried to lick and gnaw the tip back to a smooth end. As he examined his work more closely, Ermine had snatched the pages away. As things got more serious between Barry and Bea, Barry had been less free about letting her read Bea's letters. Hence Ermine's desire to read Bea's letters quintupled.

"'I can hardly wait until tonight,'" Ermine read. "'I just got a new blue dress" – damn it, I'm wearing blue, too – "I know you told me red is Grittyfloor colours, but red makes me looked flushed.'" Ermine smirked. 'Flushed? Wait 'till Mr Purple Jesus Punch gets a few drinks into you, dear. I'll remember to bring my stomach pump.

"'Anyway, I've never been to the school and can't wait to see what it's like inside. Gran tells me it's one of the finest examples of Medieval Psychotic architecture left in the world.'" Really? I'd never heard that,' Ermine said. She was trotting around the room, a few steps ahead of Barry, who was in hot pursuit. Every time she finished a page, she tossed it behind her, causing Barry to scramble around, picking it up.

'"I'm also quite looking forward to meeting your friends, particularly Ermine. I don't believe you when you say she's part Yeti."

'You know, just when I think you've sunk as low as possible, you go a little lower,' Ermine said. 'I've said it before, and I'll say it again: she seems decent, Barry. Why the hell is she dating you?'

'Gimme that,' Barry said, and finally got it. He slunk off to his room, feeling low. Ermine was right, he was a bit of a sleazoid – but Bea was his chance to improve, maybe.

Reaching into his pocket, he ran his fingers over the present Bea had sent by owl (just to make sure he got it) several days before. It gave him an explosion of warmth in his chest. Bea had sent him a small, flat piece of metal with an open palm painted on it – 'a gesture of friendship'.

In addition to his – well, Tuna's – poem (which he still had to get), Barry planned to give her something he'd seen advertised in a magazine called 'Magical Olive of the Month Club'. Every month, you'd get another olive, and instead of a pit there'd be something neat inside. Olives were the only Roman-type food he knew.

Barry put the obviously gnawed wand in his trunk. He lifted up some dress robes to make sure that the gift box with the first magical olive in it was still there; he had checked it forty-three times. Compulsion over, Barry wondered what he could wrap it in. Ermine would have plenty of extra wrapping paper; she was like that.

Barry walked into the hall, and something caught his eye. He made a mental note: remember to set aside an hour to go around the school tearing down the no-petting-with-Barry posters. He'd tell her eventually, of course – after he knew she liked him enough to forgive him for sure. Tonight at least, he planned to deny, deny, deny.

That afternoon, Barry had to swing by Radishgnaw to pick up the poem he'd paid Tuna Lovecraft to write. For five Gallons, it had better be good.

'Here you go,' Tuna said, handing it over. 'I think it's one of my best.'

Barry read the scroll, first with confusion, then with anger. Most of it was gibberish: *"'Ph'nglui mglw'nafh Cthulhu R'lyeh wgah'nagl fhtagn?'"* What the bloody hell does that mean? And who's this Riley character? I want Bea to like me, not some other guy!'

Tuna shrugged. 'Oh, don't worry about that. It's just a formalistic device.'

'Are you serious?' Barry fumed. He unrolled the rest

of the scroll, which went on for miles. 'There's loads of it!' Another name caught his eye. 'Tuna, who's Hastur the Unspeakable? Everybody's in my poem except me!'

Tuna went as white as fungi. 'You better not say his name, unless you want H. the U. to come and tapdance on your psyche. I've seen people after H. the U.'s finished with them. They have two choices of insanity: chittering or gibbering,' Tuna said. 'Sound fun?'

'No, but . . .' Barry said, calming down a bit. 'I wish you had put something soppy in there, instead of all this Yog-Sothoth stuff. I don't even know what that is . . . sounds like Asian food.'

'Artistic licence,' Tuna said. 'I wanted to give it a sort of crawling chaosy, non-Euclidean feel.'

'Well, if that's a fancy way of saying "make it suck",' Barry said, 'then you succeeded admirably.'

'Sorry you feel that way,' Tuna said, palm out. 'Pay up.'

Barry caught a glimpse of C'thulu smiling down at him, all wings and claws, tentacles and slime, and figured five Gallons weren't worth fighting over. 'Here. Merry Christmas,' he said bitterly.

Tuna's poem went straight into the rubbish bin; Barry Trotter, Clod Extraordinaire, would have to get by on charm alone. As the night's festivities approached, the boy wizard found himself pacing and nervous. He was so agitated that he knocked over the Christmas present he'd received from Dali the house elf: a tiny statue of Dali dressed as the Virgin Mary floating in a beaker of Dali's – or someone's – urine. 'Art shouldn't be something that smells,' Barry grumbled as he cleaned it up.

He decided to go and annoy Ermine. Getting into the girls' dormitories was easy; all it required was a simple *Dameedna* spell and a few words in falsetto. Barry was there in a matter of moments.

'Frankly, I'd be worried, too. She seems loads too smart for you,' Ermine said. Her roommates scurried about, getting ready. They allowed Barry to be in the room as long as he kept his eyes closed.

'Thanks,' Barry said, peeping.

'Stop peeping!' Ermine's roommate Jennifer yelled, throwing a wet cotton ball. It hit Barry right on the interrobang, and stuck there – it had been soaked in witch hazel.

Barry swore. 'Christ, Seeley! That stings!'

'Well, it wouldn't if your eyes weren't open,' Jennifer said, all cool logic. Barry had the familiar sensation of dealing with a sharper mind than his own, so he shut up.

'I still want the truth on how you snagged Bea in the first place.' Ermine turned back to her mirror – a magic eyelash curler hovered in front of her eyes. 'You nicked more love philtres from Snipe's cabinet, didn't you? That's not nice, Barry; he needs those more than you do. How's the man ever going to get laid, with his sallow complexion and greasy hair?' Ermine asked. 'And trust me, we want him nice and mellow for the A.U.K. exams.'

'J.G. Rollins wrote that, not me,' Barry said. 'You should've heard how I described Snipe. All muscles and perfect teeth, women hanging off him. I can't understand why he won't believe me . . .'

'Because you lie, Barry,' Ermine said. 'I mean, I don't mind – I don't believe anything you say, and get by okay – but other people . . . Take this girl Bea, for example. Having Tuna write a love poem for you is, well, like a lie.'

'Then you'll be happy to know that I'm not giving it to her. What Tuna wrote gave me the creeps. I threw it away; I would've burned it but I didn't want it to enter Earth's atmosphere.'

'I'm glad you're not giving it to her,' Ermine said. 'For better or worse, Bea deserves to know the real you. Take it from a real, live, female: be yourself, Barry.'

From across the room, Jennifer emitted a small shuddering sound of disgust.

Barry considered this course of action. It seemed, frankly, insane. 'We have lots in common. She's an orphan, too.'

'Really?' Ermine said. 'From the looks of this "Gran" character, I'd make sure she doesn't have a shotgun before I got too frisky.' Ermine, mid-mascara, remembered something. 'She's not magical, right? Meaning, she won't go off like a car alarm if you two started making out? Not that I think that's likely,' Ermine added. 'She'll probably come to her senses well before that point.'

'You think you're so funny,' Barry said. 'No, she's not magical. You should hear what her gran says about wizards. Most of the time, she can't even bring herself to say the word. Calls 'em "hippies" instead.'

'Well, I've worked hard on this party and wouldn't want you two to ruin it. People might think it was the fire alarm and stampede.' Ermine turned back to her eyes, which the magical mascara was making physically bigger.

'That always weirds me out,' Barry said. 'Talk about lying. How is you using cosmetics any different from me pretending to be deep?'

Ermine didn't gratify that with an answer, or didn't

have one. A jar on her dressing table caught Barry's eye. He picked it up.

'What's this?' Barry asked. '"Lamer"? Listen, Erm, I say this as a friend – you shouldn't be using any product that makes you lamer. You can't afford it.'

'That's La Mer, wee-wand,' Ermine said. 'It's makeup, and an expensive kind, too. Hey, aren't your eyes supposed to be closed?'

Jennifer threw another witch-hazel spitball at him. Barry ducked and his diamanté glasses came off. Then his wig fell off, and a falsie slipped out of his blouse to the floor. *Dameedna* was not one of his favourite spells.

'You know if you retracted your tongue once in a while and actually held a proper conversation with one of your captives, you might learn something,' Ermine said.

'About what?'

'Girls, for one thing. Life.'

Barry gave a wave of the hand. 'All I need to know is when and where, baby.'

'And Bumblemore's given you your answer, hasn't he? Never and no place,' Ermine said, with a laugh. 'At least you have your memories.'

'Yeah, well, that's better than some guy who's been in an East European Quiddit gulag since birth.'

Ermine stopped lining a lip with a tiny wand. 'Victor is an artist.'

'I can see that,' Barry said. There was a small portrait of Ermine stuck in the corner of her mirror. 'Erm, don't worry – your bum isn't nearly that huge.'

Ermine made an exasperated noise. 'Victor is an erotic magical realist.'

'Victor is perv-tastic.'

'At least he's magical,' Ermine sniffed.

'Well, that's something, coming from you, Muddley Muddington,' Barry said. 'Have you been drinking some of Dorco's Kool-Aid?'

'Just stating a fact,' Ermine said defensively. Barry's constant teasing had finally got to her.

'I'm out of here,' Barry said, getting up. He made a point of opening his eyes as wide as possible on the way out.

'Pig!' the girls yelled. Jennifer's Galloping Scrofula hex missed him by inches.

Back in his room, Barry carefully selected each item of clothing, right down to his festive crossed-sticks-of-rock-on-a-field-of-red-boxers. Nearly every combination in his closet was tried, and retried. All the stops were pulled; he'd even bought a nice new tie for the occasion. On the front it had a sedate stripe, but the back showed Valid Tumour Alarm's lead singer Art Valumord biting the head off a gnat.

Barry wasn't the only one who was nervous. Mrs McGoogle had asked Grittyfloor's two Perfects, Lon and Ermine, to help plan and supervise the party. Lon's injury restricted him to sniffing the patrons for drugs (or, rather, food). But McGoogle expected more from Ermine.

The old woman and the young one were somewhat kindred spirits. Mrs McGoogle secretly saw Ermine as a protégée, a standard-bearer for the next proud generation of pedagogy-scented celibacy. But some time during the autumn, McGoogle had got wind that Ermine had – of all things – a boyfriend. And as the You'll Ball was commonly considered a frenzy of consummation, McGoogle was determined that Ermine be otherwise occupied. So one afternoon in early December, she'd summoned Ermine to her office.

'The Headmister is a pervert, did you know that?' she barked across her desk.

'Really?' Ermine said, playing dumb.

'Oh, come off it, girl,' McGoogle said sharply. 'Surely your parents, as medical professionals, have warned you of the voracious sexual appetite of the male.'

'They're dentists,' Ermine said. 'Anything that happens below the chin is a mystery to them.' She was looking at the golden chastity belt that hung on the wall, the *Stun*'s 'Golden Spinster Award'.[37] The paper had crowned Mrs McGoogle its 'anti-page three girl' for nearly a decade running. McGoogle seemed to be prudishly proud of it.

'I'm not here to argue your parents' profession, Cringer . . . I see you're admiring my award.'

'Yes, Mrs McGoogle. It's very beautiful.' In fact, it was a cheap-looking jewelled truss-like contraption that anybody under twenty stone could've thwarted with ease. Ermine wasn't studying the award as much as trying not to smell the litterbox in the corner. Being an animagus invariably raised some really awful issues of personal hygiene.

'They don't give those out on every street corner,' McGoogle said sternly. 'You have to work for it. Self-denial, Cringer. *Decades* of self-denial and sourness go into it . . . a little fear helps, too. And thinking yourself too good for the world you've found yourself in.' McGoogle pinned Ermine with a look. 'I suspect you

[37] Winners of this Award were also given the honorific 'Mrs'. Their husband was their 'shining commitment to the uncompromising ethos of spinsterhood'.

can relate to that last one, eh Cringer? Be honest. Think yourself just a little better than all the rest?'

'No, Mrs McGoogle, I just work a bit m—'

'Don't be ridiculous, Cringer. Anyway, it's not bad to think highly of yourself,' McGoogle said. 'But there comes a time to prove it, through action.'

'Yes?' Ermine asked, eyes bright. Excelling in public was the monkey on her back. If being a keenie was wrong, she didn't want to be right.

'Cringer, I need you to form Grittyfloor's contingent on the You'll Ball Planning Committee. With Lon being more dog than boy, you'll be on your own,' she said. 'The other houses are nominating their Perfects, too – you'll have to work with Dorco Malfeasance. Can you do that?'

'Yes,' Ermine said, a bit breathlessly. Being given responsibility always gave her an incredible rush.

'Good. Meetings are the next four Mondays at four, with the School Spirit Committee.'

Ermine's heart sank. 'They're involved, too?' The School Spirit Committee was comprised of all the ghosts that loitered around Hogwash doing nothing; its (nominal) job was to make sure things like the You'll Ball weren't total catastrophes. This had been another of Alpo Bumblemore's moronic brainwaves. The Head-mister had been trying to evict the ghosts for years, but whenever he threw them out they floated back in again. So he put them to work.[38]

'Of course they are. The School Spirit Committee is a valuable—' McGoogle broke off mid-sentence as a mouse scurried across the floor. Quick as a flash, the Housemistress had transformed into a cat and pounced. But the moment she touched it, the mouse exploded with a loud bang.

Ermine smelled gunpowder, mixed with burning fur, and heard Ferd and Jorge's muffled laughter from behind the office door. They ran away in triumph, hooting and high-fiving each other. McGoogle, now back in human form, lay on the floor, muttering nonsensically to herself. Ermine saw she had wet her dress.

Gathering up her books, Ermine slipped out of the room quietly. Descent into madness is a private moment.

---

[38] Being noncorporeal meant that most of them couldn't quite remember what it was like to be alive. Those who still did resented the living bitterly; the Committee became their weapon of choice. And so the Committee, far from making dances and such more pleasant, made them even drearier. Unless, of course, there were enough humans around to keep the ghosts in line. 'The Bloody Imbecile's motion to make the dance's theme "Sandpapering Your Eyelids" is vetoed . . .'

Chapter Ten

❀

Over the next several weeks, Ermine had taken charge of the You'll Ball like few students ever had. With frightening efficiency, she had commandeered large sections of the school; one group was making decorations, while another detachment was in charge of games. Ermine herself was in charge of the evening's entertainment, and she (rather predictably) hoped to hire the Beatles. Ermine was a tremendous fan of the group, and longed to abduct one or more of its members on a semi-permanent basis.

One Saturday, with a pocketful of Gallons and dreams of kissing Paul McCartney, Ermine strolled into the Hall of Fame Talent-Conjuring Agency, conveniently located on Corleone Street in squalid downtown Hogsbleede.

'Can I help you?' a somewhat cadaverous man asked. He had slicked-back hair and a pencil-thin moustache.

'I'd like to book the Beatles for our school dance,' Ermine said confidently.

'That's going to be expensive,' the man said, taking out a binder filled with prices. 'How much do you have to spend?'

'A hundred Gallons,' Ermine told him.

He laughed. 'You're kidding! I could get you half of the Monkees, maybe,' he said. 'Ever heard of the

Troggs? They'll do all right, if it's a "party atmosphere".'

Ermine looked puzzled.

'If people are drunk enough.'

'Oh,' she said. Reluctant to give up just yet, she asked, 'How much do the Beatles cost, anyway?'

He told her; Ermine momentarily blacked out. When she came to, the man was explaining, 'See, it's not just the talent. It's also the shipping and handling, back into that time and place, into this time and place, all done in such a way so that the talent doesn't realise what's going on and go insane. When your entertainer goes insane, slipshod time travel is usually in there somewhere.'

'I wouldn't want to hurt them,' Ermine said, crestfallen. 'But I was really looking forward . . .'

The man seemed to take pity on her. 'Tell you what I'll do,' he said quietly. 'I can't give you the 1964 version for that price, but how 'bout before they were famous? I could probably swing the Hamburg version. They're a little rowdy, but they're still the Beatles, right?'

'Okay!' Ermine said. Beatles were Beatles – how bad could it be?

Ermine had walked on air for days after her coup, telling everybody who would listen that the Beatles

were going to play the You'll Ball. But there was at
least one Hogwash student who considered this to be a
terrible piece of news – and he had been the one to pay
for it in the first place!

The boost to Barry Trotter's popularity via J.G.
Rollins's books had forced Dorco Malfeasance to take
desperate measures: he had formed a rock band. 'We
Hate Music' consisted of Dorco, Panties Parkinsons,
Flabbe and Oyle. Through intimidation and bribery,
the quartet had a foothold in Silverfish, but the rest of
the school loathed them. The only good thing about the
band was that they, unlike the Who, destroyed their
instruments at the *beginning* of their performance instead
of the end. The only reason Dorco had deigned to be on
the Planning Committee was to finagle We Hate Music
another gig. Ermine knew this, and used it to her
advantage.

'Dorco, can you give me some money?' she asked
before a double-Notions class.

'How much?' Dorco asked, in that sort of pointy,
pale way of his.

'Five hundred Gallons,' Ermine said, trying not to
flinch. 'I want to book a band for the You'll Ball.'

'Why spend the money when We Hate Music can
play all night?' Dorco asked.

'Because' – Ermine searched for a suitable lie –

'because I want to make you guys look good. How can people know how great We Hate Music is unless they have another group to compare it to? But I'll get a shitty one, I promise – and we'll give you top billing. It'll be "We Hate Music" all in big letters, and then, at the bottom, tiny, it'll say, "Also, Whoever".'

'How about "Dorco Malfeasance's We Hate Music"?'

'Fine, whatever you want,' Ermine said. The boy's ego was incredible; it was almost as big as Barry's.

Dorco thought for a second. 'Nah,' he said. 'We'll just play all night.'

'Okay . . . ' Ermine said. 'But then I'll be forced to tell the *Stun* you have a half-inch whanger.'[39]

Dorco blanched, and even threw up a little into his mouth. 'You wouldn't dare!'

'I would.'

'But it's a lie!'

'Thankfully, I'll never find out,' Ermine said. 'So what about it?'

Dorco dickered her down to a hundred Gallons. She'd really wanted to get the Beatles, just to make his band look like shite, and figured that the Hamburg version would do that well enough. She also got Dorco

[39] 1.27 cm.

to sign the paper that the man at the agency gave her. It protected the agency from being sued in the event of 'any damage to the stage, bar, club, or environs; any personal injuries suffered by the performers, audience or staff; any lawsuit as the result of lewd behaviour, drug use, or overzealous roadies'. The paper was ten pages of tiny type. But Ermine wasn't worried; she'd seen *A Hard Day's Night* five times. What was the worst that could happen?

Dorco Malfeasance stood behind the microphone, facing an equal mixture of hostility and indifference. The first act, 'The S. Meekings Experience', had been a third-year from Silverfish armed with a clarinet, a distortion pedal and two hundred pounds of stage pyrotechnics. It had not gone down well.

'Hello,' Dorco said. The two syllables were packed with a kind of haughty obnoxiousness that immediately had the audience biting the palm of his hand. 'We're We Hate Music—'

A smattering of applause was drowned out by an avalanche of boos. 'We hate you!' someone yelled.

'Thanks,' Dorco said, then a burst of ear-splitting feedback threw him off his stride. There were cries of anguish from the audience. 'Uh, our first CD, "We

Can't Play", which was produced by Professor Snipe, is available in the Silverfish tuck shop.'

'It fucking sucked!' another voice yelled. This immediately mutated into a chant. '*It – fucking – sucked! It – fucking – sucked!*'

Oblivious or defiant, Dorco soldiered on. 'Thanks,' he said. 'Now we'd like to do a song my dad wrote for me called, "Soon There Will Be a Cleansing".'

They couldn't destroy their instruments fast enough; before the second verse of the third song, We Hate Music was driven from the stage by audience members brandishing pitchforks and torches.

Ten minutes later, Dorco sat in the corner, putting cigarettes out on Panties Parkinsons. The Beatles, dressed in leather, were stomping their way through an obscure ballad. One of them had a toilet seat around his head.

'God, what syrupy crap,' Dorco fumed. 'Panties, if you can't keep still, I'll stop putting fags out on you.'

'Sorry, D-d-dorkie,' Panties said. 'Ooh! I think P-p-paul just l-looked at me!'

The song ended and George spoke. 'The next song we'd like to do is called "Besame Mucho" . . .'

'. . . which is Spanish for "I'm not wearing any knickers"!' Lennon chimed in.

~ 201 ~

Chapter Ten

Paul began to croon, and Panties began to melt.

'God, you disgust me.' Fed up, Dorco waved his wand and the song changed. The avant-garde tape collage 'Revolution 9' staggered out of the amplifiers. This got a reaction. The band, already jazzed on amphetamines, began looking at their instruments as if they'd been betrayed, fiddling with knobs and yanking cords. The audience promptly stopped dancing and began booing. Someone started throwing Christmas cookies, and one hit George. That became the signal for a full-fledged mêlée, with Beatle hitting student, student biting Beatle.

In the room next door, Ermine was blissfully unaware. In a fit of high spirits, she had allowed some smuggled-in Snogging Grog to be added to the punch, and so was presiding over a display of mass-kissing unequalled since the days of ancient Rome.[40] Amidst steady liplocking, her conversation with Victor had recently turned to a nude portrait, and Ermine, always a patroness of the arts, found herself not unpleased by the idea. This passionate tête-à-tête had been shattered by a Lennon-propelled student crashing through a door. Ermine disentangled herself and scrambled to the

---

[40] Somebody tell Gran!

Great Hall, where a mighty fracas was in full force. Fists and spells were flying.[41]

'Please don't hurt the group!' Ermine said via the ancient PA. 'I paid a deposit!'

But her efforts were to no avail, and Ermine finally had to find Mrs McGoogle.

'How did this get so out of control?' Mrs McGoogle demanded. 'Why weren't you watching the performance? Where were you?'

Ermine blushed.

'I might've guessed,' the old sourpuss said. 'I expected better of you.' As Ermine wept, McGoogle called the police. Soon, a squad of Hogsbleede's Finest, clad in magical riot gear, galloped in on thestrals. They

---

[41] Unbeknownst to anyone – even the group themselves – this trip to Hogwash had an immense effect on Beatle history. In the midst of the fracas, a Pufnstuf sixth-year turned the group's drummer, Pete Best, into a badger. It took Nurse Pommefritte several months to undo the poorly made bootleg spell; Bumblemore asked for a volunteer to take Best's place in the group while she worked. A Pufnstuf fifth-year named Starkey was chosen. Bumblemore picked a random name out of a Western-themed skin magazine, and 'Ringo Starr' was born. The others liked him, so he stayed. It was a terrible break for Pete Best, but at least he wasn't a badger.

~ 203 ~

restored order via magic truncheons before anything too valuable got damaged.

'Watch out!' Cyril Broadbottom had yelled to one of the cops. 'The bloody thestral's gnawing the wood-work! Look sharp, Ermine, you're about to step in a thestral apple.'

Cyril's warning came too late, and Ermine found herself coated to the left ankle in invisible poo. And even though the beasts and their excretions are invisible to one who has not seen death – or at least sat through a really bad movie – they are not in-smellable.

This is awful, Ermine thought. I stink, I'm a failure, and the Head of my House hates me. At least I have Victor. Just then, she saw Victor snogging some skank from Radishgnaw.

'Uh, Ermeen, eet is naught whut eet look lik,' Victor said. 'I can eexplane – I was jus' looking at her with great closeness . . .'

Ermine struggled for words. 'You . . . you . . . Your cartoons are sexist!' Ermine yelled, and ran from the room. This was the worst night of her life! Crying hard, Ermine ran upstairs. All she could feel was betrayal: Victor was a dog, just like Barry – and Lon! She had really liked him, but all she was to Victor was a sexual object, utterly replaceable, to be discarded at will. She'd always tried to be a good person, to do the right thing, and this was how she was treated. Fair enough, Ermine thought through her tears, if that was the way the game was played, she'd play it. And she'd win, too. Thus Ermine Cringer, hard-bitten heartbreaker, sexual libertine, was born.

Upstairs, Barry was having a much happier You'll Ball – for the moment. He had taken advantage of the rioting downstairs to spirit Bea out of the Great Hall and into his room. Not for the first time, he thanked God for the clout that allowed him to get a single.

'Are you sure it's okay to do this?' Bea said with trepidation. 'Nobody's up here.'

'Oh yeah,' Barry said, trying to sound convincing. 'It's not far.'

They got to his door. The wipeable marker board that hung on it read 'Bea: No matter what Barry tells you, do NOT go in here!!! – Ermine.' Then, under it, written in fresh ink: 'Oh, fuck it – Erm.'

Barry wiped it quickly with his hand, giving a black smudge to his palm. But Bea had already seen it.

'That's Ermine,' Barry said, 'always kidding!'

'I don't know, Barry,' Bea said, real doubt in her voice. 'Maybe this isn't such a good idea . . .'

'Come on, Bea,' Barry said. 'You like me, right?'

'Right, but—'

'And listen to what it's like downstairs.' They could hear furniture being broken up, spells hissing this way and that, George Harrison swearing. 'You don't want your new dress to get damaged, do you?' Barry was laying it on thick – his hormones demanded it. 'We can always go back downstairs after the riot's over . . .'

Barry opened the door, and a smell of stale sweat wafted forth. Maybe this wasn't the best idea, he thought. 'Obviously, if you really want to go downstairs . . .'

Just then the mounted police arrived, to much screaming. 'Oh, well, what the hell,' Bea said, and followed him in.

Barry snapped his fingers, and several floating candles sputtered into action. This had been Ermine's idea. 'Not only is it romantic,' she had said, 'but it will hide your horrible room.'

Barry's room was horrible – not on its own, but in what he had allowed it to become. The house elves flatly refused to come anywhere near, calling it 'The Bog'. Magazines, papers, past-due bills were strewn about, after Earwig had knocked them over and shredded them. Speaking of Barry's owl, she had claimed one corner as her own, and proceeded to fill it with moulted feathers and cigarette ends she'd fished from the gutter (Earwig treated tobacco products like a falcon treated its prey – more than one Hogwesian had a butt snatched out of his very mouth by her greedy talons). Piles of dirty clothes – knickers included – had been sitting in piles for so long they were beginning to ferment. Discarded packets and scraps of food provided a rich medium for bacteria of all sorts. It was, in short, fairly standard issue.

'Sit down,' Barry said.

Bea paused; every horizontal surface had something piled on it.

'Oh, sorry, let me —' Barry said, and grabbed his Quiddit robes from the bed. As he threw them into the corner, he got a whiff. After four and a half seasons of sweat, those noble garments had never known the touch of soapy water.

'Thanks,' Bea said, sitting on the edge of the bed.

'So,' Barry said, sitting next to her.

'So,' she said.

They stared at each other, until the silence became unbearable. Barry tried to speak, and his voice broke. The second time he got it out. 'Can I kiss you?'

'Okay, if it's that important to you,' Bea said.

Barry lunged at her. Slightly alarmed, Bea moved, and Barry planted one right on her nostril.

'Whoops.' It seemed like the only thing to say. 'I didn't mean to. Sorry.'

'It's okay,' Bea said. 'I moved. Can we try it without you coming at me at a million miles an hour?'

Barry was in full embarrassment mode. 'Yes. Sure. Sorry. I didn't mean to. Sorry.'

They did it again, this time successfully. Barry noticed she tasted a little like meat. He'd always liked meat, but now he liked it even more. After half an hour, Bea pulled back and said, 'My lips are starting to hurt. Can we stop for a while?'

'Okay,' Barry said. 'Is it anything I'm doing?'

'I'm not sure,' Bea said. 'I don't really consider myself an expert at this.'

'Your lip looks swollen,' Barry said.

'Do you have a mirror?' Bea said.

'No.'

'Oh, honestly. Barry, you live like a bloody caveman, do you know that?'

'I can make fire,' Barry said sheepishly. Trying to show how useful he was, Barry said, 'It's cold outside. You could stick your head out of the window. That might make the swelling go down.'

Bea was prodding her lips tentatively, and wincing a bit each time. 'I'll pretend you didn't say that,' she said.

This wasn't going well, Barry thought. Things were so much easier when you could give Doris a Sickie and be done with it. The more you liked a person, the more nerve-racking all this stuff got. Then he had an idea.

'Hey, I have another present for you,' he announced proudly.

'Really?' Bea said, smiling. 'Barry, you shouldn't've.'

'Right,' Barry said, 'move over a little – just push those magazines off the bed.'

Bea held up a copy of *Viz*. 'Don't tell me – a subscription.'

'No, even better,' Barry said. Opening his dress robes, he pulled out his shirt and began to unbutton it. Bea got very uncomfortable.

'Barry, I don't like where this is going,' she said. 'I don't know you that well.'

'What?' Barry asked. 'Oh! No, sorry, Bea. It's not that – I mean, not that I don't – not that I do, mind you – I mean, I do, but not – oh Hell, just watch . . .'

Barry pulled up his shirt. There, in the general vicinity of his heart, was the extremely shaky word 'Bea'.

'Oh my God,' Bea said, with a slightly horrified laugh. 'Surely it's not permanent?'

Barry couldn't tell what answer she wanted, so he went with the truth. 'No. I did it this afternoon with a marker and a mirror. I was really nervous and was looking for something to do.'

'I can tell,' Bea said.

'Anyway, Bea – I just wanted to tell you, I really like you.'

'I like you, too, Barry,' Bea said.

'I mean, you're so funny, and clever, and pretty, and' . . . Barry was tucking in his shirt . . . 'and a whole lot of other things that I can't think of now, but I think of them all the time when you're not around . . .' He unbuckled his belt, to tuck his shirt in properly.

'You look weird, Bea. Are you okay?'

The room was filled with a deafening klaxon-type horn, pouring out of Bea's mouth. Barry immediately clapped his hands over his ears, then had to take them off to try to close Bea's mouth. It was frozen open, rigid. Barry could tell by her eyes that she didn't know what was happening, and was scared. Barry tried to dampen the sound with a towel, but that didn't work; Bea would suffocate. A pillow was even worse.

'Hold on, Bea, don't be scared, I'll figure something out!' Barry said. Obviously, it was the petting alarm – but that meant that—

People started pounding on the door outside.

'Open up!' Bumblemore shouted. 'Pack your bags, creep!'

The door shuddered on its hinges, and Bumblemore gave a roar of pain.

'Someone go and get Hafwid,' Barry heard the old wizard say. 'Maybe he can breathe on it!'

Frantic, Barry whipped out his wand. 'Bea, don't move. Everything's going to be okay. I'm going to rewind you three minutes,' Barry said. 'Just try to stop screaming, 'cause I have to concentrate.' Did he remember the spell? Barry hoped to God he did. A mumble and a jitterbug later, and . . .

The door gave way, and Hafwid staggered in, rubbing his shoulder.

'It's all over, Trotter,' Bumblemore said triumphantly, then stopped. There was no one in the room but Barry.

Chapter Eleven

NEVER RUN WITH
A WAND

ᏩᎠᎠᎠᎤ

'. . . and you're awake. How do you feel?'

'What happened to her?' Barry asked, sitting upright.

'To whom?'

'To Bea, you idiot! Where did she go?' Barry said impatiently. 'She disappeared, I must've cast the spell wrong.'

'Maybe instead of "rewind", you cast a "fast-for-ward". It's not impossible, I've done it myself.'

'No,' Barry said. 'That would've left something – bones, ash, something. There was nothing left.'

'Perhaps she went too far back,' Ritalin said. 'Perhaps the spell took her past her own birth.'

'*That* doesn't sound good.'

'It's not,' Ritalin said. 'The human body cannot take such strains. It gets confused. And when the body gets too confused, it shuts down.'

'Oh my God,' Barry said. 'I killed her.'

'Perhaps you did. How do you feel about that?'

Barry, distraught, continued speaking rapidly. 'I didn't mean to kill her! But I must have, by accident. Why didn't I remember that before? It's as if as soon as I realised what I'd done, I tried not to know it.'

'Understandable. In your shoes, I'd be consumed with guilt and horror at my own actions,' the doctor said. 'Of course, that's just me.'

Barry was quiet for a long time. Finally Ritalin cleared his throat nervously and said, 'You're still on the clock, you know.'

Barry paid no attention. Looking up at Dr Ritalin, he asked, 'Do you think that's why I can't get any older?'

'Yes, I do,' the doctor said. 'And what's more, I think I know what you must do. I don't think you killed her, Barry—'

Barry brightened. 'You don't?'

'— I mean, she might as *well* be dead—'

Barry got glum again.

'— I think you put her in a nether state. An afterlife, if you like.'

'Like Heaven, you mean?'

'I don't know,' Ritalin admitted. 'I've never died. But you must find her in the afterlife – or in the pre-life, but

I think the two are connected. You must travel to the afterlife, find her, and set things right. Bring her back.'

'But how do I do that?'

'Again, I'm just spitballing here, but I think you've got to snuff it,' Dr Ritalin said, as if this were the most natural advice in the world.

'What, now?'

Ritalin pondered. 'In the past, I guess.'

'I'm confused,' Barry admitted.

'Try to relax into it,' Ritalin said. 'It's simple: we regress you to the episode you just recalled. Then, after Bea winks out, you must die as well – follow her across.'

'Wait,' Barry said. 'If I die under hypnosis, will I be dead in real life as well?'

'No, no, no,' Dr Ritalin said, chuckling slightly. 'No more than if you died in the midst of a dream.'

'Right,' Barry said. 'Then what? How will I find her, much less bring her back?'

'Search me,' Ritalin said. 'All I know is, you must cross over somehow. After that, you're on your own.'

'Ermine won't like it. After all, Bea's my ex-girl-friend.'

'Oh, hardly,' Ritalin said. 'A few kisses . . .'

'Shut up,' Barry said, his pride wounded. 'You're sure this is the only way?'

'I think so, but remember I'm viciously incompetent,' Ritalin said. 'Barry, after all our sessions, all you've relived, and all I've seen, I think you must find Bea, your first love.'

'But she wasn't, really,' Barry said. 'Girlfriend, yes, love, no. I mean, maybe if we'd kept going out, but as it was ... We hardly dated, really.'

'Okay, okay! What are you, some kind of lawyer?' Dr Ritalin said. 'Whenever this book gets some sort of drama going, you just ruin it.'

'Sorry,' Barry said. 'I'll shut up.'

Ritalin continued: 'She is the key to breaking yourself out of this temporal rut. Forces beyond your control – God, your own subconscious, the author – have imprisoned you in Time, as punishment for what you did to that poor girl. And you will stay young until you go back there and make things right. My professional opinion, and keep in mind I don't say this often, is that the only way for you to get well is to kill yourself. Barry Trotter, you must die.'

'Can I get a second opinion?' Barry asked. 'Just kidding. Put me under again – let's go for it.'

Within moments, Barry found himself back in his fifth-year bedroom. A pile of clothes lay where Bea had stood. Roused by the alarm, there was a pounding on the door.

'Trotter, let me in,' Bumblemore said. 'I know you've got a girl in there!'

'I haven't!' Barry said. 'I've turned gay!'

There was a pause, then: 'Then you've got a boy in there! Doesn't matter, let me in!' Bumblemore said. 'Everybody get out of Hafwid's way.'

Barry didn't have much time; if they found him with Bea's clothes, there would be an hour's interrogation, at least. By that time, Bea might be anywhere. He had to die, fast.

'Terry, are you around here?' Barry called. He looked under the bed. There was a note that read, 'Got tired of waiting. Kill you tomorrow, L.V.'

'Great! The *one* time . . .' Barry trailed off, thinking hard. He looked around frantically for some method of self-extinguishing; it had to be fast, and foolproof. He didn't want to wake up in the infirmary two days from now, groggy and pissed off, having to whisper out some line of b.s. that explained Bea's clothing. Then he would still be alive, and everybody would think he was a transvestite.

Wait – wasn't Serious always telling him never to run with his wand? He pulled it out of his pocket, and started running. Round and round he went, holding his wand in his right hand and waiting for something lethal to take place.

'Him, her, or it, Trotter; it doesn't matter – just start packing!' There was a definite note of triumph in the Headmister's voice.

Barry ran faster. He felt really stupid.

The door burst open, and Hafwid staggered in, rubbing his shoulder. Bumblemore was right behind. He was followed by Colin Creepy, editor of *The Hogwash Haunt*.

'Smile, Barry!' Colin said, and took a picture. Barry's expulsion would be the biggest story ever.

'Huh?' Distracted by the flash on Colin's camera, Barry's foot caught on the edge of his rug and he tumbled forward. Oh, right, Barry thought, in the last split-second. You'll put your eye out!

In fact, what happened was much worse (or in this case, infinitely better): as Barry hit the floor, the wand not only punctured his right eye, but continued on into his brain, killing him quite dead.

'Creepy, keep taking photos,' Bumblemore said, when he saw Barry crumple. 'I'll split the rights with you fifty-fifty.'

Meanwhile, back in Dr Ritalin's office, Barry lay motionless on the couch. After describing the wand piercing his brain, Barry's voice trailed off; his breathing grew shallower, then stopped altogether.

'Barry, what do you see now?' Dr Ritalin said. There was no reply.

'Barry, are you dead?' Still getting no response, Dr Ritalin leaned over and listened for Barry's breathing. There was nothing. Smiling, the doctor grabbed Barry's right wrist and felt it. There was no pulse, either.

Dr Ritalin leapt up and began doing a little jig around the cramped office, kicking books and papers out of his way as necessary.

'He's dead! He's dead! I finally killed him! I'm going to be rich! Or richer, as the case may be,' Dr Ritalin sang, to a tune made up on the spot. 'First come the commemorative magazines! And then the limited edition books! And then all the T-shirts, and plates, and God-knows-what! I'm going to make billions! Barry Trotter is finally dead, and who's happy? Me! Me! Me!'

Grabbing his wand, Ritalin aimed it at his head and mumbled an incantation. Slowly his features scrambled themselves, then reorganised into their proper arrangement. There, standing in the middle of the room in full dress regalia, was Lord Valumart.

Chapter Twelve

BARRY TROTTER
SNUFFED IT AND ALL I GOT
WAS THIS LOUSY T-SHIRT

൸

Despite Headmister's best efforts to celebrate in relative
quiet, Barry's funeral became an incredible circus. The
school was hung with black bunting, the bats were
allowed to gambol about freely, and all the ghosts were
happily taking bets on when Barry would make his
appearance.

'*Of course* he'll haunt the school,' Barely Brainless Bill
said at dinner one night. 'They won't take him in the
one place, and even Hogwash is better than the other.'

Before the body was even cold, Bumblemore had
bullied Colin Creepy into slapping together a five-
Sickie 'Commemorative Edition' of the *Haunt*, which
Valumart's minions hawked far and near. Along with
laughable articles like 'Trotter Devoted Much Time to
Schoolwork, Needy', and a word-jumble revealing

gruesome details of Barry's death, there was a map of the school and a schedule of funeral services. Expecting a titanic crush of fans, the Hogsbleede Chamber of Commerce announce plans for a parade. 'Something tasteful and restrained,' Hogsbleede's mayor said, 'like Carnival in Rio.'

As the Scottish hills echoed with the screams of a thousand Brazilian waxes, Lord Valumart worked tirelessly, eyes aglitter with greed. First, he turned the Magic Bus into a shuttle service from London. Then he covered the school's lawns with stands to milk the mourners. Grieving fans could soothe themselves with everything from souvenir shotglasses to 'authentic shards of the Death Wand'.

As the day approached, Bumblemore was filled with trepidation. He feared that his fraudulent sombreness would fracture under the world's scrutiny, revealing the giddy glee he felt inside. As a last resort, the Headmister had released a statement saying, 'As we all know, Barry was a very shy person, and valued his privacy, so please stay the bleeding hell away from here.' No one listened, and on the appointed day, over 250,000 Trotter fans ran through the Great Hall, viewing the body at a trot. It was laid out under glass like a dictator or saint.

Bumblemore had spared every expense in making

sure that Barry looked his best. The boy wizard's face still wore the 'Oh, shit!' look he had in his last moments; even the Death Wand still protruded defiantly from the boy's eye socket. (In a pitiful attempt to spruce her friend up one last time, Ermine had knitted a small pennant and placed it on the end.[42]) Every thousand mourners or so, another fan would fling him or herself on to the catafalque, sobbing hysterically and claiming that Barry had promised they would get married – before or after fathering a child.

After a few hours of this, it became clear that the whole apparatus couldn't take the pounding. Lest it crack open like a rotten egg – and probably smell just as bad – a velvet rope was put up. Hafwid was stationed next to the coffin. 'Hay, freek,' Hafwid growled at a flatheaded boy who had uncapped a marker and was moving towards the casket with intent. 'Don' draw on tha'. I eat bigger things than you fer tee.'

'Sod off,' the boy said, sticking out his tongue.

Hafwid took one step towards him. The boy screamed, and scrambled out of the door.

This gave Hafwid no pleasure; he was furiously hungover. 'Ennybody got ennything ta drink?' Hafwid

---

[42] It read, in small, knobbly letters, 'We Miss You.'

said to the throng. A lot of people did. Hafwid drank it all, then got noisily sick.

'It's grief, probably,' one fan said to another.

Barry wasn't watching this post-mortem pandemonium. He was – well, exactly where he was will have to wait a moment. One thing is for sure: he wasn't alone. Lots of people die every day. In fact, Barry was joined in the afterlife by none other than his pal, Lonald Measly.

Here's how it happened: several days before the funeral, Bumblemore had begun the systematic ransacking of Barry's belongings.

'Christ, this is what eBuy was *made* for!' Bumblemore said. 'Cringer, stop crying. He's not going to need Gallons where he's going.'

'But – but could we at least use the money to set up an award or something?' Ermine sniffled.

'For what? "Biggest Git"?' A house elf was trying to get Bumblemore's attention. 'God yes, frisk the body!'

With the Headmister distracted by greed, and Ermine by grief, Lon had been allowed to wander around Barry's old room unsupervised.

'Lon, don't lick the bloodstain,' Ermine scolded. 'That's sacrilegious.'

Just as any three-year-old will immediately discover all the electric sockets in a room, Lon immediately turned up the chocolate wand that Bea had given Barry as a Christmas present. Within minutes, the dog-boy had gorged himself on so much chocolate that he killed the canine portion of his body. Unfortunately for Lon, this was his brain.[43]

Having company in the afterlife was a comfort to Barry, as was missing the rest of fifth year, especially the A.U.K.s. He had Accumulated plenty of Useless Knowledge over his life, but there were no tests on the minutiae of Valid Tumour Alarm. And taking the W.E.T.s instead – *Wizard Equivalency Test* – would've been a major embarrassment. So all in all, death was treating Barry pretty well.

Several weeks before his death, Barry had whiled away a Divination class by drawing a little smiley face on the end of his wand. This was the last thing he saw while alive. Leering tinily, it shattered his glasses and made friends with his right eye. Then everything went black.

Barry was floating in darkness. Muzak seemed to be playing, songs like 'Theme from "A Summer Place"' and 'Girl from Ipanema'. Barry found that he could control

[43] Whenever anybody asked about Lon, Bumblemore told them that he had 'sent him to live at a school far out in the country, where he has lots of other dog-boys to play with and is very happy'.

the speed of the songs with his mind, or whatever he had now that he was dead.

After an interval of uncertain length, a film began to play. Two absurdly unknown actors capered and joked.

'Now that you're entering the afterlife,' said the blond one, 'be polite – don't forget to turn off your mobile! And don't talk during the movie!'

'That's right!' said the brunette one, oozing false cheer. 'Take it from two guys in Purgatory . . .'

'Actually, just Los Angeles,' the blond one quipped.

'Zip your lips! Courtesy counts!' they chorused, then shuffled off to oblivion.

Then there was a short movie, where all the events of Barry's life were re-enacted. The actor playing Barry was sweating profusely, and kept flubbing his lines.

'Boo! Get off the screen, wazzock!' Barry said. Obnoxiousness at the movies was a proud tradition.

'Shh!' somebody hissed. Who was that? Who was watching *his* life? Barry looked around, but couldn't see anybody else in the dark, so he continued to watch. The only comfort was that the girl playing Ermine was even more inept. Wait 'til I tell Erm, Barry thought, forgetting where he was. Lon, played by a toy Yorkie, had a few excellent comic moments. Strangely, the film had been edited so as to make Terry Valumart the hero.

Barry realised why at the end – his company, Valumart Enterprises, had made the film.

When the movie of Barry's life was over and the lights went up, Barry found himself sitting in a theatre. There were a few people sprinkled about.

'What the hell are you doing here?' Barry asked a nebbishy-looking man eating popcorn. There was a massive wound in his chest, and occasionally some popcorn fell out of it. Yuck, Barry thought.

'I like to watch the movies,' he said. 'After mine was over, I just stayed.'

'So did I,' said a woman with long black hair sitting next to him. 'You know, every time I see your chest, I'm glad I took pills.'

'My chest would be fine if you hadn't shot it!' the man said.

'Let's not fight. Fighting's what got us here in the first place. I didn't much like that last one,' the woman said. 'Was that you?'

'Yeah,' Barry said.

'Too bad,' the guy said. 'Pretty boring.'

'Everybody's a critic.' Barry stalked up the aisle towards what, he didn't know.

'See? He thinks you're an arsehole, too!' the woman said. The lights began to dim; Barry didn't stay to watch.

The moment Barry walked through the door at the top of the aisle, everything went black again. Moments (hours? days?) later, he found himself at the end of an immense queue. This didn't seem fair – didn't these people know who he was? Apparently not.

He was in the biggest room he'd ever seen. It was like some sort of Olympian train station, drab and gloomy and built for use. The ceiling – if there was a ceiling – loomed somewhere above, long past the point where the room's feeble light allowed one to see it. The room was filled with the murmur of a big crowd trying to be quiet, all the coughs and chuckles and whispers blending into a single soft sound.

Thousands of people long, the queue – and five more like it – radiated out from the room's centre, like the arms of a six-pointed starfish. Up ahead, impossibly far away, there appeared to be a round, glassed-in booth. Above it was a sign that Barry couldn't make out; he would have to get closer, and the way the line was moving, that could take days.

His right eye itched. Barry raised his hand to scratch it, and bumped into his wand. Without thinking, he grabbed the wand and pulled; it exited his eye socket with a soft pop. Shouldn't that have hurt? Barry thought, looking for a place to wipe the wand's end. He decided on the pink linen jacket of the man directly in front of him. It already had a bunch of rose-like gunshot wounds on it. Barry could see them slowly closing up before his eyes.

Several people were suddenly standing behind Barry. Even though the line was still moving very slowly, not being last any more made him feel better. He shuffled to his right a bit and tried to peer up ahead. Where was he? Why were they waiting in line? Could he jump the queue?

'If this is Heaven, it sucks,' Barry said aloud, mostly to himself.

The man in the pink linen jacket looked over his shoulder and said simply, 'This isn't Heaven; it's just check-in. You should listen to the loudspeakers.'

Barry adjusted his ears; sure enough, a pleasant female voice of authority was repeating a recorded message. 'Welcome. This is check-in. Please be patient, and have your ID available when you get to the window.' Barry felt for his wallet – it was still there.

'So why isn't this line moving any faster?'

The man laughed. 'Do you have somewhere you need to be?'

This guy irritated Barry. He decided to write 'Kick Me' on his jacket in eye gore. It would take a steady hand and delicate touch, but he had for ever.

Barry looked around. He saw a few babies and felt

sorry for them. To his delight, he also saw Lon. Lon, chocolate smeared around his mouth, was two lines over, and further ahead. Barry decided to join him.

'See ya,' Barry said.

'Hey!' the man said. 'Pushing in means five more years in Purgatory, kid!'

When Barry got to Lon, his old friend started jumping around licking his face.

'Easy, Lon – I'm glad to see you, too,' Barry said, then to the people who were staring, 'He's just excited.'

'Barry, Barry, Barry, Barry!' Lon said. 'I'm so happy to see you! Except—'

'Except what?' Barry asked.

'Promise you won't get angry?'

'I promise,' said Barry, lying.

'I ate your chocolate wand, Barry,' Lon said.

'It's okay, Lon, really—'

'No, it's not, Barry. I did a bad thing.' Lon unzipped his fly.

'Lon, no! *Don't* pee on yourself.'

'But I want to! I need to show you how sorry I am!'

'Later, maybe,' Barry said. 'It's no big deal.'

Lon stopped. 'Are you sure?'

'Yes, I'm sure. It's okay.'

'Okay,' Lon said. Looking around, he asked, 'Barry, where are we?'

'Check-in, whatever that is.' He heard the loud-speaker again and asked, 'Do you have the tags Nurse Pommefritte put on you?'

'Yes,' Lon said. They had his name, the address of Hogwash, and the date when he had last had his injections.

'Good. Hey, look at that,' Barry said, pointing. 'It's like the one at the Ministry of Magicity.' They'd moved close enough to see that the kiosk was roofed by a glorious, golden fountain. Jets of water spurted around a group of connected statues; the biggest, obviously a wizard, was planting a kick on the backside of a house elf, who was planting a kick on the backside of a Muddle.

'It's so beautiful,' Lon said, lip quivering.

'Do you remember that time we went to the Ministry, before you were a dog? Do you remember chaining yourself to the— Lon, wait – what are you—'

Lon had sprinted towards the fountain, with Barry lagging far behind. 'Lon! Come back!' As Lon climbed the kiosk and leapt into the water, Barry realised what was going on: Lon wanted to bite the stream of water.

'Lon, stop! It's *not alive*! We're going to lose our place in line!' The crowd, grateful for any distraction, started hooting and clapping as Lon rolled around in spastic canine delight.

Barry finally reached the kiosk. The people inside it were trying to ignore the cheering outside, as well as the thumps coming from above. Barry slid in front of the man at the head of the queue.

'Excuse me,' he said to the office person. 'I don't mean to push in, but my friend just jumped into your fountain. Can I go and get him?'

'Is that what that thumping is?' the office worker said. 'I thought it was an earthquake.' Looking over Barry's shoulder, she could see the formerly quiet queues deteriorating. With every splash from Lon and whoop from the crowd, the room seemed to get a little brighter and more colourful, and the people in the kiosk were plainly concerned about what might happen next. The afterlife depends on order, and once a party started . . .

'Thanks,' Barry said, and hauled himself up to the roof. Lon was on all fours, biting streams of water and barking.

'Come on, Lon,' Barry shouted. '*Come!*' He chased Lon for a while, much to the delight of everybody but himself. Soaked, Barry finally grabbed Lon's collar and hauled him out. After they both climbed down, the thousands of people standing in line broke into applause. Barry smiled, and waved – then Lon shook himself, spraying scores of people with water.

As people swore at Lon, a balding man with a toothbrush moustache inside the kiosk tapped on the glass with a coin.

'You two, come here,' he said. Barry and Lon presented themselves. Barry wrung out a shirttail.

'We can't have everybody riled up,' the man said through a hole in the glass. 'We have to keep everything running smoothly, or else magical folk have no place to go when they die. Don't want ghosts,' he said. 'Ghosts mean the system's fouled up. Lots of paperwork with ghosts. If I get you two processed, will you sit in the waiting area quietly, and stop causing all this ruckus?'

'Okay,' Barry said.

'What about him?' the man asked.

'He'll do whatever I tell him. Mostly.'

'All right, then. Can I have your identification?'

Barry pulled out his wallet. To his horror, it contained precisely three things: the fake thousand-pound note that he'd swiped from Bumblemore's office, a picture of Bea, and a novelty business card that read 'FBI – Female Body Inspector'. 'Uh, Mr—'

'Abercrombie,' the man said.

'Mr Abercrombie, all I have is this,' Barry said, handing over the card.

Abercrombie sighed. 'Is it so much to ask for people to die with ID?' he said wearily. 'Okay, we'll do it from

~ 231 ~

fingerprints.' Scratching his neck, which had shaving
bumps on it, Mr Abercrombie fed the business card into
a machine. He looked down at a computer screen, and
hit a button. A printer somewhere in the kiosk whirred
to life.

'Can I ask—'

'I'm sorry,' Abercrombie said, 'but if we allowed
questions, we'd never get anybody processed.' He
pointed behind Barry. 'Your friend is licking that
woman's head wound.'

Barry was mortified. 'Lon!' he hissed. Lon stopped
what he was doing and walked over. 'Stay here, Lon,'
Barry said. '*Stay.*'

A woman sitting next to Mr Abercrombie gave a
gravelly swear. 'Bernard, my chit-maker is down. Can I
use yours?' She was a small, rosy woman of uncertain
age, but Barry pegged her as older, judging by the
sweetness of her perfume.

'Certainly, Loretta,' Mr Abercrombie said. 'On condition that you never work next to anyone but me.'

Loretta had a surprisingly girlish laugh. 'Oh, Mr
Abercrombie, you're a devil.'

'What number do you need?'

'Sixty-nine,' Loretta said, giggling. 'I didn't plan it, I
swear.'

He handed her a small golden object. She took it, and

pulled on the windowshade. It sent up with a snap. 'V. Nemeth! Victoria Nemeth!' she said through the speaker.

Imagine that, Barry thought. Flirting in Purgatory. I wonder if people —

'Okay, Mr Trotter,' Mr Abercrombie said. The pile of printed pages had grown to a stack several inches thick; he had fastened the pages together with three golden rings. 'You didn't waste time on Earth, did you? Quite a file for somebody so young,' he said.

'It's a little more complicated than that, but thanks.'

'Don't thank me until it's judged. Could be nothing but bad, and we both know where you'll go then.' Another office-type machine whirred, then Abercrombie handed Barry a nametag: 'Trotter, B.' Then under that, 'Awaiting Final Assignment'.

'Stick this on your shirt, and have a seat in the waiting area,' Mr Abercrombie said, indicating a massive wedge-shaped phalanx of uncomfortable, putty-coloured chairs behind Barry. 'Listen for your name; someone will call you after you've been evaluated.'

'Thank you,' Barry said, beginning to sweat. There had to be a way out of here, he thought. If they looked through that stack, he was headed straight to ... Besides, he had to find Bea.

'Mr Trotter!' Abercrombie called after him. 'Wait for your friend.'

Barry and Lon found their way to two empty seats and sat down.

'Did I ever tell you about the time I spent the night in Heathrow?' Barry said to Lon. 'This is even more depressing than that.' Lon didn't answer – he was passing the time by picking a hardened piece of gum from underneath the plastic chair.

Barry examined his surroundings more closely. The section was packed – as were all the others – with people in various stages of healing, patiently waiting to be called. Every ten seconds or so, a name would be called. The person would walk up to the kiosk, where he or she would receive a golden chit with a number on it. The person would walk to that numbered doorway on the outer wall, step through the curtain and disappear.

Barry counted quietly, using the 'addition' Bea had taught him. Seventy-two curtained doorways ringed the gloomy, dusty chamber. If there was a way out of here, Barry thought, those had to be it.

'Lon, stay. I'm going for a stroll,' Barry said.

'Okay, Barry,' Lon said. He popped the ancient gum in his mouth. 'Yum, grape!'

Barry ignored his rising gorge and walked down the row to the aisle. Then he strode down the aisle to the back wall, all the way ignoring the dirty looks and rude comments of those people he'd cut in front of. He noticed that there were uniformed men with tiny, shrunken wings and truncheons patrolling the outer walls of the room. At first glance, the cops appeared to be shuffling, but upon closer inspection Barry could see that their tiny wings were lifting them a few inches off the ground. He guessed that they – some sort of angel-in-training? – were trying to discourage exactly what he was trying to accomplish. Getting out must be really good, Barry thought.

At the back edge of each section of the waiting area there were vending machines and a magazine rack. Unfortunately, the magazines were all tattered beyond belief, and the sweets in the machines were even older. Barry browsed for a while, catching up on tidbits like Elizabeth Taylor's third marriage ('Liz: This One's for Keeps!') and that latest fashion craze, the miniskirt.

Back against the rack, Barry slyly peered over the top of his magazine. The doorway directly opposite him had small golden letters above it, reading 'Asgard'. He looked fifteen feet to the left and read: 'Limbo'. The one to the right said, simply, 'Hell'. I'll stay away from that one, Barry thought.

A cop strolled over. 'Hey, mate,' he said. 'No dawdling. Just get your magazine and go back to your seat.'

'Sorry,' Barry said. 'I've never been here before. What's that over there?' Barry pointed to his left, towards a wall full of scaffolding, covered with tarps of blue plastic to keep the plaster dust down.

'They're expanding the waiting room,' the angel-cop said. 'They're expecting a big rush sometime soon. Now, back to your seat.'

'Thanks.' A lot more dead wizards? Barry walked – slowly – to the nearest aisle. Looking back at the wall under construction, he noticed that the doorway closest to it was labelled 'The Underworld'. If he could sneak in under that tarp, there'd be no way an angel-cop could nab him in the two or three steps between the edge of the scaffolding and the Underworld, wherever that was. It might be perfect, Barry thought. It was doubtless full of criminals, and maybe this fake thousand-pound note would buy him some real information as to where Bea might be.

When Barry returned to his seat, he had even more company. Actually, this wasn't so surprising; every witch and wizard on Earth had to pass through sometime.

'Beany!' It was Serious Blech, and he still couldn't

remember Barry's name. Barry looked about, craning to see around the horse that was standing in front of him.

'Baggy, it's me! Serious!'

'Where?' Barry said. 'Wave or something.'

'I can't – I'm the horse!'

'I can't wait to hear this,' Barry said, not really wanting to know.

'Come over and I'll tell you,' Serious said.

'Serious,' Barry asked, 'how can you talk when your mouth isn't moving?'

'I'm talking out of the other end,' Serious said. 'First of all, and I'm really sorry about this, but I lost all your money . . .'[44]

❊

---

[44] Barry was the first, and as it turned out, only, major investor in Serious Putty, Ltd. In an attempt to capitalise on his fame – as a white-collar criminal, but fame nonetheless – Serious had tried to manufacture and sell the first ever toy for tedious, dreary children: Serious Putty, Beige and inert, it did nothing. It even smelled boring.

'Think of it, Barry,' Serious had said. 'The world is full of uninteresting people – all of whom were kids, once. But every toy is designed to be amusing and fun. What the world needs now is a truly lacklustre toy!' Actually, it hadn't, so Barry lost all his money.

'. . . so Big Julie comes by the house one morning and says, "If you don't pay Jesus Frankenstein the money you owe him by the end of today, I'm gonna come back and break your kneecaps!" Scary, right? I turned the house upside down and found something like seven Gallons – leaving 449,993 to go,' Serious said. 'I had a couple of beers, and started thinking, Could I get by without kneecaps? Then my house elf, Trayter, came up with a great idea: I could pay off the loan by selling my organs,' Serious said. 'So that's what I did. Everything was going great, until . . .'

'Until what?' Barry asked. Talking to a horse's behind was incredibly distracting.

'Well, I got a little carried away. I looked at the price list, and thought, Let's go for the big-ticket items, you know? Make it back in one operation, no muss, no fuss.'

'You are so stupid,' Barry moaned.

'I sold my brain, spine and heart. By the time I realised what I'd done, I was on the operating table, and Trayter was sawing away,' Serious said. 'Remember, Bernie: always read the fine print.'

'What difference does it make now?' Barry said. 'I'm dead.'

'I'd like to hear about that,' Serious said. 'Every corpse has a story. Anyway, I think this is a golden opportunity. There's a market here, Bogey. Under-serviced, evergreen. With your capital and my brains – you do have some capital, right?'

Barry evaded the question. 'So how did you get to be a horse?'

'Now that's interesting. After we realised what was going to happen, Trayter told me about this spell he could cast, sort of flinging my soul into whichever living being was closest. It sounded good to me,' Serious said. 'I didn't have a lot of options. Trayter had been keeping a horse in his room for a while. He brought the horse in, and after I signed the house over to him, Trayter— Wait . . .'

'Trayter screwed you, didn't he?'

Serious stamped his feet and whinnied.

'Well, at least you were a horse,' Barry said. 'That must've been fun.'

'It would've been, except that I was still a human being inside. I was still attracted to women. Trayter sold me almost immediately to this farmer,' Serious said. 'After I put the moves on his wife, he had me put down – thought I was possessed by the Devil.' Serious chuckled, then asked, 'How did you die?'

'Nothing big,' Barry said. 'I stuck my wand in my eye.'

'I told you not to run with it,' Serious said.

'I did it on purpose,' Barry said defensively. 'I need to find a dead friend of mine.'

'A girl, obviously,' Serious said, and Barry admitted it. 'What, does she owe you money?'

'No,' Barry said acidly. 'You're the only person who ever owes me money.'

'Right, I know that, and I'm going to pay you back – with interest – just as soon as we set up our business,' Serious said. 'We have to think of something to sell.'

'Serious,' Barry said, 'if you think I'm investing in any more of your dumb schemes . . .'

'I think you'd be a very wise man indeed,' Serious said. 'How'd dog-boy end up here?'

'Chocolate,' Barry said. 'Listen, I'll make a deal with you: if you help me find my friend, I'll think about giving you some money.'

'What's her name?' Serious asked.

'Bea Thompson.'

'Just a first initial, eh? That might be tough,' Serious said. 'But I'll do it. Between you and me, I don't think my file's going to be too good. When you've made and lost as much money as I have, it's hard to end up in Heaven. Do you have a plan?'

Barry said, 'I was thinking of sneaking behind that scaffolding over there.'

Serious looked over Barry's shoulder to the tarp-clad wall. 'Okay. Why?'

'Then when the guards aren't looking, sneak into that doorway, right there.' Barry pointed behind his hand.

'What's so special about that doorway?'

'It's the Underworld,' Barry said.

'Oh, I don't like the sound of that,' Serious said. 'What if we ran into Big Julie? Or Jesus Frankenstein?'

'What could they do to you?' Barry said. 'And even if they died at this moment, they'd have to sit out here for decades. Look.' Barry indicated a woman sitting a few feet away. A spider had spun a web between her head and the arm of the bench.

'I see your point, Breathy. What about the guards?'

'They've got to change shifts some time,' Barry said. 'Union rules. Here's what we're going to do . . .'

Precisely on the hour, just as Barry had predicted, the angel-cops started to swap over.

'Let's go,' Barry said. 'Lon, hold on to Serious's tail.'

Acting meticulously casual, the trio sauntered down the row to the aisle, then over to the vending machines nearest the scaffolding-covered wall. They didn't know what the penalty was for trying to escape, but they were already dead, so how bad could it be? Checking to see

~ 241 ~

that nobody was looking, they slipped behind the
plastic tarp, one by one, first Serious, then Lon, then
Barry.

'Wow,' Serious said. Even amid the clouds of plaster
dust, they could see that the extension was massive –
easily double the size of the current room, and that was
just the visible portion. Teams of angels wearing
hardhats moved about; some hefted jackhammers,
others were doing carpentry, making the newly hewn
space into a proper room.

'No time to gawp,' Barry said. 'Somebody might see
us.'

The three moved quickly over to the other side of the
tarp. Barry went to the front. 'When I run,' Barry said,
'we all run.' Carefully, Barry stuck his head out. The
guards were in place, but none were close enough to
stop him – so he made his dash.

A guard saw him. 'Stop!' he yelled, then blew a
whistle. The room was suddenly filled with a great
fluttering of wings.

Taking a deep breath, Barry plunged through the
curtains. Lon followed. As the guards converged upon
him, Serious thought for a second. There were so many
money-making opportunities here – all these bored
people, trapped with nothing to do. But there might be
even more people on the other side of the curtain ...

As usual, greed won out. 'What the hell,' Serious said, and clopped through to whatever was waiting on the other side. The angel-cop's hand missed his tail by inches. Using the horse's bottom, Serious blew him a raspberry.

Chapter Thirteen

AH, UNDERWORLD!

The last thing Barry expected to find on the other side was more people. And yet here they were, all jostling and BO and complaints. There was a crowd of griping shufflers decked out like Bea's gran in togas and sandals. Barry moved into the crowd, well away from the entrance; he didn't want an angel-cop to be able to reach through and pull him back.

It was gloomy – felt like twilight – and they were all standing on the banks of a steaming, roiling river. The atmosphere was oppressive: humid and dank, like the Tube in August or the inside of a particularly ripe-smelling compost heap. Barry pulled off his warm dress robes, revealing jeans and an 'I'm With Stupid' T-shirt.

'What's this all about?' Barry asked the fellow closest to him. He was translucent, which meant that he probably knew something.

'Your clothes are strange,' the man said. 'Why do you call me stupid?'

'Uh . . . it's a form of greeting in my country.' Barry was in no mood to take crap from ghosts. Barry saw Lon come through, and wondered how good he would be in a fight.

'Ridiculous!' the man sniffed. 'Preposterous! How dare you, an impudent young fool just off the slab, insult the garb of noble Rome?'

Jackpot! Barry couldn't believe his luck. 'Right, right. I'm sorry. I blame it on the modern age.'

'I accept your apology. Have things got worse?' the man asked gleefully.

'You wouldn't believe it,' Barry said. 'What is everybody doing here?'

'None of us has money for the ferry,' the man said. 'Hey!' Apparently being translucent didn't make getting goosed by Lon any more fun.

'Who's in charge?' Barry asked.

'That man, I suppose.' He pointed towards a hippie-ish-looking fellow leaning against the prow of a bark. Engrossed in a book, he was extremely scraggly, and scratched himself frequently.

Barry saw Serious step through the curtain into the gloom. He waved.

'Hey, Lassie! Over here!' Barry said. Serious walked over.

'Lassie was a dog,' Serious said when he got there. 'I'm a horse.'

'Excuse me, but' – the fellow Barry had talked to pulled on his sleeve – 'that horse talks out of his—'

'We know,' Barry said.

'Mister, got any gum?' Lon asked.

Barry felt for his wallet. 'Guys, come with me,' he said. With Lon and Serious in tow, Barry pushed to the head of the group. Being dead had made him even more assertive. Crowd members made various noises of protest. Barry took out his wallet, and pulled out the thousand-pound note.

The ferryman, who was evidently used to tuning out the hubbub, was reading a book entitled *Basic Database Management for the Dead*. But Barry's money caught his eye.

With a practised motion quicker than that of any mortal man, he grabbed the note and stuffed it into his pocket. 'Get in,' he said.

'Hey, Sharon,' a dead person said, 'that's plenty for all of us to get across.'

'It's Charon, tit,' Charon said. 'Ask this bloke. It's his money.'

'Can I get change?' Barry asked Charon. There was

a chorus of boos, and someone shouted, 'Let's throw him in the river!'

Barry happened to look over just in time to see a skeletal piranha leap out of the river, clicking its teeth like castanets. 'Okay, okay!' he said. 'This one's on me!'

Amidst the claps on the back, Barry hoped Charon didn't look too closely at the Queen on the note – at least until they were across.

The water of the Styx was utterly foul – brackish, almost pudding-like in consistency, with chicken bones and crisp packets and used condoms floating in it. Every so often, a bubble would heave itself to the surface, and the river would give a great, gassy belch. Lon barked incessantly at these.

'Hey, man, tell your hound to knock it off,' Charon said.

'Shut up, Charon!' said a shade. 'He paid his fare like the rest of us. Go ahead and bark, weird person!' The dead were a democratic lot.

Charon grumbled something inaudible and unflattering, then continued talking to the shades clustered around him. 'Yes, it's a steady job, but there's nowhere to go. No room to move. Think Pluto's dyin' anytime soon?' Charon made a sound of disgust with saliva and his teeth. 'Not a chance. That's why I'm studyin' the computers.'

Some of the shades laughed.

'Oh, go ahead,' Charon said. 'Laugh it up. But that's a career, not like ferryin' you sorry lot back and forth. You work in an office, with air-conditionin' and fresh water. There are no infinite-toothed piranhas, and very few demons to speak of. Plus, once or twice a year, you get to go to conventions, too. Know how many people would show up for an Infernal Ferryman convention?'

'How many?' Barry said. Apparently boredom was a big part of the whole Underworld experience.

'One!' Charon said bitterly. '*If* you held it in Vegas! Otherwise, I'm not goin'!'

Barry, Lon and Serious stepped off the boat. Charon stuck his palm out. 'A tip is customary.'

Barry looked at him. 'Are you daft? I paid you a thousand pounds!'

'Cheapskate,' Charon grumbled and shoved off. A fading voice came a bit later: 'People like you have ruined this business!'

'Shut up!' Barry and Serious chorused.

'That bloke was a barrel of laughs, wasn't he?' Barry said. Lon barked, and they turned around.

'This one's even funnier,' Serious said.

In front of them had appeared a massive black dog, growling, with hackles raised. Each of its three, blunt, muscly heads had a mouth filled with fangs. Slavering with stinking, acid-green, probably poisonous spittle, the fearsome beast looked at the three wizards in a blatantly 'which one shall I eat first' way.

'What the Hell?' Barry murmured.

'Indeed,' Serious said.

'We paid our fare!' Barry said to the dog. It made no movement, continuing to weigh their relative succulences.

'He won't let us in because we're not ancient Greeks or Romans,' Serious said. 'We don't have the chit. I've read about him. His name is Care-Bear something.'

'Bugger!' Barry said; to have escaped the waiting room and crossed the Styx only to end up as dog food . . . what a disappointing book this was turning out to be.

'I could outrun it,' Serious whispered.

'Speak louder,' Barry said. 'I'm at the front.'

'I said, "I could outrun it,"' Serious said, and leapt rightwards. Care-Bear moved so quickly to block his way it seemed the creature could teleport.

'Okay, I can't,' Serious admitted.

'Not fair!' Barry said, trying not to look at the three pairs of burning yellow eyes, and more rows of fangs than seemed legal. 'I mean, if you want to kill us, fine, but where's the fun in that? *You* know you can kill us. *We* know you can kill us. Why not give us a sporting chance?'

'You do realise you're talking to a dog, right?' Serious said.

'Got any better ideas?' Barry said with irritation, then continued his pitch. 'I mean, really, think about this: we're just some guys trying to get into the Underworld – not escape, mind you, but get *in*. Why should you care if we want to subject ourselves to eternal torment? Maybe we're masochists. I think it's pretty small-minded of you to sit there in judgement on our sexual orientation.'

'Yeah,' Serious said, half-heartedly. He didn't think whatever Barry was planning would work, but then again they were still breathing.

Barry's continuing exegesis of the sexual politics of masochism aside, the fact was he didn't have a plan. But his blathering on did distract the beast a bit. As Barry talked, Lon had seen a small squeaky-bone made of soft plastic (left there by a Greek hero) and made a run for it. Infernal yes, but Care-Bear was also a dog, with all the weaknesses that the canine flesh is heir to. He was similarly enchanted, and sprinted for the bone.

'Lon!' Barry yelled. 'No!'

This action was so completely unexpected by the three-headed guardian of Hades that Lon actually made it to the bone unhindered. Now in possession of his prize, Lon was determined to keep it, and that meant escape. So he took off towards where they had come, back to the river.

'Lon! Come here—'

Serious flicked his tail, whopping Barry on the head.

'Are you crazy? Let's go, before the dog comes back.'

'But Lon—' Barry looked towards the river. Actually, Lon seemed to be holding his own. He and Care-Bear were running around in circles, dashing in and out of the water, splashing Charon, who was bringing some new arrivals. The next moment, it was no longer about the toy; Lon and Care-Bear were now running figures of eight after each other. They had each found a playmate.

'You're right,' Barry said. 'Let's go.'

The way cleared, Barry and Serious entered through the towering ebony gates of the Underworld. Inside, they found themselves in a meadow the colour of ash. It stretched for miles in every direction under a leaden sky.

Barry looked at – and somewhat through – his hand.

The longer he stayed here, the more washed-out he became. 'I miss colours,' he said.

'Me, too,' Serious said.

Pushing through the grey fields, they eventually found a path, which made the going easier. All around them, spirits clumped and separated, slashing through the air like a flock of bats. Presently, the grasses seemed to thin out a bit. From his elevated position on Serious's back, Barry could see something interesting: up ahead, there was the convergence of three paths.

'A crossroads,' Barry said. 'It's like where you go to sell your soul to the Devil for cool guitar chords or something.'

'The Devil's already got us,' Serious said bleakly. 'Or would've, if we were in the Christian Hell, instead of the Roman one.'

The moment the pair reached the convergence of the paths, they felt a small explosion.

'Shades!' boomed a voice, as the smoke congealed into human form. 'I am Hecate, goddess of witches and denizen of the Underworld. Though you may be weirdly dressed, that will not save you. Prepare to meet your doom!'

'What are you going to do, kill us?' Serious mumbled.

'I heard that, wise-arse,' said the goddess, who had

taken the shape of a wizened – but still strangely
GMILFy – crone swathed in black velvet.

'Er ... O, Hecate, do not kill us,' Barry said,
dismounting Serious and bowing his head. 'We are in
search of someone, a young witch untimely taken from
the upper world ... A person pure of heart unfairly cast
down—'

Hecate interrupted. 'Wait. I *know* you,' the goddess
said. 'You're that wizard that blew our cover! Barry
Wossname.'

As one, all Barry's pores opened in fear. 'Oh no, that
wasn't me,' he stammered. 'You must be thinking of
somebody else.'

'I don't think so,' she said. 'The papers are slow, but
they get down here eventually. Let me see under your
hair.'

'Is that really necessary?' Barry said; her glower told
him it certainly was. He lifted his fringe.

'Aha! I knew you were that idiot,' Hecate said. 'I've
been waiting for you, my fame-addled chappie! It's
because of you that thousands of years of lovely secrecy
went down the ol' porcelain pipe! Now every witch and
wizard is being bugged by a mob of Muddles, asking to
learn magic. Nobody can get any proper incanting
done. They're always invoking me, complaining, saying,
"Hecate, please smite the irritating school friend of my

daughter so I can finally do some work," or "Hecate, please force all the neighbourhood kids to leave flaming bags of dog turds somewhere else this Halloween." That book has caused no end of troubles, me lad.' Hecate conjured a rubber glove, which she pulled on to her hand with a snap. In a trice it was glowing like molten steel. 'Prepare to start paying the price, Mr Wizard. Trousers down, please.'

'Wait!' Barry exclaimed, terrified. 'It wasn't my fault! What about the author?'

Hecate waved it off. 'Reviews are punishment enough.' She took a step further. 'Prepare for a prostate exam you'll never forget.'

'Wait!' Barry said, scrambling behind Serious. 'Female doctors make me uncomfortable!'

'Nice try,' the goddess said. 'Should've thought of that before you got famous.'

Barry crouched behind Serious's buttock, trying to make himself small and put some horseflesh between himself and the angry goddess's burning glove. Just as Barry was tensed and ready to run, Serious cleared his throat and gave a whinny. Since he wasn't a real horse, it was a fairly pitiful attempt. And it came from the wrong end, which caused the goddess to exclaim, 'Impudent animal! I will deal with you next!'

Barry saw the look on Serious's face and said, 'No, Goddess. I think he was trying to placate you.'

'Farting is no way to placate the divine, worm,' Hecate said. 'If that were so, Christians would hold services after brunch, instead of before. Now, stop cowering. This is going to hurt you a lot more than it is me.'

Barry stood up, momentarily annoyed. 'How do you figure that?'

Serious was trying to form his features into the picture of equine seduction, but between being another species, and controlling it from the other end, he wasn't having much luck. But he had caught Hecate's eye. He whinnied again.

'Your horse definitely has wind,' she said. 'Look at the face he's making.' Hecate pointed to Serious, whose mien did suggest confusion and/or health problems. Still, something in the mix attracted the goddess.

She looked at Serious for a moment, pondering. 'Tell you what, boy,' she said. 'I'll offer you a trade. This stallion here, in exchange for your—'

'Yes!' Barry said, trying to smile. 'Take him! Just put away the hot glove!'

The glove stopped glowing, and Hecate took it off with another snap.

'Barry!' Serious hissed. 'Come over here!'

'What?' Barry said, keeping a smile frozen on his face.

'I've never had sex as a horse! What if I'm gay?'

'Any problem?' Hecate asked.

'Yes!' Serious said loudly.

'Nope!' Barry said, even louder. 'He's just a little colicky.'

'Does he have any papers?' Hecate said.

'Of course,' Barry said. 'But I lost them. He's a thoroughbred, it's obvious. Take him, he's all yours.'

'Very well. This character will join my harem, to pleasure me when I am in mare form.'

'Whatever you say,' Barry said. 'I'm sure he's very, uh, adept.' Serious whopped Barry with his tail.

'What makes you say that?' Hecate said, conjuring a sugar cube and feeding it to Serious.

'Um . . .' Barry searched for something. 'I used to read the *Kama Sutra* to him.'

'Barry, I don't know the *Kama Sutra*,' Serious said quietly.

'Shut up! You'll think of something,' Barry mumbled, face close to the horse's butt.

'Now, shade, begone, before I change my mind,' Hecate said.

'But Goddess – before I go, can you help me find the person I seek?'

Hecate grabbed her brow. 'You know something? You're even more annoying than all the supplicants say you are. Hand over the picture.' Barry did so.

'She came through here not too long ago,' Hecate said. ''Course I know her, she's a witch. One of the few ones nice enough not to bother me all the time.'

'Pureblood or Muddle-born?' Barry said. 'Just curious.'

'Pure. She's a *real* thoroughbred.'

Barry said, 'Do you know where she is now?'

'Go and see Persephone. She liked this girl – they talked about books and things,' Hecate said. 'Me, I don't care for that kind of crap. Every book I read, witches get a bad rap. One gets tired of the stereotypes. Anyway, go down that path' – Hecate pointed – 'and ask Persephone. For all I know, they're together right now.'

And with that, both the goddess and her new consort disappeared.

'Bye, Serious,' Barry said, trusting that his godfather could hear him somehow, and started walking.

Standing on the crest of a hill, Barry looked around – asphodel for as far as the eye could see. Off in the distance, a herd of unbaptised babies grazed. Just for fun, Barry yelled. Spooked, the babies crawled away at breakneck speed, raising a great plume of dust across the prairie.

Laughing to himself, Barry descended the hill; at the bottom the path split into two branches. One signpost read, 'Suicides This Way'.

Barry paused. If one was going to be a stickler about it, he *had* killed himself. But it wasn't like he was depressed or anything. Furthermore Barry didn't think suicides would be much fun to hang out with. He decided to keep on the main path, and make up an excuse later if necessary.

Barry hadn't walked very far when a shade appeared and started giving him the high-pressure sale.

'Listen, pal,' the shade said to Barry, walking beside him. 'I just got a bunch of souls. The genuine article, fell off the back of a truck.'

'Oh yeah?' Barry said. 'Sounds illegal to me.'

'No, no, no, no, no, no,' the shade said. Barry fixed him with a dubious look. 'Okay, yes.'

Barry walked a little faster; the shade kept up. 'I've got a friend topside who . . . anyway, the point is, if you wanna get back early – and who doesn't, right? – you got to have one of these. You can either wait for a thousand years like the rest of the suckers, or—'

'Look, pal,' Barry said. 'Save your breath – I didn't die yesterday.' Of course Barry *had*, but what the shade didn't know couldn't hurt Barry. 'I'm looking for a girl named Bea Thompson.' Barry pulled out his wallet, and showed the shade Bea's picture.

'Looks young,' he said.

'She's fifteen, like me. Sort of.'

'What do you mean?' the shade said.

'I mean, I'm really thirty-nine, but in my mind I'm fifteen again and I'm looking for another fifteen-year-old down here so that I can be thirty-nine for good. I'm really still alive.'

'That's what they all say down here.' The shade sniffed. 'Oldest story around.'

'Believe what you want.' Barry took the picture back.

'Good luck,' the shade said. 'Hope you find her. The afterlife's too long to spend alone. And if you change your mind about these souls, I'll be here.'

Barry quickened his pace. Just because he had an eternity to look for Bea, that didn't mean he wanted to hang around. It was creepy here. Grey. Ashy. And everybody got on his nerves.

All around was eye-high asphodel. Just as Barry began to wonder if he'd be able to see Bea, if he ever found her, the foliage started to thin out again. Here and there black poplars had claimed bits of space; and some areas actually looked freshly mown. The ground rolled a little, with gentle hills here and there. It seemed almost settled – certainly pleasant, as afterlives went.

There was a water-cooler just off to the side of the path. Two shades stood next to it, siphoning drinks into paper cups and downing them. It looked good; after walking for a while, Barry was thirsty.

'Either of you have an extra cup?' he asked. A shade gave him one. 'Thanks,' Barry said. He got out Bea's picture and gave it to the shade. 'I'm looking for this girl. Seen her? Name's Bea Thompson.'

'Oh, nobody uses names around here,' the second shade said.

'It's very informal,' the first shade said.

'Well, does she look familiar?' Barry started to fill his cup.

'Oh dear,' said the first shade. 'I wish you'd asked five minutes ago, before I had a drink.'

'Why?' Barry said, cup to his lips.

'This water's special,' the second shade said. 'It wipes away all your memories.'

'Yeah!' said the first, laughing. 'We drink to forget.'

Barry, cheeks full, did a spit take, spraying the shades.

'That's not the way it works,' the second one said. 'You have to swallow it, not just spit it. I think – I'm not sure.'

'Yeah, thanks though. It was a nice thought,' said the first. 'Whatever it was.'

Barry, spooked, took the photo back and walked away quickly, feverishly trying to remember things.

'Nice guy,' the first shade said.

'Which guy are you talking about?' the second shade said.

'I forget,' the first shade said.

Barry hadn't forgotten anything. In fact, as he walked he found that, if he really concentrated, he could remember things that hadn't really happened. This was normal.

Rounding a bend, Barry was just recalling that time he had sex with seven luscious supermodels when there, sitting crosslegged under a tree, was Bea.

Suddenly embarrassed about his thoughts, Barry tried to think of puppies as he ran towards her. 'Bea!' he shouted.

Bea, who was reading a book, turned and saw Barry. 'Oh, hey,' she said.

This made Barry reconsider the hug. 'That's it? Just "hey"?' He stopped at a polite distance and sat down. 'I've been looking all over for you.'

'I haven't gone anywhere since I got here,' Bea said. 'Thanks to that spell of yours.' She closed the book, and put it atop a small pile of books that lay next to her. 'So – are you dead?' she asked, with perhaps a note of hopefulness in her voice.

'No,' Barry said. 'I mean, yes. In my mind, at least. I think I'm not. But I am here, so . . . really I'm not sure.'

'I don't get it,' Bea said.

'That makes two of us,' Barry said. 'I've found that it helps to let your mind go kind of slack . . . This doesn't look so bad,' Barry said, looking around. 'At least there aren't any insects.' Bea didn't respond, so Barry asked a question. 'What are you reading?'

'It's a book about the multiverse,' Bea said. 'It's a theory in physics that says that sixty-four multiple universes are all happening simultaneously.'

'Sounds neat,' Barry said, all perky incomprehension. 'All I remember about physics is that Italians can't hear radio broadcasts, something like that . . . Wow,' Barry said, hefting the book, 'it's heavy!'

'I hadn't noticed,' Bea said.

Yep, Barry thought, she's definitely mad. 'So . . . read a lot?'

'Yes,' Bea said. 'As you might've noticed, there's not much to do. When I finish one, I just throw it into the air and a different one comes down.'

'Erm . . .' Barry mumbled, searching for more small talk. It was suddenly a long afterlife.

Bea misheard. 'How is she? Sorry I never got a chance to really talk to her – seemed like an interesting girl.'

'Oh, she's great.' Now came the sticky part. 'Married to me, actually.'

'Those two statements seem mutually exclusive,' Bea said. 'Anyway, aren't you a little young for marriage?'

'No – I mean, yes. I mean – what do I mean? I mean, I can understand why one might think – I'm not as old as I look, I have a disease—'

'Yes, called ignorance.'

Barry let it go. 'Right. What I'm trying to say is that I'm really thirty-nine, and my doctor suggested that I kill myself—'

'Some doctor,' Bea said coolly.

'– and come down here and get you, so that I can start ageing again,' Barry said. 'God, this is hard to explain.'

'And you, with so few tools.'

Barry just took it. 'So I'd like to take you back . . . uh . . . upstairs,' Barry said. 'Are you game?'

'I don't think you can,' Bea said. 'I think this is permanent.'

'Come on, Bea,' Barry said. 'Let's try! What could it hurt?' Barry saw her considering, so he pressed the point. 'You died so young, and stupidly, and didn't ever really have time to do all sorts of great things. I mean, who wants to wait a whole thousand years?'

Bea got up. 'Okay, we'll try,' she said, brushing off her trousers. 'I don't think you'll be able to do anything, but I'm a little sick of reading at the moment.'

'Are you just going to leave the books there?' Barry asked.

'Yeah,' Bea said. 'Every once in a while, the goddess Persephone comes by with a little cart.'

'Hey, are she and Hecate, like, gay?'

'Why do you ask? Simple prurient interest, or are you thinking of dating her? Because if she were to ask my opinion,' Bea said, 'I really can't recommend it. I'm only telling you.'

'No. We just met Hecate, and she seemed . . . randy. Open to experimentation,' Barry said. 'In fact, she took my friend as a love-slave.'

'Well, magical people are irresponsible below the waist,' Bea said. 'As I found out, to my chagrin.'

Wanting to change the subject, Barry pointed to the books. 'Are any of those about computers?'

'No, why?'

'Can we get one?' Barry asked. 'It might come in handy.'

'Sure,' Bea said. 'Start tossing.'

'You don't mean that,' Barry said.

'God,' Bea said, 'I had forgotten what rarefied levels of conversation one inhabits with you, Barry. I mean, "start throwing the books into the air".'

They did so. About five minutes later, Barry caught *Learning C++: Royal Road to Riches*, and with that they started back.

About halfway there, Barry said to Bea, 'I suppose you're pretty pissed off with me.'

'You suppose!'

'Well, I apologise.'

'You apologise?' Bea said, suddenly fuming, now that the pretence of politeness was over. 'I should hope you would! I come to your school, hoping to have a nice time, and not only do I miss all the dancing and the Beatles, whom I enjoy, but before the night is half over I end up dead! Then, if that weren't bad enough, I had to sit in a field for God knows how long!' She smacked Barry on the ear.

'Ow!' Barry said. 'Crap, Bea! That really hurt!'

'I don't care. I wanted it to hurt,' she said. 'What did my gran say?'

'I faked a letter from you, saying you'd run off and joined the Visigoths.'

'Never would've done that,' Bea said. 'Personal hygiene is too important to me. Was she sad?'

~ 265 ~

'I don't think so. I think she knew that I would bring you back eventually,' Barry said. 'All that prophecy stuff.'

'Well, I'm glad you're trying to put it right, but I still think you're a wanker,' Bea said.

'Bet you believe I can do magic now,' Barry said, trying to salvage a victory.

Bea snorted. 'I always knew you could do magic, dipstick. I was teasing you. Now that I've found out I'm magical, too, I'm even less impressed.'

'Come on, Bea. This is by far the most mature thing I've ever done,' Barry said. 'Give me credit.'

'I'll give you credit when we get out of here,' Bea said.

'Did somebody say "get out of here"?' an unearthly voice said.

Barry and Bea turned around. A beautiful woman of approximately twice normal size stood there. She wasn't happy.

Barry started to speak.

Bea elbowed him. 'Shut it,' she whispered. 'Oh, hi, Goddess. This is an old friend of mine, Barry Trotter. Barry, Persephone. Persephone, Barry.'

'How do you do?' the goddess said. 'Are you that fellow Hecate is irritated with? She says that horse you gave her has erectile dysfunction.'

Bea leapt in. 'Goddess, listen: Barry's the reason I'm here. I was out with him on a date, and, well, I'll spare you the details. I died. He killed me.'

'Men,' Persephone muttered bitterly.

'Yeah,' Bea said, chuckling. 'What can you do?'

'Beat this punk to a pulp,' Persephone said. 'Would you like me to?' Barry really started to sweat.

'I assure you that was my first idea, too,' Bea said. 'But then Barry explained how he had killed himself specifically to come down here and bring me back. That changed how I felt. A bit.'

'I see,' Persephone said. 'Well better late than never.'

'That's what I said!' Barry exclaimed. Persephone smiled, and Barry's stomach dropped back into its normal slot. Then the smile disappeared.

'But you know the rules, Bea. Once you're here, you can't leave early. You have' – Persephone counted on her fingers – 'nine hundred and seventy-six years left until you can go back. Even I can't leave early.'

'I know, Goddess,' Bea said, 'and normally I wouldn't even think of it. But after Barry got here, and explained his really stupid plan—'

'*Really* stupid,' Persephone said, laughing.

'– I thought, Well, what better way to cheese off Pluto than to escape from the Underworld? What do you think of that? We were just on our way to see you,' Bea lied.

Persephone thought for a moment, a smile still on her face. 'That *would* really chafe his biscuits,' she said.

'Could you possibly consider it a blow for woman-kind everywhere?' Barry said. Bea trod on his foot, hard. Persephone saw it, and laughed again.

'Young wizard, you certainly have a way with the ladies,' she said. 'But you're right. It would be a blow of sorts. And frankly, I don't think Hecate *wants* you here.' She rearranged her raiment; Barry swore inwardly – he had been getting a small glimpse of boob. 'I'll let you go as far as the river, after that you're on your own.'

'What about Pluto?' Bea asked. Pluto was in charge of the Underworld, and had tricked Persephone into spending part of every year there. It was sort of like an anti-holiday.

'Don't worry about Pluto,' Persephone said. 'I'll keep him busy.'

'How?' Bea asked.

'Dear,' Persephone said somewhat wearily, 'if you have to ask, then I'm glad you're going back. You didn't have enough fun the first time around. You just walk to the Styx as fast as possible, and I'll lie there and think of Rome.'

'We can take it from there,' Barry said, holding up the book.

'That's good,' Persephone said. 'Because I can't help you across the river. Charon's an old crab – an eternity in the service industry will do that to anybody . . . Now, get going,' Persephone said. 'You know, Barry Trotter, for a loser I find you strangely winning.'

Chapter Fourteen

THE MID-AFTERNOON
OF JUDGEMENT

༄ ༺༝༻ ༄

Barry's fortunes had definitely changed: Care-Bear, doubtless cavorting with Lon, was nowhere to be found. And the computer book made Charon actually happy to take him and Bea back across the River Styx.

Dusting themselves off, Bea and Barry walked out of the Underworld and back into the wizards' waiting room.

'What in the Hell . . . ?' the angel-cop closest to them said. 'I've never seen somebody walk out.'

Barry heard him. 'Not a nice place to visit,' he said to the angel-cop, 'and I wouldn't recommend living there, either.'

'Oh, don't listen to him, it's not as bad as all that,' Bea said. 'It grows on you.'

They found some empty seats and sat down.

'Now what?' Bea asked.

'Now we wait,' Barry said. 'They're weighing all the stuff I did on Earth.'

'I'm not responsible for that!' Bea said quickly.

'I know. Calm down, spaz,' Barry said. 'When they call me up there, that's when I'll tell them about you and how this was all a big misunderstanding.'

'I'd prefer to speak for myself, if you don't mind,' Bea said.

'Fine,' Barry said. 'I'm going to get some magazines. Would you like one?'

'Are they still really old?'

'Probably a little older.'

'No thanks,' she said. 'Unless you find one with crosswords in it.'

As Barry walked to get a magazine, the idea that he was being judged – and could be enjoying his last few moments outside of Hell – didn't bother him so much. I mean, nobody *likes* the idea of endless torment, but going back and getting Bea had squared things a bit. As for the rest of his life . . . He was the person he was, and if that damned him for all time, well, he'd just have to write nasty letters to the appropriate authorities in between sessions of molten lead gargling.

After what seemed like an eternity – and may well have been – Barry heard a voice on the loudspeaker: 'Barry

Trotter – Barry Trotter, please step up to window fourteen.'

'Come on,' Barry said to Bea. Bea smoothed her hair nervously as they walked up the aisle.

It was Mr Abercrombie again. 'Mr Trotter,' he said, 'I'm not supposed to comment on files, but I must say that you've got your soul's worth.'

Barry didn't know what to say. 'Thanks?'

Mr Abercrombie looked at Bea. 'Miss, you'll have to wait your turn. This is extremely personal and confidential.'

Bea turned to go and sit back down. 'Wait!' Barry said. 'Mr Abercrombie, this is Bea Thompson.'

'Is she your sister?' Mr Abercrombie said.

'God, no!' Bea said.

'She was my girlfriend – can I say that?' Barry looked at Bea.

'Yes, for about two months. Until you killed me!'

'By accident! By accident!' Barry said. He turned to Mr Abercrombie. 'Can she stay here while I find out where I end up?'

'Well, why her, out of all the legions?' Mr Abercrombie said. '"Plays more doctor than the Royal College of Surgeons."' He chuckled. 'That Alpo Bumblemore certainly has a way with words.'

The mention of Barry's old enemy galvanised him.

'Listen, just tell me I'm going to Hell and be done with it. I've already hauled my arse all over the Underworld to get Bea here out, and—'

'Glad to hear you're so well-adjusted to your fate. Most people kick up an awful fuss,' Mr Abercrombie said. 'Wait – what was that you said about the Underworld?' Mr Abercrombie frowned. 'Don't tell me you were part of that unauthorised descension – some people got fired over that, you know.'

'See, Mr Abercrombie, it's very complicated.'

'*Quelle surprise,*' Bea said drolly.

Mr Abercrombie just sat there looking at the pair of them.

'I'm a Roman,' Bea said, as if that explained everything.

Mr Abercrombie turned to Barry. 'Okay, Mr Trotter. As much as I'd like to sit here and chat—'

Abercrombie's finger was on the chit-maker. It's now or never, Barry thought. 'Bea was an old girlfriend of mine, who I had to cast a spell on, only I did it wrong, because I never pay much attention in class, which I'm sure you already know from my file. It was a time-reversal spell, and I went too far, not a lot too far, just – at least sixteen years.'

'Whoops,' Mr Abercrombie said.

'Right, no kidding! I felt such an idiot! Anyway, Bea

died, and being a Roman, went to the Underworld,'
Barry said, talking fast. 'Now, fast-forward twenty-four
years—'

'Whoa,' Mr Abercrombie said.

'No, wait, it makes sense,' Bea said with amazement.
'Sort of let your mind go slack.'

'— I'm thirty-nine, and really famous, and Bumblemore's gone, and so is Valumart, and life is great. I'm
married and have two kids, who are excellent most of
the time – well, some of the time – but I have this awful
pain-in-the-arse disease that won't let me get any older.'

'Lucky you,' Mr Abercrombie said. Under the
circumstances, Barry decided to let it slide.

'Youthenasia, it's called. I go to this doctor, and
through hypnosis he and I discover—'

'Wait,' Mr Abercrombie said, flipping through
Barry's papers. 'This isn't Ernst Ritalin, is it? I got
worried once I saw his name in your file. He's
practically filled this room with people under his care.
The man's not going to have fun when it's his turn, I
can tell you that.'

'Yes, it was him,' Barry said. 'He had this theory that
if I went back and undid the wrong I did Bea all those
years ago, maybe I could age again.'

Mr Abercrombie paused. 'So you killed yourself on

purpose, sneaked your way into the Underworld, found her and brought her back here?'

'Yeah,' Barry said.

'I see.'

Barry put on what he hoped was his most ingratiating smile. 'I was sort of hoping you'd give her a do-over.'

'And you don't want anything for yourself?'

Barry thought. 'No, not really. I've had a pretty good run.'

Mr Abercrombie thought for a second. Then he pushed some keys on his chit-maker.

Crouching close to the window, he said quietly, 'That's worth an exception, I think. And Ms Thompson seems to have been an innocent bystander if there ever was one.' He handed over two pearl-coloured chits. 'Here you go,' he said. 'One each, to send you back. But I better not catch you two down here for at least another thirty years.'

'Thank you so much!' Bea said. Barry was speechless, having the old brain-out-of-gear problem again. 'Bar-ry.' Bea enunciated each syllable, elbowing him.

'Sorry,' Barry said. 'Thanks a lot.'

'Put it in your right hand,' Mr Abercrombie said.

Smiling, Barry and Bea each took a pearl chit and closed their eyes. In a moment, they were gone.

Chapter Fourteen

Behind the glass, in the neighbouring seat, Loretta was looking at Mr Abercrombie. 'You old softie,' she said, smiling.

'Well, I'm a sucker for a pretty face,' Mr Abercrombie said. 'I'm going on a break – want anything?'

Chapter Fifteen

THE GREAT CHASE

꧁꧂

Lord Valumart was still doing a loose-limbed mambo of triumphal ecstasy when Barry abruptly sat up.

Blinking, the ex-boy wizard smacked his lips and scratched his still nine-year-old head vigorously. When his eyes adjusted, Barry was greatly puzzled to see Lord Valumart.

'What are you doing here?' Barry said. 'Where's Dr Ritalin?'

Startled, Valumart turned. '*Schiesse!*' he yelled in a strangled voice. 'Don't you ever die?' He leapt on to Barry, fastening his gloved hands around Barry's throat.

'Is this part of the therapy?' Barry croaked. 'C'mon, get off.'

He received no answer except Valumart's tightening grip. The two men struggled, Valumart continuing to lament his lot. 'Of all the snot-nosed punks in the world to be enemies with, I had to pick this one ...'

Realising this attempt was in earnest, Barry reached for his wand. It sat on a nearby end-table, just out of reach. Valumart saw this, and choked Barry harder. With the flexibility of a nine-year-old body, Barry was able to stretch a bit further. He grabbed it.

'Uh-oh,' Valumart said, and with good reason. The next moment, a large boxing glove made of pink vapour shot out from the end of Barry's wand and socked He-Who-Smells right in the stomach. Valumart let go, and fell to the floor, sucking air.

Rubbing his throat, Barry gasped, 'You can tell Dr Ritalin I'm not paying for this session!'

Valumart scrambled to his feet and backed away. 'You stupid fool,' he said, wand raised. 'There never was any Ritalin. It was always me.'

'Don't lie,' Barry said. 'Ermine would've never allowed you to work at Hogwash!'

'Oh, I gave the stupid cow some sob story about being down on my luck. I told her that Bellettrist L'étrange embezzled all my money.' Valumart laughed. 'As if.'

'Nobody insults Ermine!' Barry fumed, voice coming back. 'That's my job!'

'Stupid cow, stupid cow, stupid cow!' Valumart said. 'Your wife is a stupid cow!'

'You're so lame,' Barry said. 'No one likes you, not really. They just want your money.'

'Talk about the pot calling the kettle black!' Valumart said. 'Anyway, you're about to be dead, so I don't care what you think.'

'Typical,' Barry snorted. 'You did all this, just to kill me?' He shook his head. 'How idiotic. Don't you ever get tired of yourself? All the rest of us do.'

'Idiotic?' Valumart smiled. 'You still don't get it, do you? Because of this little scheme, I was able to sell nearly four million Muddle pounds worth of Barry Trotter death paraphernalia.' Valumart sneered. 'T-shirts, pennants, commemorative plates, a Christmas ornament of your head that plays "Taps" when you push its nose – it was a goldmine. And after twenty-four years in the sleaziest, most destructive investments I could find, that money was worth over a hundred million pounds! Your dying was the best thing that ever happened to me – and you had to come back to life and ruin it.'

'What do you care?' Barry said, looking for an opening to zap the Dork Lord. 'You're still obscenely rich.'

'That's right. No thanks to you!' Valumart said. 'I

sent you back in Time, back to the Underworld. I never imagined that you would come back alive, and even more irritating than before. Well, now you're finally going to die for good!'

In a lightning-quick motion, Valumart traced a figure in the air. Suddenly all the photos of Dr Ritalin with various insane celebrities flew off the wall and came straight at Barry, spinning like angry frisbees. Barry dived to the floor, covering his head as the pictures exploded against the far wall. This spell, *Makepictures-flyatsomeonethenexplode-io*, was not very common, but it was handy in the right circumstances.

After the glass had stopped flying, Barry looked back at the shattered, smoking sideboard. then he turned to Valumart and said, 'Very nice. I suppose a picture really *is* worth a thousand words.'

Valumart grimaced. 'Your quips don't even make sense.'

Barry got a sly smile on his face. 'Maybe they do, and maybe they don't. But can you withstand ... *this*?' Barry pointed his wand at Valumart, and muttered an incantation. A small flag bearing the word 'BANG' on it unfurled pitifully from the wand end.

'Damn it!' Barry said. He slid a plastic panel on the side of his wand, and looked at it – the battery was nearly dead. 'That can't be possible ...' Barry couldn't understand. By changing his life, had he become less magical?

'It appears your vaunted magical powers are waning, Trotter,' Valumart said. 'You've become too well-adjusted, I fear.'

Barry knew what he had to do: run. 'Okay, Valumart,' he said, edging imperceptibly towards the office door. 'You've got me. But before you kill me, I've got one final request.' If he could only keep Valumart talking until he reached the doorknob . . . 'I want you to recite the dictionary.'

'Nice try, Trotter, but I won't fall for your little gambit, whatever it is,' the Dork Lord said. 'Yes, it's ironic. By going back and saving that girl, you've become a decent person, not the irresponsible clod we all knew and disliked,' Valumart said, permitting himself an unspeakably evil laugh. 'Not so impetuous, not so greedy, not so selfish . . . So nice – and about to become so dead.' Valumart set the dial on his wand to 'kill'. 'Well, at least you'll go to Heaven,' he said. 'Save a seat for me.'

'You? In Heaven?' Barry said. 'Don't make me laugh.'

'It's already arranged, Trotter,' Valumart said. 'A little cash to the right people can do wonders. Do you have any final codicils you'd like me to ignore?'

'Yeah ... bite the wax tadpole!'[45] Barry said, throwing open the door, and flinging himself into the hall.

'*Aveda Neutrogena,*' Valumart screamed, but missed. As Barry spilled on to the linoleum-covered stone, a bolt of greenish slime splattered against the far wall harmlessly. As some students stopped to put the moisturising lotion on their hands, Barry disappeared into the seething mass of teenagers. Crouched down to rob Valumart of a clear shot, Barry scrambled madly down the hall like a crab in heat. Behind him, Valumart was heaving people out of his way.

'*Achtung, Schweinkinder!*' Valumart bellowed.

'Hey, mate, watch the hands!' A Radishgnaw fourth-year smacked the Dork Lord across the face with her backpack, which had a collapsible cauldron in it.

'*Ach —*' Valumart fell, momentarily concussed.

Up ahead, Barry's mind was working frantically. What was wrong with him? Why couldn't he do magic? Was Valumart right? Was he too decent, too nice, now to harness the great irresponsible power that made every spell work? Spotting a frail first-year toting an

---

[45] This is a funny little piece of history, like the interrobang. Coca-Cola's original attempt to translate its name into Chinese resulted in this phrase being plastered all over the country. I've always thought it made an excellent insult, don't you?

armload of books, he decided to test the theory. With a deftness borne of practice, Barry knocked the boy's books to the floor. A term's worth of papers spilled out too, and were stepped on by the hordes marching all around.

'Arsehole!' the boy yelled after him.

'Okay,' Barry said, still running at full speed. He pointed his wand at the sliding stairway. 'Here goes nothing.'

Miraculously, the stairway slid where Barry wanted it.

'Son of a witch!' Barry laughed. He ran down the stairs, looking for more opportunities to cause trouble and recharge his magical power. As soon as they spotted him, students cleared the centre of the stairs, cowering near the edges.

'Trotter! *Halt!*' Valumart said from the top of the stairs. Bracing his wand on his arm, He-Who-Smells aimed and fired. It missed, but not by much; Barry could smell the shoelace burning on his right shoe. He couldn't afford another shot, so Barry pounded the banister in a way that Ferd had taught him way back when. The stairs went flat, and tens of people lost their footing. They all slid down to the bottom with Barry, shielding him from Valumart's wand.

The bottom of the stairs looked like the aftermath of

a very tiny, but fierce, battle. Extricating himself from the wailing jumble of injured students and damaged belongings, Barry sprinted for the front door. Valumart leapt over the banister three floors above and floated downwards, shooting as he went. As Barry's hand touched the knob, a blast of pure necrotising magic whizzed over his shoulder – if he stopped to open the door, he'd be toast.

Hemmed in, Barry ran into the Great Hall. The house-elf staff were having their dinner, and weren't pleased by the interruption.

'You can't come in here,' said Fistuletta. 'You know the rules – we're eatin'. You can't come in for a half-hour yet.'

Barry veered widely to slam into an elf carrying a full tray of food. It sprayed all over. He ran into the kitchen.

'He did that on purpose,' the house elf said.

'Didn't even say sorry, neither,' another one griped.

'I always thought he was a wanker,' Fistuletta said to the general agreement of everyone at her table. 'I say we put some dragon poo in his food.'

Before anyone could move, Valumart walked in. 'Vich vay did he go?' Then he saw the elf sprawled in front of the doors, unconscious amid the spilled food. 'Ah.' As he walked toward the kitchen, Valumart said, 'I vould advise everyvon to stay out here, no matter vat you might hear. I expect a fair bit of screaming and et cetera.'

In the kitchen, the elves were preparing that night's meal. Cooks with filth-caked hands were tapping cigar ash into soups, booby-trapping salads with large, stringy bogeys, and painstakingly hiding small bits of spoiled meat in otherwise edible entrées.

Barry whizzed by at full speed, trying to upset as many pots and pans and possible.

'Hey, you!' hollered a cook plucking an owl (much of the school's meat came from kidnapped familiars). 'Get outta here!'

Valumart appeared in the swinging doors. Barry grabbed a plate and slung it, discus-style, in Valumart's direction. It missed by a mile, but with every bit of destruction, Barry's stores of magical energy increased. The only question was, could he be destructive *enough*?

'Pardon me,' Barry said, grabbing the hand of a nearby kitchen worker and jamming it into a boiling pot of spaghetti sauce. The elf screamed; he'd be able to reconstitute his hand, and Barry needed the mayhem.

'You must leave!' another cook shouted. 'Take your fighting outside!' Barry threw a potholder at him (every little bit helps).

A bolt of evil purple energy shot towards Barry, so

close that he could feel the static charge his hair. Barry dropped down and hid in an open cabinet.

'Fuck this, I quit,' a house elf said at the sight of such obviously lethal magic, and he was joined by everybody else in the kitchen save Barry and Lord Valumart.

'Come out, Barry,' Valumart said. 'I . . . I vas just kidding.' The Dork Lord crept around the room, listening for clues to Barry's hiding place. 'I know I seemed unfriendly earlier but it's chust . . . I forgot to take my medications . . .'

Barry realised he had to move; this was a small room, and both doors were behind Valumart. He could try to evaporate, but what if he didn't have enough magic left? And what if he could evaporate, but not condense? Ending up as a nomad fart didn't sound like fun.

Barry searched his pockets for something that would save him. A wallet, some keys, the defective homing umbrella from the Tiki Shack – he'd brought it to the session to help him remember the details of his fifth year . . .

'Trotter, this becomes tiresome,' Valumart said. 'Vy can't ve discuss this like responsible adults?' Valumart lost his temper, grabbing a spoon and throwing it. 'So I CAN KILL YOU!'

The spoon clattered to a stop right outside Barry's cabinet. He heard Valumart's bootsteps falling closer

. . . closer. Valumart was standing in front of Barry's cabinet. Through the half-opened door, he could see from mid-ankle to mid-thigh. He had to reach above the boot . . .

'I feel that you are close, Trotter, very close. It's almost as if I can smell you,' Valumart said. 'You know, now's probably as good a time as any to say: I'm not the only von with a body odour problem.'

Barry grabbed Valumart's leg, and jammed the toothpick end of the homing umbrella into it.

'Ahhh!' Valumart bellowed in the universal language of pain. Reaching down to extract the umbrella, the Dork Lord unfurled it – and was sent crashing into the ceiling, and through to the classroom above.

'Cyril Broadbottom,' Barry heard Snipe sneer, 'what do you think you're doing, being smashed beyond recognition by Lord Valumart hurtling through the floor? Five points from Grittyfloor!'

Barry knew he didn't have much time. He scampered out of the small door the elves used to come in and out of the kitchen without disturbing anyone. Outside in the sunshine, Barry ran. As a stitch in his side started to throb, he heard Valumart land heavily somewhere behind him. Damn, he could use some magic now! Barry glanced at the indicator on his wand – still not much, but better.

'Halt, *Schwienehund*, halt!' Valumart huffed and puffed, out of shape.

Ten feet away, two boys in Silverfish Quiddit uniforms were walking away from the school's front doors, each carrying a mop. Valumart was closing fast, so Barry sprinted towards the smaller of the two.

'Gimme that,' he said, roughly pushing the boy to the ground and taking his mop. With a kick, Barry was airborne.

'Ha, ha!' The other boy pointed, laughing at his teammate's misfortune. 'What a wuss!'

Valumart biffed him so hard on the back of the head the boy lost a tooth. 'I'll take that mop. Don't expect it back.'

Barry flew towards the Silverfish practice, hoping that he could lose himself in the game, or at least be shielded by the players. Catcalls and insults flew thick and furious as Barry swooped and dived. Valumart stayed a half-second behind; after all, his mop had more weight to carry. Scanning the air furiously, Barry began to sweat – was this the end of the line? No; he saw a glimmer of gold, and dived towards it. Grabbing the sneetch firmly, he popped it in his mouth – this bit of flying would take two hands – and pushed the cheap mop as far as it would go. The entire Silverfish Quiddit team followed; the deposit on a sneetch was expensive, and Barry knew it. He also knew that the students would be better flyers than Valumart, so they formed a splendid protective barrier.

After ten minutes of this, however, it became clear that Barry wasn't really getting away; Valumart could, and would, fly as long as he did, and eventually pick him off with a lucky shot. He looked at his wand; every moment the angry squad followed him, he got a little more magical power. When his wand had crept up to a sixteenth full, Barry decided it was now or never. Jumping off the mop and spitting out the sneetch, Barry began to fall . . . He'd have to time this perfectly . . . Just before he hit the ground, he waved his wand and evaporated. A brief quack echoed throughout the Forest.

As the Silverfish team dispersed to catch the sneetch, and Barry's mop ploughed into a remote part of the Forsaken Forest and exploded, Valumart flew to a stop. Still covered in plaster dust, He-Who-Smells pulled out a small device.

'You can run from the Dork Lord, Barry, but you can't hide.' Then, with the sound of a quack, he evaporated too.

As a team of surgeons worked on the brain of an

accident victim, Barry Trotter condensed himself in the corner of Trauma Room Four.

A nurse shrieked and dropped a bag of blood.

'What the—?' a surgeon said, turning and knocking over a tray full of instruments.

'You can't be in here!' shouted the anaesthetist.

'Just passing through!' Barry said, then got an idea: he leaned over and spat into the man's open head wound. That would get him enough magic to evaporate again. Just as the medical team converged on him with hatred, he did so.

Moments later, Valumart appeared, tripping over a ventilator and unplugging it from the wall.

'It's him!' the nurse cried. 'He's back!'

'*Guten Tag*, I vas—'

The two surgeons, several nurses and the anaesthetist fell on the befuddled Valumart, getting in a few good whacks with the gas bottle before the bruised Dork Lord could scramble out of the room and evaporate to safety.

Travelling at random to throw off his pursuer, Barry appeared in the midst of the trading floor of the New York Stock Exchange. Seeing how the transatlantic jaunt had drained his wand, he knew what he had to do.

Waving his hands wildly, shouting out 'Buy!' and 'Sell!' nonsensically, Barry made two complete circuits of the trading floor before security cornered him. He had pauperised hundreds of traders, bankrupted a large hedge fund and got two CEOs fired. 'Cool,' Barry said, looking at the indicator on his wand. As the cops told him to come out from behind the water-cooler with his hands up, Barry evaporated again.

As luck would have it, Lord Valumart appeared right where Barry had been.

'*Guten Tag*, fellows,' he said. 'Haff any of you *Herren* seen a man —'

The jittery security guards opened fire.

'*Schiesse!*' Valumart cried, and evaporated again.

'Goddamn it!' Barry kept catching glimpses of Valumart, appearing just as he was disappearing. How can he keep up? Barry thought. Desperate, he stretched the chase even further.

With a loud quack, Barry popped into the middle of a circumcision ceremony in Turkey. The noise caused the blade to slip. Just as the baby's relatives converged, Barry evaporated again.

'Take it from me,' Valumart said, thirty seconds behind, 'it's not vat you have that counts, it's vat —' The boy's family and friends pelted him with stones, and Valumart was off to Egypt and the Sphinx.

'You just missed him,' the Sphinx said. 'He wrote his name on my forehead.'

'I'm afraid zat's pretty typical. That's vy I'm going to kill him.'

'Well, good luck with that,' the Sphinx said. 'Really.'

Meanwhile, Barry entered a Polish monastery, just as a tour was starting. 'Around seven hundred and fifty years ago, the local cemetery had been filled to capacity by a terrible plague. So the brothers of this Order were forced to do something new . . . and astonishing,' the guide said, Barry edged close to the railing. 'They decided that one monk, a talented artist named Brother Balthazar, should take the bones of the dead and arrange them. Balthazar arranged them in a geometric display both macabre and beautiful, something that would simultaneously please the eye and remind the soul of its coming judgement.'

A bank of lights flicked on, and thousands upon thousands of bones came into view, each one placed precisely to create a magnificent vista – an astonishing, if bizarre, work of art. 'There are over ninety-five thousand individual bones here,' the guard said. 'It took Balthazar nearly thirty years to complete, but as you can see it was worth it.'

The rest of the tour group murmured in amazement – then horror, as Barry leapt the guard rail and dashed to the display. Before the guide or any of the Brothers could reach him, Barry had pulled out several femurs, an essential tibia, and a precisely balanced scapula. The entire portion came crashing down; and the vibrations from its collapse brought the rest down, too, one after the other like collapsing dominoes.

Valumart appeared to find the Brothers in a very un-Christian mood.

'*Bitte*, fellows – did a man chust come through here, about so high, vith glasses—'

'Oh, you know him, eh?' one particularly huge monk said, cracking his knuckles. 'Friend of yours, eh?'

'Vell, no actually, you see—' Valumart found it hard to put his and Barry's complicated relationship into words.

'Since he broke our bones, we're going to break some of yours,' said another Brother, equally huge. 'Right, Brother Viper?'

'Right, Brother Crusher.'[46]

Valumart left without his wallet, but with all his own bones intact.

There comes a time in every man's life when he's got to stop running, Barry thought. Plus, my lips are really

---

[46] This Order of monks was particularly popular among ex-convicts.

chapped from all this evaporating. He had some magic left in his wand, but what was the use?

When people talk about the way they want to die, they always mention 'dying at home'. Suits me, Barry thought, and condensed himself back into the small living quarters that he shared with Ermine and Fiona at Hogwash. As he waited for Valumart to arrive, Barry looked over all the mementoes of his life: pictures of the Order of the Penis, all young and randy and full of anticipation; some strands from his mop, which he had destroyed drag-mopping over the Forsaken Forest; the Chamberpot of Secrets.

He picked up the Chamberpot with a smile – and was instantly teleported to a chemist's down in Hogsbleede. Swearing, Barry remembered that Fiona had mischievously transformed it into a Portalpotty earlier in the year. With all the stuff that had happened since, he'd forgotten to deactivate it.

Standing there in the women's hair-care aisle, Barry had an idea. 'Holy shit!' he said. 'It might work!' A Muddle matron gawped at him, mouth open. 'What are you looking at?'

With a quack, he reappeared in the bedroom. Did he have enough magic left in his wand? There was no time to answer that question: a very bruised and bedraggled Lord Valumart immediately appeared.

'Okay . . . Trotter . . . Qvit vith the silly stuff . . . time to die,' Valumart panted.

Barry didn't respond. He had the Chamberpot completely covering his face, and was mumbling quietly into it.

'Vat are you doing mit that Chamberpot?'

Barry lifted his head up. 'Wouldn't you like to know?'

'*Ja!* Actually, *ja* I vould like to know,' Valumart said. 'Zat is vy I asked, because I vould like to know, *Dummkopf*.'

'Here,' Barry said, 'I'll show you.' He took a step towards Valumart.

'*Halt!*' Valumart said. 'Do not come any closer. Chust toss it to me.'

'Okay,' Barry said. 'But if you drop it, Ermine's going to be really cheesed off.'

'I von't drop it,' Valumart said. 'I vas captain of Hogvash rugger, vay back vhen.'

'Are you su-ure?' Barry taunted, in a sing-song.

'*Ja*, I am sure!' Valumart said impatiently. 'Just commence with the tossing!'

'Okay,' Barry said, and tossed it into the air.

'I von't dr—' The moment the Chamberpot touched Valumart's hands, the Dork Lord was teleported. However, Barry hadn't sent Valumart to the ladies' hair-care aisle of Boot's – he had reprogrammed the Chamberpot to take Valumart to the centre of the active volcano located right next to the school! Amazingly, this awesome geological feature, such a rarity in Scotland, had never been mentioned before in any Trotter book. It simply hadn't come up.

Leaning out of the window, Barry watched the tiny form of Valumart, sun glinting off his helmet, plummeting into the volcano, screaming. He-Who-Smells was incinerated instantly.[47] The mountain gave a vast rumble, spewing a great cloud of ash into the air, then a sound not unlike a belch. Then all was quiet again.

Despite the ash raining down on him, Barry watched the crater for a while. Naturally, he expected Lord Valumart to clamber out again, mad as hell and covered in soot, just like in the cartoons. But this wasn't a cartoon, it was reality. Slowly it dawned on him: the Dork Lord truly was no more.

Barry didn't feel much, one way or the other – no rush of triumph, but no real sadness either. Yes, Valumart had been a pain in the arse, but without him how interesting would Barry's life have been? There

---

[47] And very cinematically, we might add. If anyone's interested in the movie rights . . .

probably wouldn't have been a single Barry Trotter book . . .

Barry whistled, happily but with no discernible tune, as he left the room and walked down the hall to deliver the news to Ermine. It would be fun to tell her that she'd hired Valumart by mistake.

He passed a group of weeny first-years. They could grow up in a world without Valumart, he thought happily – then remembered what Bea's gran had foreseen, and the vast extension he'd seen in the wizards' waiting room. Can we avoid the smackdown between Muddles and wizards? Was Valumart the cause? Barry wondered. Or was it inevitable, caused by violence and stupidity on both sides? Only Time – and the sales of this book – would tell.

Chapter Sixteen

ERMINE EXASPERATED

❦

Worn-out, with a soot-covered head, and still smelling vaguely of Boot's, Barry walked into Headmistress Cringer's office.

Ermine was at her desk, marking a stack of papers from her class on Environmental Magic. The topic was the life and career of the famous wizard Gareth the Granola-y. Back in the 1970s, Gareth had invented a way of casting spells that produced less smoke. Lower-emission magic was great, no doubt, but things always came out a little weird. Food conjured this way always tasted a bit like tofu, and anything plastic would often biodegrade suddenly without warning. People like Ermine conjured smokeless anyway. People like Barry figured that people like Ermine made up for them.

The Headmistress smelled her husband before she

saw him. Looking up, she was confronted by something more smudge than man.

'Playing with the volcano again, I see,' Ermine said, and went back to marking. 'What did you throw in this time?'

Barry opened his mouth, but his wife cut him off. 'No, don't answer, I don't want to know. All I can say is, it's lucky somebody's prepared to do a little work around here.'

Barry went to a chair and sat down heavily. Pulling over a waste-paper basket, he began brushing the cinders out of his hair.

'Where have you been?'

'In a session with Dr Ritalin,' Barry said. 'He says I'm cured.'

'Really!' Ermine said, looking up. 'You know, you do seem to have a growth of beard again. Although that could be ashes.'

'No, it's hair, I think. Ashes don't get ingrown,' Barry said, touching a sore spot on his neck. 'By the way, Ritalin told me to tell you he's gone on a sabbatical.'

Ermine was surprised. 'How odd – for how long, did he say?'

'From the way he looked, for ever.' Barry tried to sound nonchalant.

The Headmistress was incensed. 'Bloody hell, Barry! I knew you'd drive him away!' she yelled.

'It was Valumart,' Barry said, not wanting to wait any longer. 'Ritalin was Terry Valumart in disguise.'

'You're insane!' Ermine said. 'I suppose you're going to tell me he was trying to kill you again.'

'Bingo.'

Ermine looked like she was about to burst a blood vessel. After taking a moment to calm down, she said in a low, angry voice, 'I never thought I'd say this, but now I really understand what Bumblemore was on about. There's something really wrong with you, and it's not this age stuff, either! You just bollocks things up. And—'

'Breathe, Erm, you'll pass out.'

'At least I wouldn't have to look at you!' Ermine continued. 'And it must be genetic, because Nigel's just been caught with his hand up another student's smock.'

'Dangerous habit, that,' Barry said. 'I'll talk to him.'

'You'd better — and Fiona, my God, what a little hellion she's been.'

'More pranks?'

'Yes!' Ermine said. 'I was all set to get her to see Ritalin, and now you go and—'

'Erm, you worry too much,' Barry said, taking a

priceless crystal ball off her desk and tossing it up in the air. 'They'll grow out of it. I'm living proof.'

'Barry, don't. I just got it in the post. It once belonged to Thrasyllus.'

The ball slipped out of Barry's hands and hit the floor with a smash.

'Out! Get out!' Ermine yelled, and Barry ran.

BIBLIOGRAPHY

Anonymous, *A Child's Treasury of Profanity*. New Haven: Yale University Press, 1991.

Bacon, Canadian, *Alchemy for Medieval Dummies*. London: Argent Vive, 1125.

Bumblemore, Alpo, *Some Call Me Git*. Hogsbleede: ValuBooks, 2002.

Cringer, Ermine, *Arm-Hair Styling Dos and Don'ts*. Hogsbleede: ValuBooks, 2002.

Drabble, Edith P., *Toilet-training Your Zombie*. Port-au-Prince: Nosferatu Books, 1993.

——, *The Zombie Gardener*. Port-au-Prince: Nosferatu Books, 1995.

——, *Zombie Home-Repair*. Port-au-Prince: Nosferatu Books, 1996.

——, *Undead . . . and LOVING IT! 1001 Small Businesses Involving Zombies, From Catering to Child-Care*. Port-au-Prince: Nosferatu Books, 1998.

Edwards, Timothy, *How to Tell a Faerie from A Leprechaun Without Getting Slapped*. London: Wee Folk, 2001.

Fnord, Edith, *Writing Without Verbs: Gateway to the Imagination*. New York: Scribbler's, 1984.

Grunk, Esmeralda, *Pixies: An Unexpurgated, Uncompromising Look at the Boringest Creatures on Earth*. New

York: Minuscule Press, 1963.

Hoenzollern, Hans, *Slightly Incorrect Latin*. Oxford: Little Knowledge Press, 1933.

Ignatz, Ignatz I., *Barry Trotter – Magician or Madman?* New York: Fugue State, 2000.

D'Endicott, Prunella, *Beaubeaux: C'est Magnifique*. Paris: Maginot, 1999.

——, *Hogwash: School for Sin*. Paris: Maginot, 2000.

——, *Schadenfreude: Den of the Torpid*. Paris: Maginot, 2001.

Killington, Pansy, *Cold Feet: The Sonja Henie Story*. Lake Placid: Triple Axel, 1961.

Lucre, Og, *Perspire and Grow Rich*. New York: Avarice Unlimited, 1997.

Moody, Red-Arse, *I, Error*. Hogsbleede: Smudge and Mackle, 2001.

Nottington, Clarabella, *Teasing Theory and Practice*. London: Psyche!, 1994.

Oggler, Oswaldo, *How to Receive Pornography Via Crystal Ball*. Onan & Co., 1977.

Ptomaine, Henri, *Commedia della f'Arte*. London: Pardonmoi, 1973.

Quixotic, Marcy, *Your Cat CAN Type!* Manchester: Purr & Knead, 2001.

Raisinbread, Herschel, *Ignoring Magic*. Cambridge: Cambridge University Press, 1969.

Bibliography

Stimple, Avid, *The World According to Gorp: Half Giant, Half Pile of Trail Mix, All Superstar!* Hogsbleede: ValuBooks, 2003.

QUESTIONS FOR READING GROUPS

'Pleasure shared is pleasure doubled,' the old saying goes. Why not meet up with other *Barry Trotter* fans and discuss what you've just read? Here's why not: it would be boring and stupid. Still, you could tell your parents that's what you were doing, and avoid a lot of sticky questions.

1. Clearly the author is not a well individual. What are some childhood traumas that might make a person compulsively write parodies of Harry Potter?

2. On page 91, Ermine says, 'Outside of a dog, a book is Man's best friend. Inside of a dog, it's too dark to read.' Since when did *she* grow a sense of humour? Do you think it's all right to steal jokes? If not, what should the punishment be?

3. Some people shouldn't write books. Other people shouldn't read them. Name four things that you could do with *Barry Trotter and the Dead Horse* instead of reading it. What would you have rather done than read this book?

4. If you got this book as a gift, do you think the giver was trying to tell you something? What? Is *that* very nice?

5. Whole chunks of this book simply don't make sense. What do you bet the author was drunk?

6. The Barry Trotter series is centred upon the struggle between Barry and Lord Valumart, between not-very-good and kinda-sorta-evil. And let's be honest, it's just not that fascinating. Do you think that's why there hasn't been a movie yet?

7. The Trotter series has been called 'a significant addition to the literature of flatulence and excretion'. Should the author be proud of this? How about his mum?

8. In the character of Ernst Ritalin, the entire concept of mental health is undermined. Which other literary figures could use a trip to the psychiatrist? Which ones should simply get a good bang on the head with a hammer?

9 When he was younger, the author often claimed to have written famous books – 'under a pseudonym, of course' – to impress girls. Why do you think this never worked?

10. Do you think people will look back at this book and say, 'That's when the New Dark Ages began'? Why or why not?